WALKING WITH

Born in Hull in 1942, and educated at the university there, John Baker has worked as a social worker, shipbroker, truck driver and milkman, and most recently in the computer industry. He has twice received a Yorkshire Arts Association Writers' Bursary. His three previous Sam Turner novels, *Poet in the Gutter*, *Death Minus Zero* and *King of the Streets*, are available in Vista. John Baker is married with five children and lives in York.

WALKING WITH GHOSTS

John Baker

VICTOR GOLLANCZ

LONDON

First published in Great Britain 1999
by Victor Gollancz
An imprint of the Cassell Group
Wellington House, 125 Strand, London WC2R OBB

A Gollancz Paperback Original

A catalogue record for this book is
available from the British Library.

ISBN 0 575 06643 1

The quotation on page 42 is taken from the poem
'Daddy' by Sylvia Plath, first published in *Ariel*, by
permission of Faber & Faber Ltd.

Typeset by SetSystems Ltd, Saffron Walden, Essex
Printed and bound in Guernsey by
The Guernsey Press Co. Ltd, Channel Isles

99   5 4 3 2 1

'I've said goodbye to haunted rooms and faces
in the street.'

Bob Dylan

I would like to thank Anne Baker, Peter Fjågesund and Simon Stevens for their helpful criticism. It is also necessary to say that any offended sensibilities are the responsibility of the writer alone.

This one, like the others, is for Anne.

1

Sam had problems with insurance. You could only insure the things that didn't matter. Houses and cars, the material trivia of life: things that could be replaced. New for old. You couldn't insure people. Not really. The insurance companies said you could, but it wasn't true. When you lost someone you loved they'd make a cash settlement. A bunch of fifties to replace flesh and blood. Courage, spirit, laughter. New fifties, though. Crisp, new ones, to replace an old love.

Jill Sheridan opened the door of her office and came across the reception area towards him. Sam got to his feet and took her hand. She was thirty-seven, lean machine, dressed in a navy Hermès suit, classic cut, with a white silk blouse showing at throat and cuffs.

'Jill. Looking good, as usual.'

She stood back to frame him from a different angle. 'You look like shit, Sam. Had a bad night?'

He grinned and shrugged his shoulders. Followed her into her office. The brass plate on the door: JILL SHERIDAN – CLAIMS ASSESSOR. Behind her desk was a picture window that looked out over York. The skyline dominated by the Minster. In the distance the blue smudge of the North Yorkshire Moors.

She stood close to him and they took in the view together.

'Different to the last place,' Sam said.

'Yes. It felt strange at first, but I'm getting used to it. At least it's not haunted.'

Sam laughed. 'There must be a ghost in every other building in this town. Romans, Vikings, Normans. They all had their day, and they've all left the odd strangler behind.'

'There's one in your office, isn't there?'

He laughed again. 'Celia and Geordie keep bumping into a shady Victorian lady on the stairs. But I haven't seen her since I gave up drinking.'

She waved him into a chair and went behind a desk that housed only a telephone/fax/intercom gismo. No pen or pencil, no notepad. Polished wood and the box of technological tricks. 'Thanks for coming. Can I get you something? Coffee, isn't it?'

'Yeah. Unless you've gone over to the powdered stuff.'

She punched a key on the intercom. 'Holly, will you let us have a couple of filter coffees, please? Mr Turner'll have his black and strong, no sugar.'

'Your memory's holding up,' Sam told her. 'But how do you work in here? No PC or terminal. What happens if I ring in with info? You can't even take notes.'

Jill smiled. 'Always the practical Sam. Whatever happens on the telephone is recorded. Holly intercepts the tapes and does the necessary. If there's something that needs my action, she prepares it and puts it in front of me.'

Sam shook his head. The year before he married Dora, he'd been keen on Jill, and they'd had a brief affair. He could date the beginning of the end of that affair from the time he'd heard her say that she'd 'actioned' something. That, and the fact that his clothes never seemed to suit hers. Wherever they went he'd felt like a poor relation. Nice woman, though. When everything came to an end he'd missed her for days.

'Why did you call?' he asked.

'I've got a job for you.' A hint of a smile passed over her face, as if a secondary thought had come to mind, unrelated to whatever it was she wanted to communicate to Sam. A memory of some kind? 'It's rather complicated.' She hesitated, avoided eye contact for a moment. 'But I've heard you're having a bad time. If you don't want to take this one on, I'll understand.'

'We need business, Jill. I'm not the only one in the office.'

'What I've heard, Sam, you're not *in* the office at all.'

He shook his head. 'Exaggeration. I can't get in as much as I'd like. But everything's covered. There's Geordie and Marie, Celia, all raring to go.'

Jill Sheridan looked over the desk at him. She looked into his eyes, and Sam looked back. 'I mean at home. How is she, Sam?'

He blinked a couple of times. Sighed. 'She's in pain some of the time. Other times she's calm, coherent. We talk a lot. Talk through the night.'

'I'm sorry,' said Jill.

'There's nothing anyone can do. Sometimes it feels like we're the only two people in the world. It's a special time.'

There was a knock on the office door, and Jill's PA entered with a tray, jug of coffee, cups and saucers. Sam watched her legs and behind as she served the coffee, wondered briefly how many legs and behinds he'd checked out in a long career. And then his thoughts returned to Dora, and he wondered what it would feel like to be a widower all over again.

When Holly left the office, Jill said, 'I want you to handle this job yourself.'

'I'll give it all the time I can. I'm not gonna promise anything, Jill, except you'll get the same attention you did in the past. This time it might be Geordie who handles it, or Marie. Maybe both of them, instead of me. But at the end of the day you'll get better service from us than you'll get from anyone else.'

She smiled. 'I wouldn't dream of giving it to anyone else.'

'So what've you got?'

'Edward Blake.'

'I thought that was all over. You mean you haven't paid him yet?'

Jill shook her head. 'You remember the story?'

Sam showed her the palms of his hands. 'Only what was

15

in the papers. You'd better fill me in. I never thought I'd be working on it.'

Jill spoke with a clear voice, as if she was making a presentation. 'Edward Blake is a political lobbyist. He came to prominence in the eighties, and made money under Thatcher and Major. In the spring his wife, India, was kidnapped. But he didn't go to the police. According to Blake he received a call from the kidnapper, and paid a ransom of twenty-five thousand pounds. But India was not released, and nothing more was heard from the kidnapper.

'When Blake *did* call in the police, a search was launched, but nothing was found. There was no real evidence to confirm that she'd been kidnapped, apart from Blake's story, and the police thought she'd run off with a lover. They reasoned that India and her lover had stung Blake for the twenty-five. Anyway, the whole thing died down, the newspapers found another cause to stick on the front page. We had several weeks of minor royals in and out of each other's playpens. But then, three months later, India Blake's body was found in a box in a garden allotment shed near the racecourse. She had been left to starve to death. The police took Edward Blake into custody, held him for a time, and seemed fairly convinced that he had been behind it. Especially when they discovered that he'd insured her for two and a half million pounds the previous year.'

'You still think he did it?' asked Sam.

Jill shrugged her shoulders. 'We want you to look into it. Two and a half million pounds is a lot of money. But if you say the man's kosher we'll pay out.'

'The police have written him out of it?'

Jill nodded. 'He has finished helping them with their inquiries. There was a time when they were convinced he did it. But since the DNA tests they've left him alone.'

Sam finished his coffee and looked at the jug. Jill moved it closer to him. 'She was pregnant, wasn't she?' he asked.

16

'Yes. Only just. The presumption is that she was raped by the kidnapper. What is certain is that whoever the father was, it wasn't her husband.'

'Is that all you've got?' Sam said. 'Why haven't you paid the guy?'

Jill shrugged. 'It smells,' she said.

'These things always smell a little,' Sam said. He sniffed. 'Yeah, there's a real whiff, but it's not like it makes your nose fall off. I bet if it wasn't two and a half mill you'd have paid him by now.'

'Oh, sure, Sam. Of course we would. But I'm hoping that if we pay your daily rate for a couple of weeks, we might save ourselves a lot of money.'

She walked to the lift with him. 'I hope Dora'll be all right,' she said.

Sam didn't say anything.

'She's lucky to have someone to take care of her.'

Sam smiled. 'You don't need taking care of, Jill.'

'I know,' she said. 'It's a bitch.'

She touched his arm as he stepped into the lift, dug out the soft smile, the one with the hint of concern in it, and flashed it at him as the doors closed between them.

Sam looked at his reflection in the full-length mirror that made up one side of the lift, and shook his head. Why didn't they just pay the guy? Jill acted like it would be coming out of her personal bank account instead of corporate funds expressly put aside for the purpose.

Still, why should Sam Turner worry? It meant work for the business, paid work. And the thing was about work from Jill, she paid well, and she paid quickly.

The job would consist of straightforward leg work, interviews with the dead woman's associates, maybe a little surveillance on Edward Blake. Sam wouldn't need to get too involved himself, Geordie and Marie could handle it easily enough.

Two weeks, maybe two and a half. He'd be able to spend more time with Dora.

It would have been too complicated to go into with Jill Sheridan, but Dora, Sam's wife, had known the murdered woman. They hadn't been close, but Dora had been upset when India Blake had disappeared, and shocked when the dead body was discovered. Dora had followed the case closely, sometimes reading extracts from the newspapers to Sam when he got home in the evenings.

He stopped in at Betty's for coffee instead of going straight to the office. Sam was still surprised that he was married at all. He'd watched himself getting closer to Dora, talked himself out of it a dozen times, then watched himself making up his mind to go through with it. He and she had recognized the lawlessness in each other. That's what they called it. Whatever it was, they shared a bond.

And now she was falling apart.

He had watched his wife at night rowing out into a fjord. Before the disease took her strength, they had stayed in a wooden cabin near Tromsø, courtesy of a satisfied client. He remembered her strength. The water was slate grey, with a faint touch of blue. There was a line of silhouetted trees on the opposite bank, edged with scarlet, but fading out into pink and blue. No sound. Total silence. She'd pulled away from the shore with strong, rhythmical strokes. Sculling across the glassy surface of the water. She was a silhouette. In the distance an oyster catcher had called out in the wilderness.

2

You were a child then. You were a girl in pigtails, thin, your ribs and collar bones sticking out of you like primitive scaffolding. You did not fit. And they told you over and over that you did not fit. And you believed them, because they had all the answers, and even if they had not told you you would still have known that you did not fit, because they all did fit, and you were different. *Not fit to . . . Not fit for . . .*

What was it all about? That time? Your childhood? You should be able to make sense of it. You feel a deep need to look there for the meaning which has reverberated throughout your life. The meaning, or the lack of meaning.

You knew he was dying. He had been dying for as long as you could remember. They took you into a curtained room and pushed you towards his bed, and he was your father, your dying father, and he was thinner than you. Badly shaved, prickly and yellow, with hollow jaws, and stinking breath and long gnarled fingers with calloused nails that should have been shorter, and you had to let him hold your hand and go so close that it looked as though you kissed his cheek. Though you never kissed him. Never once; only brushed your lips so close to his face that your heart thumped against your flimsy ribcage. My God, Father, you think now. If you'd known, if it had been possible for you to know then what you know now, then you would have kissed his lips. His dry, flaking lips. And he would not have died so soon, for your lips then were like a knot of juicy grapes, the spittle of the vine. And your lips now are like his were then, and you are kept alive by love.

You are confused. You are grateful, but you are confused. The world has gone through so many contortions. And it is not because you are so old. It is rather because everyone else is so young. It is because the thing that crouches inside you is so elemental, so mindless, so ageless beyond age, so weighty and cud-chewing, so liable to charge an imaginary rag. You have to keep it at peace. You have to dominate it. You are a matador. You have to pray.

You have the facility of perfect recall. You are a daughter of the earth. You can remember the details of your mother's womb, your reluctance to leave its warm-sea-saltiness, your horror at that first tug-of-war. Since then you have become a virtuoso of birth. Now, for as far as your eyes can see, there stretches an infinity of sand.

Sam's hand smoothes your brow. His two eyes are twinkling in the darkness above you, slightly out of horizontal, like Aries. It is night and you are coming back. The pains are dulled again. You have come through another tug-of-war. The desert is still there, waiting, but here in the oasis the night is cool.

'There,' he says. 'It's better now.'

And you feel your head nod assent, and your lips rustle as you try to speak. Sam moves above you and you feel his fingers pressing the sponge to your mouth. The cold water is like light, it sends messages of hope to every nerve in your body. You do not tell him when you have had enough, you do not flicker your eyes or alter the tempo of your breath. He takes the sponge away. He knows.

You can feel Geordie's dog, Barney, settled at the end of the bed, by your feet. And you wonder about Geordie. Where he is, what he's doing.

Your fingers move on the quilt and Sam takes your hand in his own and you hope he can see the smile that is like a song in your blood, and any doubts you might have sink away, down through the mattress, down further through the floor, as his chuckle unfolds itself into the room.

'It's past, isn't it?' he says. 'You're feeling better.'

You move your lips and he gives you the sponge again, and finally you can speak: 'What time is it?'

'Four o'clock. The night is young.' He chuckles again. 'Can you sleep now?'

'Where's Geordie?' you ask.

'At home in bed. It's late.'

You close your eyes. Yes, you can sleep. You let yourself slip away. Sam is holding your hand. He has a grip of you. It is four o'clock in the morning. You are no longer confused. You are grateful.

As a part of history, you are connected with events and people of the past. On the day you were born Rudolf Hess invaded Scotland by parachute; clothes rationing was already in force. The previous year the British army was evacuated from Dunkirk, three hundred and thirty-five thousand, four hundred and ninety men huddled on the beach under constant attack; and the following year the siege of Leningrad was lifted. Lady Day had her first taste of hard drugs. You were destined for history.

Your mother was a historian, a secret historian. Her account of the Great War is still among your papers in the bureau. You have failed to edit it for more than thirty years. The truth is, you never wanted to edit it because it was hers. You were jealous of her, as she was jealous of you. Her only achievement, as far as you are concerned, is that she was a cousin of Dylan Thomas (and your earliest memory is of being kissed by him).

'I was kissed by Dylan Thomas,' you have told almost everyone you ever met. 'He went down on one knee and kissed me on the cheek. I remember being tickled by a day's growth of beard, and the smell of figs on his breath. He was a relative on my mother's side, somewhat removed, but he visited us when he was in the neighbourhood.' You have been a snob about that.

In truth, you don't know if you remember it or not. You don't know if you remember Dylan Thomas, or if what you remember is your mother's memory. Because she told everyone the same story: 'Dylan Thomas kissed Dora, you know. She was small at the time, but she still remembers, don't you, Dora? His bristles and a figgy smell, typical childhood observations. He was my cousin, you know, a regular visitor whenever he was in Wales.' You are like your mother. You have become more like your mother as you have grown older. The last ten years have been a nightmare in that respect. You would not have believed it possible. You feel like her. You turn your head when someone speaks and in a flash you recognize the gesture. It is your mother turning her head. She lives in the tone of your voice. Your characteristics, gestures, inflections of speech, they are all inherited. You are reverting to form. Everything you rejected, burned, left behind; it is all reconstituting itself. You have not escaped. You have run away, but you have not escaped.

You laugh because you can see now what you were running from. It is life's oldest comedy. Your mother was not so bad. She was like you. A Swansea girl, born and bred. When you laugh at her you are laughing at yourself.

You were special. You were a special child born into a special family. A respectable family. A middle-class family. You had advantages. The house had more rooms than people. A mile away the working classes lived in black shams lit by candles. Further away still lived the miners who communicated in grunts. The miners who lived on roots, and who made Mother tug you into her skirts when they passed in the street.

Already when Dylan Thomas published *Deaths and Entrances* you could read and write and converse about the world, you were more knowledgeable and wise than any miner or any miner's son or daughter. You told all Mother's visitors about the Sydney Harbour Bridge. 'A triumph of engineering.' You described the treasures of Tutankhamun.

22

You were a precocious child. Everyone patronized you; but even the adults were a little scared. You could see it in their eyes.

Everything in your childhood was special, but more special than anything else was your education. For your mother the highest learning was history. You spent seven years in a class with five other girls under the personal tuition of Miss Masefield ('Not, like my namesake, a poet; though, believe me, young ladies, poetry has been for me the most edifying inspiration of my life.') Miss Masefield hated children and loved knowledge, and her mission in life was to wed the two together. As a child you watched her grow haggard with the struggle.

Apart from Joan, the other girls in the class were stupid. Joan was your cousin, and like yourself, an only child. You agreed to be sisters on the day an atomic bomb destroyed Hiroshima, and you still think of her as your sister now. Together with Joan you looked at the photographs of the wedding of Princess Elizabeth, and years later you reminded Joan that Lady Day was serving a prison sentence when the princess and her prince walked up the aisle. Lady Day had taken a cure earlier in the year, but then got herself arrested as a user in Philadelphia. She was sentenced to a-year-and-a-day at the Alderson Reformatory in West Virginia. Joan's something big in Women's Lib now. She became politicized late in life, about the same time you were beginning to turn to God.

Joan made it to Oxford too, only she did not stay the course. It was different for you. You were a sticker. You clenched your teeth in the face of the humiliation, the patronage, the sheer bloodiness of a masculine preserve. There was not a day, not a single day at the University when you were allowed to think of yourself as other than a woman, a poor relation of man. Hesketh-Darwin-Jones, your tutor in the history department, was struck dumb by the swish of a skirt. He had chosen academia in preference to the military or the church to avoid the female sex; and, lo, the establishment had betrayed him. He was dumb. He never spoke a word to you in three years. He coughed and stammered and constantly rearranged the features of his face, he pointed at books and scribbled unreadable notes, but he could not speak. Now you can laugh about it. Almost forty years have passed.

Lady Day died when you were in that place. Her life came to an end before you'd ever heard her sing. She slipped away before you'd heard her name. It was years later that you were penetrated by her haggard voice with its plaintive cry. The Classical and the Gothic were your teachers then; it was to be some time before you discovered 'What A Little Moonlight Can Do'.

And it was at Oxford that you met Arthur. The one place in the world that your mother thought you would be safe from miners was the one place where you met a man with coal dust in his eyes. Arthur. He had coal dust in his soul. Mother never knew. Until her dying day she thought he was the son of a country parson. She should have married him instead of you, she would have managed him better. She would have appreciated his aspirations. That was something you never did, Dora, because while he was climbing up the social scale you were intent on climbing down it. You were searching for the working classes while he was trying to forget them. What a funny couple you were. What a hilarious duo. How you mauled each other. How you marked each other.

And yet it could have worked. You could have sacrificed yourself as other women did. Arthur wanted you to sacrifice yourself and you refused because you thought your own life had meaning, import. You were full of . . . history. The English Civil War was more important to you than a miner's son with coal dust in his eyes. You judged his aspirations spurious and let him go. He would never understand why. He did not have the insight. He was a miner's son. A philosopher, an economist, an idealist in his way. Arthur, the father of your children; a child himself who wanted that you be his wife first and last. Arthur, who reminded you of your vows. Arthur who, in truth, did not want much, but who sought it from you who could not give.

And if his aspirations were spurious, Dora, what about your own? Did you really think it possible that they would give you a Chair? You? A woman? A married woman? A divorced woman? A woman with children? And the working classes; did you think they would listen to you? Yes, you thought all that, and more. You thought you had the answers. You thought your generation would change the world, but in the end you fell back on gin, long black cigarettes, all-night parties, and, and . . . you are not at all like your mother.

But then, Dora, then? Can you salvage anything from memory? You were married on the fourth anniversary of the assassination of Jack Kennedy. It was winter, snow on the ground. You were a virgin. A lecturer at the University of Leeds, stubbornly pushing your department into accepting more female students. Even then seventy-five per cent of entrants were men. Arthur was climbing the ladder in the Scientific Civil Service. There had been a hard frost overnight, and the bushes and trees were decked with crystals. It was the happiest day of your life.

Remember? It is your day. A long white underskirt in silk. The dress fastens high up the neck with those tiny buttons. Lace. Oh, dear God, Dora, remember all that lace? Mother is crying into huge, starched handkerchiefs all morning. Half an hour before the car arrives she blurts out her guilt: 'I should have broken your hymen. Dora, darling, forgive me.' She is inconsolable. Her own mother had done it for her when she was three months old. It saved so much pain. She had worried about it, on and off, for years. 'It didn't seem so important at the time, but now . . .' She searches for another starched handkerchief and blows. She is a whale on the morning of your wedding to Arthur. A spouting whale. The ditches in her face powder run with tears.

Poor Dora. You do not know what a hymen is. You have pursued history to the exclusion of everything else. You do not think about this hymen. If it was important you would know what it was. Nevertheless, it stands there all day, in one of the tributaries of your mind, this unbroken hymen that makes your mother cry.

You do not worry about sex. You are a virgin, but you have read Emile Zola. And Arthur is experienced. He has been with prostitutes; twice. What could possibly go wrong? It would be different if Arthur was green. But he is . . . well, another colour.

White, actually. His body is powder-white. You realize in the bedroom when his shirt comes off that you have never seen his body before. It is flesh-white; divided vertically in front by a line of black hairs that originate way below the belt and fail hopelessly to blossom on his chest. His back is divided too, but horizontally. The shoulders are matted black, with the same long hairs, but below the shoulder blades the white skin is barren. You avert your eyes when he lowers his trousers, and only look back again when he is completed by pyjamas. Your silk nightgown is pale blue. You feel naked in it.

Neither of you speak. There is an atmosphere in the room. You have created that atmosphere. It has grown out of your subconscious. Something wonderful is going to happen. You are trembling. Arthur is climbing on top of you in the bed. Why does he not kiss you, Dora? Why? He is tugging at the stuff of your nightgown, pulling it, stretching it, grunting and tugging, kneeling above you, forcing his knees between your thighs.

When he has spent himself he rolls away and weeps. It was the first time for him. It was a lie about the prostitutes. You comfort him, tucking your body into the curves of his, wrapping your arms around his flesh-whiteness. You wipe

26

his tears away with the palm of your hand, blow into his ear, cover his neck and face with kisses. He groans softly, like a big bear, and falls asleep. The surface of your body is prickling, you can feel the blood gushing through your breasts and thighs, you spread yourself in the bed and bury the memories of the day in your feelings. Arthur begins to snore.

3

William had forgotten everything. He was standing in Parliament Street watching the screen of a mute television through a shop window. There was a smear of perspiration along his top lip and his heart was beating rapidly. Off to his right a brass band was playing Sousa's 'Hands Across The Sea'. It felt like they had been playing it for ever. To his left a couple of girls were involved in a game of chess on the municipal 'board', which was marked out by coloured paving stones. One of the girls was lugging a black plastic bishop along the length of the diagonal. Her friend seemed to be composed entirely of breasts. William felt a surging hatred inside him that threatened to obliterate the second girl from the face of the earth. This was not a new experience for him, he had felt the same way before.

William recognized the street, but he didn't know why he was there. He looked at the clock above Marks and Spencer's. Eleven o'clock. Morning. He must be here for a reason. This had happened twice lately. It was as if he was sleep-walking. He'd wake up, and have no idea how he'd got to wherever it was, or what he was doing there. If he stood perfectly still and waited it would come back to him.

Worrying.

Worrying when a part of a person wasn't functioning properly.

He inspected his clothes, tried to remember putting them on in his room that morning. Clean clothes, neat. Jacket, grey; with a white shirt, maroon tie. His black slip-on shoes had been polished to a high shine. The creases in his trousers were straight and sharp. He'd pressed them before he came out. He remembered that.

It was all right to stand here and pretend to watch the television. If people passed by they wouldn't look at him. They wouldn't know that he wasn't functioning properly. They'd think he was watching television.

No one would dream that he had had blood on his hands.

William smiled. He could fool people. When he was functioning properly he could fool people easily; but when he wasn't functioning properly he could still do it. He had a genetic propensity.

Some memory remained. He knew who he was. Knew he was directed.

A bead of sweat dripped off his eyelid and sprayed salt into his eye. He wiped the eye and looked around. The people passing by went about their business. No one looked twice at William.

The picture on the television changed, credits moved up the screen, and a series of adverts began. You could order a CD or a cassette of the world's favourite love songs. They were only available from one address in London. Next there was a new scouring pad that moved by magic, wiped up the kitchen and the oven by itself, made everything clean and bright.

Bright.

Light.

That was it, that was what William was supposed to be doing in the town. Bright. Light. He was here to buy candles.

The band stopped playing, and the players brought out satchels and bags and flasks of coffee. That's what happened if a person waited. You got a break. The world which seemed as though it had no purpose suddenly took on meaning.

William turned away from the shop window. He walked past the girls playing chess, the one with breasts still disturb-

ing him, flashing images of violence through his consciousness. He controlled himself and made his way along
Daveygate to the wax shop.

He found the candles. Ten centimetres long, cream-col-
oured. He took one of them to the counter, where the young
female assistant was smiling at him. He didn't return the
smile. 'I want three hundred of these,' he said.

The girl's eyes widened. 'I don't know if we have that
many,' she said. 'I'll have to ask the manageress.'

'They keep them in the back,' William told her. 'In boxes
of fifty.'

The girl disappeared into the stock room, and a couple of
minutes later she returned with four boxes of candles. The
manageress followed with another two boxes.

'You were right,' the salesgirl said.

William didn't need a woman to tell him he was right.

One day he had followed the maternal-looking manageress. She had collected a toddler from a childminder before
going to a flat in Fishergate, where she lived with a man.
The man went out drinking in the evening, stayed out late.
And while he was out the manageress was alone,
unprotected.

He paid for the candles in cash and when the girl had
packed the boxes into strong plastic bags, he carried them
back to his flat. He lived alone now. With the ghost of his
father.

Bright. Light. It was a miracle how he had been reminded
of his purpose. Like a voice. As if someone had spoken to
him.

4

Geordie was first into the office that morning. He put the water on to boil and spooned ground coffee into a blue jug which Celia had bought to replace the one he'd broken the previous week. Celia was visiting Dora, staying with her while Sam came into the office. But Marie would be in as well, so that meant three of them. He put five measures of the coffee into the jug. No point drinking it if you couldn't taste it. That was Sam. That's what Sam would say.

He looked through the audio tapes while he waited for the kettle, and dug out *The Very Best Of The Mamas And The Papas*. He stuck it in the machine and pushed the PLAY button. 'California Dreaming'. That'd do. Sam liked his music to have matured.

What Sam had said on the phone last night was that there was a new job. But what he'd also said was that he wanted Geordie and Marie to handle it between them. He'd want reports, but essentially they were gonna do it on their own. Make the decisions, everything. What did Geordie think about that?

'Oh, sure, why not? We've been involved in enough cases by now. We know what to do. It'll be a piece of bread.'

'Cake,' Sam told him.

'Piece of cake?'

'Yeah, like falling off a twig.'

But then after Sam rang off and Geordie got to thinking about it, he wasn't so sure. He'd talked to Janet about it, and Janet thought he shouldn't worry. Just do it.

'But what if we make a mess of it? How long's it gonna be before we get another chance? And we could lose business – I mean if people hear how we screwed up this job, we might never get any other jobs.'

'Geordie,' Janet had said with her patient voice. 'There are never any guarantees that things are going to turn out right. You just do the best you can. That's what we all do. The best we can. And if that turns out not to be good enough, then that's how it is. We learn by our mistakes. But if you make a mistake it doesn't necessarily mean it's a disaster.'

'Yeah. Sure,' he said. 'And it'll be good experience. When Sam dies, eventually. I don't mean he's gonna die soon, or anything like that. He could live for years yet. Could live to be over a hundred. But when he dies or retires, I might have to take over the business, me and Marie together. Then I'll remember this time, when Sam gave us this chance.'

But he didn't sleep all night. Lying next to Janet, breathing in the scent of her, feeling the closeness and warmth of her body, watching the fluorescent numbers on the digital clock by the side of the bed. At half-past three Janet got up and said she'd make him a cup of cocoa.

'I thought you was asleep,' Geordie told her.

'How can I sleep when you're just lying there not moving and not breathing right?'

'Jesus,' said Geordie, pulling on a dressing gown, and following her down to the kitchen. 'I thought I was breathing perfect.'

The Mamas and the Papas moved on to 'Dedicated To The One I Love', and the kettle boiled and switched itself off. At the same time Marie arrived, and Geordie told her that it was synchronicity.

'Don't think so, darlin',' she said, hanging her coat and scarf on the stand. 'Synchronicity only happens to Jungians.' Marie had lost weight over the last year. You would still regard her as big, but it was more to do with the size of her bones than the amount of fat she carried. Geordie couldn't work out if she looked better for it. She did look better for it, but she looked better because she felt good about herself for losing the weight. She didn't really look better because she was slimmer. Geordie had liked her when she was rounder and softer, but he didn't say so. It might be sexist.

She took a copy of Val McDermid's *Blue Genes* out of her bag and put it on Sam's desk.

'Have you read the *Rubáiyát of Omar Khayyám*?' Geordie asked.

'Not this week,' she said. 'I read it when I was your age, along with *The Prophet* and *Jonathan Livingston Seagull*. Now I'm older I've moved on to social realism.'

'Celia gave it to me, and me and Janet've been reading it in bed. "The moving finger writes; and having writ, moves on."'

Marie tapped her head and took up where Geordie had left it, ' "Nor all thy piety nor whit shall lure it back to cancel half a line . . ." '

' ". . . Nor all thy tears," ' concluded Sam, coming through the door, ' "Wash out a word of it." Thought I might be in the wrong place, coming up the stairs there. The Mamas and the Papas and Omar Khayyám. Nearly turned round and went home till I smelled the coffee.'

'I thought you liked the Mamas and the Papas,' said Geordie, kneeling down to fuss with Barney, his dog, who'd been sleeping over at Sam's house. 'It's one of your tapes.'

'I like them,' said Sam. 'I liked them thirty years ago. Twenty years ago I still liked them. But there comes a time when a man thinks he ought to listen to something else. You listen to the Mamas and the Papas for thirty years, there's a possibility you could end up getting stuck.'

'So what're you listening to instead?'

'Christy Moore.'

'Never heard of her.'

'Him. I'm listening to all the Irish music I can get my hands on.'

Barney moved over to his basket by the side of Geordie's

desk. The smell of coffee and sixties' music meant they were going to be here for some time.

Marie handed Sam the book she'd left on his desk. 'You'll enjoy it,' she said. 'Female PI.'

'And that's another thing,' said Geordie. 'Reading books by women. I've never seen you do that before.'

'I've been working my way towards it slowly,' said Sam. He looked at the book, held it at arm's length. 'This is the fulfilment of a life's ambition.'

Marie laughed.

Geordie scowled. He didn't like change. He didn't like more than one thing to change at a time. And he certainly didn't like anything to change at all after a sleepless night. 'Anyway,' he said. 'What's the score? You gonna tell us about this job?'

Marie poured the coffee, and Sam sat at his desk to outline the history of the case of Edward and India Blake. Marie sat in the clients' chair, and Geordie perched on the edge of Sam's desk, making notes as he listened to the story.

'So, you want us to collect background information?' said Marie, when Sam had finished. 'See if we can come up with something new, something to tie the husband in?'

'Yeah, or anybody else,' Sam said. 'We're being paid to find Edward Blake guilty, but if we're gonna be on the job anyway, and if Edward Blake's innocent, it would be nice to nail the real kidnapper.'

'That's not gonna be easy,' said Geordie. 'Edward Blake, yes, if we can find something that ties him to, say, the allotment shed. But we haven't got anything else to go on. No other suspects.'

'That's true,' said Sam. 'But if, for example, India Blake was having an affair, and her husband found out about it. That might explain why she was pregnant. And it might also be a motive for Edward Blake to kill her.'

'I would've thought two and a half million pounds in insurance money was enough of a motive,' said Marie.

Sam shook his head. 'You never know,' he said. 'Murders are committed for all kinds of reasons. Something that one person would shrug off as insignificant, might easily make another man reach for a knife. And the two and a half million insurance money is chicken feed compared to what she was worth.'

'She was some kind of heiress, wasn't she?' said Marie.

'Furs,' said Sam. 'A great great grandfather started out as a trapper, and by the time India was born the family was worth something like ten million. Conservative estimates put Edward Blake around fifteen million better off since his wife went to heaven.'

'So if he did it, and we can prove it, he'll still get away with it,' said Geordie. 'So much money, he'll hire the best lawyers in the world, and they'll talk him out of trouble.'

'You don't wanna work on this one?' asked Sam.

'Yeah, I've been up all night thinking about it. Anyway, is that what you want us to do? See if we can prove she was having an affair?'

'Just go through the motions,' Sam said. 'See where the investigation leads. I don't know if she was having an affair. After you've talked to the husband, to people she knew, her friends, you'll start to build up a picture of her, of their lives. Then you'll feel yourselves being nudged in this or that direction. You'll develop a nose for it, and you'll find yourselves following a scent you never thought of before.'

'I can't wait to get started,' said Marie. 'It's gotta be more interesting than serving process orders.'

'Yeah, and checking credit references,' said Geordie. 'I hate that. And you never know if the stuff you get off computers is right. I've read about cases where people can't get a mortgage, or whatever, because the computer says they don't pay their debts. But it's because the people who put the info in the computer got it wrong. Is that true, Sam?'

'Yeah. It happens.'

'So that means we could be stitching people up. We give

somebody a bad credit ref, which is what the computer's come up with. And then the guy can't get a mortgage, has to spend the rest of his life in a cardboard box; dustbin liner instead of a duvet.'

'Maybe you're in the wrong line of work, Geordie,' said Sam. 'You could go into politics, or join the civil service.'

'Hell, no, Sam. I like the job well enough. Don't wanna do anything else. I'm gonna be a private eye for the rest of my life.'

Sam went home to relieve Celia. Marie went out on the job, and began the task of talking to friends of the dead woman. Geordie stayed in the office, wanting to finish up several odd jobs he'd been working on over the last few weeks. Get everything out of the way before he started on the murder inquiry.

'Hell, what do you think, Barney?' he asked his dog. 'D'you think we could find out who done it?'

Well, why not? The woman, India – how the hell did somebody get a name like that? There's probably people in the world called Australia, Africa, Greenland, maybe. But maybe not, Greenland. He'd heard of someone called Israel once, and the guy who lived next door to him and Janet was called Irish. The woman didn't put herself in a box in an allotment and starve herself to death. Somebody put her in that box. Somebody did it to her, and left her there. So there was someone who knew all about it. Everything. Just because the police hadn't been able to find him, or her – no, it would have to be a man. Just because the police hadn't solved it, it didn't mean that Geordie and Marie wouldn't be able to do it.

There must be clues. The guy must've left something behind that tied him to the scene. If they could find whatever that was, and crack the case . . . 'Wouldn't that be something, Barney?'

Barney got out of his basket and walked over to Geordie,

nuzzled against his leg. He didn't understand about murder, he was only a dog. But he could take all the attention he was offered. If it meant appearing to be interested in a murder inquiry, so be it.

Geordie was filling out a job sheet. Working out the hours he'd spent trying to repossess a car, so that Celia could send out the invoice, when a tall guy with a full beard and tinted glasses walked into the office. 'The boss Shamus about?' he asked.

Geordie looked at him. He must be around forty years old. His suit and shoes were clean. He had a faded red shirt, and a string tie that was pulled down, the top button of the shirt unfastened; black wiry hair which had been combed at least once that day. If you looked at the details the guy was neat and tidy. But the overall effect was scruffy. Must be the beard. Yeah, that was it, the beard had never been trimmed. Somebody should tell him. Maybe he didn't have any friends.

'No,' said Geordie. 'You missed him. He was in earlier.'

'Shit. OK, I'll blow, catch him later?'

'Is it important? If you tell me what it's about I'll probably know the answer.'

'Yes. I mean, no. It's not desperate. I don't want to hire you. I was looking for a favour.'

Geordie made his eyes open wider. He'd seen people do it in movies. It was like an invitation to the other person to keep on talking. And it worked, too.

'OK,' the guy said. 'My name's J.D. Pears. People call me Jaydee. I'm a writer. Write mystery novels, and I'm looking to get a slant on the private dick business.'

'Are you famous?'

The guy had a shy face, which he'd coloured pink and he brought it forward to cover the face he'd first arrived with. 'I'm not Dick Francis, but I'll brace him one of these days.'

'OK, you can ask me about that,' said Geordie. 'The private detective business. What d'you want to know?'

J.D. pulled out the clients' chair and nodded towards it. 'OK if I sit down?' He didn't wait for an answer. 'It's not so much that I've got questions,' he continued. 'What I was hoping for was some hands-on experience. Like if I could be with one of you when you're on a job. For a few days, a week, two at the most. Do you think that would be possible?'

'I don't know,' Geordie told him. 'I'd have to ask Sam. I mean, I wouldn't mind if you followed me around. I'm gonna be involved in a murder inquiry for the next couple of weeks. But lots of stuff we do, it's confidential. I don't know what Sam'd think about a stranger following us around. Specially if you're gonna write it down in a book.'

'No, I wouldn't do that,' said J.D. 'Not so's you'd recognize it, anyway. I write fiction.'

'I've read Raymond Chandler,' Geordie told him. 'And there was a book by Elmore Leonard, Sam lent me. D'you know them?'

J.D. smiled. 'Not personally. I know their work.'

'I'm reading *Omar Khayyám* at the moment.'

The writer shook his head. 'Can't say I've come across that one. Is it Chandler or Leonard?'

'No,' Geordie said. 'It's like a poem. Really old ... poem ...'

But J.D. Pears was laughing. 'Sorry,' he said. 'It was a joke. Bad joke.'

Geordie smiled. 'Yeah,' he said. But why did people make bad jokes? Geordie thought if you were gonna make a joke you ought to wait until you could make a good one. 'Would I know any of the books you've wrote?'

'You might. There's a series about a policeman who's a food connoisseur. *Bloody Broccoli* was the first one. The last one was *The Camembert Killer*. Just published this month.'

Geordie shook his head. 'Can't say they ring any bells,' he said.

J.D. looked miffed, made a pout inside his beard. 'They've had good reviews,' he said.

'Yeah,' said Geordie, taking pity on the guy. 'I don't read many of those kinds of books. Sam reads 'em, and Marie, they're always swapping them. They'll've heard of all yours. Me and Celia read more poetry, classics, literature, know what I mean?'

J.D. nodded.

'I'll make a bargain with you,' said Geordie. 'I'll get one of your books for Sam's birthday, and if you sign it at the front I'll give Sam a bell and ask him if you can get some hands-on experience by following me and Marie around on the murder inquiry. How's that grab you?'

5

Sam moves across the darkened room. He draws back the curtains. Holding it in one hand, his long fingers gripping the rim, he brings the loaded tray to the bed. He looks younger than he should. He wears a T-shirt tucked into the waistband of his jeans. You try to sit up in the bed and he helps you with the pillow, kissing your cheek in the same spot that Dylan Thomas's lips might have been.

'You're smiling,' he says.

'I'm happy.' Your voice is like dry dough. It is not easy to be young and beautiful when you are old and ugly. You make a sour face at the cracks in your voice.

Sam pulls the cardigan around your shoulders, and you wonder what happened to that pale-blue nightgown, quickly doing sums in your head. He was still in his teens the night you wore it for Arthur.

'Can you manage this?' he points to the tray. It is loaded with cornflakes, toast, marmalade and coffee.

You clear your throat before answering. The coffee is the best thing you have smelled in your life.

'You should eat,' he says. 'Try the toast.'

You nibble a crust. He is right. You should eat something. Though your body only wants the coffee and a cigarette. Sam pours milk and cornflakes into the bowl for himself, and he eats, watching your face over the rim of the bowl. He offers you a spoonful and you suck the milk and leave the wet cornflakes behind. He shakes his head, his lips pursed, his eyes wide and twinkling. You open your mouth and take the cornflakes. You cannot resist him. You are an old fool to fall for a man his age, but you like being an old fool. It is better than being a young one.

There is a searing pain under your arm and you catch your breath. The tendons on each side of your jaw strain and lock against the spasm. A few of the cornflakes fall on to your chest.

'What is it?' Sam is on his feet. His hands on each side of your face, but it is over.

You tell him. 'A false alarm. Just a twinge.' Your voice is a croak. You smile at him and he sits. He collects the flakes from your chest and eats them. He doesn't like wasting food. There are people starving in Africa.

The coffee is good. Not too hot. It tastes better because it's forbidden.

You point to the pot and Sam pours another cup. You ask him for the cigarettes and he makes his disapproving face, but gets one anyway. He lights it for you and passes it over. He strokes your face with the palm of his hand, and lets it run on, over your neck. You feel something move beneath the skin, like a small egg, and you watch Sam's eyes, because he felt it too, but he does not let on. Your body is covered with those eggs now. You are no longer surprised by them. You hate them, but they no longer shock you.

'Did you sleep?'

'Yes.' You lie with a smile on your face, knowing that Sam knows you are lying, and knowing that he knows that you know ... He pinches your cheek between forefinger and thumb and shakes his old-young head, his face weighted with irony.

'Do you want to try again?'

'No, Sam.' You won't sleep. Not what you regard as sleep, not the bottomless ocean which is a kind of freedom. Sleep now is like a wet bog; you lie on the surface of it, and it sucks and blows, unable to claim you.

Sam's eyes are tired. Has *he* slept? 'I'll get the chair ready,'

41

he says. He places it by the window and smothers it in blankets. Then he pushes the curtains back, draping one of them over the sideboard so you can see the entire street. He carries you across the room effortlessly. Lifts you from the bed like a small child, cradled in his arms. You were never heavy, Dora, but, dear God, look at you now.

'Won't be long,' says Sam, taking the tray, running down the stairs. You remember Sylvia Plath, something about the street brings back a line . . . *Poor and white, barely daring to breathe or achoo* . . . and you want to rush to your books and search for the memory, bring the poem back to your chair by the window and read it aloud to the empty street. You move your head slightly to watch a woman with a child locking the door of a house over the way. You have never seen her before. They have repopulated the street.

The people who lived in that house in 1970 – what were they called? – won the neighbourhood prize for the best-kept garden. The house was made up like Noah's Ark. You were pregnant with Diana and waddling about on the last road to motherhood. History had been put aside in the interests of biological necessity – Arthur's phrase – and you had moved to York with his job and your widening hips. It did not seem like promotion, really, moving to York, but it made him happy, and that was important. Arthur had to be happy, he had been in a war, defending the Suez Canal. He had been in the desert, making the world safe for democracy.

You waddle to church with him every Sunday morning. In the church they sing, 'Eternal Father, Strong to save', which is the only thing that keeps you going. Arthur pretends to like it all, the entire service. He falls heavily to his knees to pray, while you thank God that Diana, growing inside you, precludes you from that humiliation. If God had not already been established, Arthur would have invented Him.

When Diana is three months old, Arthur is sitting in his

42

armchair after church. You are cooking. Diana is crying and Arthur is reading titbits out of the newspaper aloud. The sauce is getting lumpy. You decide never to go to church again.

'What?' says Arthur, later, when Diana is quiet and the washing-up finished.

'I don't believe in it any more,' you tell him.

'But our child. Our . . . our civilization.'

'I'm sorry. It seems ridiculous to me.'

He looks at you as if you have shot him. His face runs to wrinkles with the effort of comprehension.

'You go on your knees to pray,' you tell him. 'And you go on your knees for sex.'

Arthur's lips turn blue. He lurches to his feet and rushes over to the draining board, taking you by the shoulders. You cannot imagine what has happened for a moment. You see his arm go back and the flash of his fist and then you are on the floor and the coffee cups are breaking around you and your eye is beginning to close. The room is swimming, and you look up at Arthur who has become huge, standing astride you, looking down, his fists clenched by his side.

'Don't talk to me like that again,' he says. He thunders out of the room, and you reach for the door of the cupboard to pull yourself up. You do not know what you have said. You had only begun your speech about knees. He should have let you get to the part about washing the floor.

You hear her for the first time. You turn on the radio and there she is. She sings, 'I Don't Know If I'm Coming Or Going'. You walk out of the house with her name on your lips. That is all you have. You don't know she is a black woman. You don't know she is dead. You don't know that her voice will haunt you for the rest of your life. Lady Day. You will name your son after her.

The trouble with Arthur was his need for violence. He was the son of a miner. He had been in that war. It was not

43

easy for him. He could never be sorry about it. There was always justification. Violence to him was a kind of love. And you were his wife. And he loved you. In his way.

And you loved him. And you *did* love him, Dora, in spite of the beatings. It wasn't as if he beat you every night, or even every week. Only when you crossed him. Only when he realized that he had been wrong. The rest of the time you could love him. For a while, at least. A long while. Some years. Hoping all the time that he would change. That he would begin to see your world, as you strove to see his. Hoping that he would see the futility of the violence, that he would recognize that he could not hurt you, even if he killed you. And it was too many beatings later before you realized that you were not a wife at all. That you were a symbol. A hated symbol. That you had been replaced in his mind by some *thing*.

You held your breath too long in those days. You should have raged. You had every right to rage, Dora, while Arthur was squeezing the life out of you. While he appropriated all the life forces that came into the family, all the forces of renewal and regeneration, and grew stout and red-necked. You should have gone underground, poisoned his food, sawed through the leg of his chair. It would have been worth it. He would have seen you then.

But you were a traditional girl, like your mother before you. You believed that Arthur should come first, that he should get the best cut of the joint, that his ideas and aspirations were more informed, more valid. You believed in sacrifice, Dora. You were a mystic.

There was a more or less hazy conviction that if you gave your life to him, he would, like God, give life back to you. But for Arthur there was no mysticism, only duty. And he was short on that. Arthur went through life explaining everything. He left a trail of destruction behind him.

After Billy was born you decided to leave him. How long after Billy was born? A week, Dora? An hour? Perhaps it

44

was the moment of birth itself, the child being an image of release. Suddenly it was possible to throw everything off, to leave yourself vulnerable. Then it would be up to you. But it was not courage. It was desperation that drove you to leave. You had seen yourself in a mirror, seen your hopelessness, the dark rings around your eyes, the pathetic smile. You could not afford to lose more weight. The midwife had shaken her head at your lies.

If it had been courage, Dora, you would have left at once, but desperation kept you going for another five years. Five years in which Arthur grew larger, more dominant every day. Five years in which you furiously fuelled your hatred of him. Five years in which you grew bolder, more reckless, in which you listened and did not speak. It was during that time that your body coddled the seeds which now swim as eggs and discs beneath the skin. Without those five years you would still be healthy, Dora. You would still be young for Sam.

6

Marie Dickens had drawn Edward Blake, the husband. She had not spoken to him on the telephone, but dealt with his secretary. The first story was that his appointment book was full for the next two weeks. But when, at Marie's suggestion, the secretary had consulted her boss, it turned out that his itinerary was not as rigid as it had appeared. Marie's appointment was fixed at three-thirty that same afternoon.

She used the ladies room before going in to see him. A hair had appeared on her left cheek, and she plucked it and flushed it down the drain. Where did they come from? Facial hairs, Jesus. Didn't they know she was a woman?

He was a tall man, three or four inches over six feet, broad shoulders. His suit was silver-grey, tailored well to hide a paunch; conservative tie and shoes. He had a small but immaculate collection of chins. His hair, which was plentiful, was a couple of inches longer than you would expect. Vanity, thought Marie. And a sexual magnetism about him which he did nothing to disguise.

His smile was disarming. It activated well over half a century of laugh lines, but in no way diverted one from the serious and deep-brown hue of his eyes. The man's ace, however, was in the timbre of his voice. Marie had never quite worked out if that professional voice was a gift from God, or something that was developed. Many politicians had it, some broadcasters and actors, and the best doctors and salesmen. It was designed to put you at your ease, take you off guard, so that you could be severely shafted from the rear.

Marie sat down.

'I thought you might have brought me a cheque,' he said. He could have smiled again, then. It was hard to tell.

'Not part of my brief, I'm afraid, Mr Blake.'

'But, off the record, of course, can I look forward to early settlement now the police have dropped the case?'

'As I said, that's not my department. But I have been led to believe that our investigation is not to be protracted unnecessarily.'

'Good,' he said. 'How can I help?'

'I have to ask some personal questions,' Marie explained. 'And I'm also going to have to talk about your late wife, India. I don't want to upset you in any way, but—'

'Just ask,' he interrupted. 'During the time I was in police custody, any feelings I may have had were completely shredded. I assure you I won't be upset. My only desire is to put the whole sorry story as far behind me as possible. I'll answer all your questions as fully as I can.'

'Did your wife have any intimate friends?'

'I'm sure you can do better than that,' he said. 'Good Lord, a private investigator with a sense of delicacy. This really won't do, Ms Dickens. What you mean is, was my wife having an affair? Did she have a lover? Isn't that what you're saying?'

Marie nodded.

'No. India was a faithful wife. She did not have a lover.'

'But would you have known? Many cuckolded husbands are the last to suspect.'

'Is that the voice of experience?' A hard edge had come into his tone, and he checked that now. 'I'm sorry. I try to be objective, but it still gets to me. My wife was eighteen years my junior, but I believe she loved me. You may well think I'm an old fool who's deluding himself, and you are, of course, free to hold any opinions you wish. But I'm sure you'll take your investigation into other quarters, as did the police before you, and I doubt very much if you'll turn up any evidence to the contrary. My wife was faithful, and she was murdered by a kidnapper who was clever enough to avoid capture. I know that is not a very satisfying solution for you, and I assure you that it is not for me, either. But it is all we have got, Ms Dickens. And unless the kidnapper decides to come forward and identify himself, it is all we are likely to have.'

'What about the insurance?' Marie asked. 'Why did you insure your wife for such a large sum at that particular time?'

'My financial adviser had a heart attack. I had liquid funds to dispose of. An insurance policy seemed a good idea.'

A very good idea, thought Marie. Especially in retrospect.

'I bought a small house as an investment at the same time. And a car. All during the same week. You can ask my secretary for the accounts when you leave. I've asked her to give you access to anything you think pertinent.'

She was a middle-aged secretary with a blue rinse and a tired smile. Definitely not a steroid enthusiast. Marie didn't have to ask to discover that the woman had three children (all girls, to her husband's eternal disappointment) before retraining and returning to work. This was her fourth job during the second phase of her working life, and Marie foresaw that the woman would have several more in the future. It was impossible to stop her talking. She was like an amplifier: tuned in to her own internal stream of consciousness and broadcasting out to the universe.

She found some of the documents Marie needed, but couldn't put her hands on the bank statements covering the week when Edward Blake had taken out the insurance policy on his wife. 'Goodness, I had them earlier,' she said. 'Mr Blake thought you'd want to check them, and I made a point of getting them ready. You know how it is, I'll find them as soon as you've gone. Probably be looking out of the window to see if your car's gone from the car park.'

'You could fax them to the office,' Marie told her, giving her a card, trying to make a getaway before the woman worked up a second steam.

When she got back to the car park Marie checked the car for tracking devices. Women like the blue-rinse secretary always seemed to know where to find her. Once inside the car she let the engine turn over while she sat with her forehead on the steering wheel, her eyes closed. 'If there's a god,' she said, speaking into the far reaches of the cosmos, 'please don't let me end up like that.'

Dr Simon Cod met Marie at the entrance to his office in the York District Hospital. He was a full head smaller than her, maybe forty years old. He had a broad smile, carefully cultivated to hide every one of his feelings. To Marie's knowledge he never took it off. Perhaps, if a person was to go to bed with him, get really intimate, he might remove it then? Marie didn't know, and she didn't intend to find out. A night with a guy that short, and for what? So he could stop smiling for a while? Christ, right after breakfast he'd look just the same as he did every other day of his life.

The smile was there now, on his face, and it really was very good. You wouldn't know it was a mask unless you spent some time with him. He had all the earnestness of a Lada salesman.

'Marie,' he said. 'Still playing at being a detective, I see. Such a shame, when you have good qualifications, excellent experience. You're sadly missed in the department.'

That was another thing. It wasn't just the smile. The sad little bastard was patronizing, too. But Marie could play that game.

'It was you who gave me the idea, Simon. Pathology is a kind of detective work, isn't it?'

'Pathology? Yes, I suppose so. Post-mortem certainly is, and I think that's why you've come to see me.'

He led her into the office and retrieved a large file, which he flipped open. 'Mrs India Blake, deceased.' He sighed, looking down at a photograph of the woman, taken a few weeks before her abduction. 'Such a waste.'

Marie looked over his shoulder. India Blake had been a striking woman. She was thirty-six, but could easily have passed for someone in her late twenties. The photograph was taken by some fashionable professional, and showed a beautiful woman wearing a thirties' style coat with heavily padded shoulders. The coat was open, revealing a black lace blouse and a skirt with a cut to die for. The gaze of the woman was upward, past the left shoulder of the photographer, nonchalant, wistful, as though the camera had caught her unawares, in a private moment.

Behind her was a parapet, and beyond that a series of rooftops. It could have been taken on the city walls, or the roof of the Minster, but Marie didn't think so. Maybe the photographer had a penthouse studio somewhere?

Cod handed her a list of substances found in and around the allotment shed. 'That's a list of everything we've identified,' he said. 'The second column shows where it was found, and the third column is a guesstimate of the approximate quantity.'

The next photograph had been taken inside the allotment shed shortly after the corpse had been found. If you looked really hard you could have identified her by the hair. There was no face left. The bugs and crawlies had got inside her eyes and stripped the flesh from her nose. Her lips had gone, as had most of the tissue from the inside of her mouth. There was still some flesh on her forehead and chin, creamy coloured, like full-fat cheese, but with black marks.

The body had been concealed beneath the flooring of the shed. A couple of teenagers looking for somewhere to screw had disturbed the flooring and found something that put a strain on their relationship before it ever got going.

'*Piophila casei*,' Simon Cod told her. He held up a cellophane bag. Inside was a small fly. 'Known as the cheese skipper, because it's a pest in stored cheese and bacon, which to its simple mind is dead meat. This is the adult variety. She appears quite early on a dead body, but her larvae are never apparent before two months, and often take between three and six months to show themselves. There were no cheese skipper larvae on the body of India Blake.'

Marie peered at the fly, but didn't find it very interesting. 'OK,' she said. 'So this, *thing*, tells us that death occurred less than two months before the body was discovered. So she was alive for about a month after she disappeared?'

'Right. But, speaking biologically, death is more of a process than an event. Different tissues and organs die at different rates. We also found these.' He showed her another sample. 'The pupa of *Diptera*, blowflies to you. The adults are usually the first to arrive, they colonize the natural openings of the body, the mouth, nose, eyes, ears, vagina, penis, anus, and any injury sites.'

'Yuk,' said Marie.

The doctor smiled. 'Yuk, indeed, Marie. Having said all that, they usually concentrate on the head area, or on open wounds. But in the case of Ms Blake there was a heavy infestation of the vaginal area. This would lead us to suspect some injury in that area, maybe the result of a rape, perhaps something worse.'

'You don't know?'

'There wasn't enough tissue left to know, but the circumstantial evidence leads us to speculate.'

'Anything else?'

'Yes, these little chaps' – he indicated the pupa of the blowflies – 'tell us almost to the day when she died. Give or take a day either side, she had been dead for three weeks.'

'No longer?'

He shook his head.

'But she was missing for three months. How long does it take to starve to death?'

'She didn't starve to death. She dehydrated. She was

undernourished, too. There seems little doubt that she was abandoned there. Whoever put her in the hole left her with no food or water.'

'How long?' Marie said.

He shook his head. 'A week? She wouldn't know much about the last couple of days.'

'But why keep her alive for two months, longer than that, and then leave her to die?'

'You asking me?' said the doctor. 'I thought you were the detective.'

'And the pregnancy,' said Marie. 'How old was the foetus?'

'Sixty to sixty-five days. It was developing in very bad conditions. But somewhere around there.'

'A couple of months. About the same time she was kidnapped?'

'Yes. Just before or just after.'

He sat at his desk beaming at her as though he'd invented her. Christ, she thought. Dr Simon Cod. Not exactly a traffic stopper. When Marie had worked at the hospital he'd sniffed around her as if she was a bitch on heat. He was the kind of guy, when he wasn't around any more, you missed him like a cold sore.

She glanced at the list of substances found in and around the allotment shed. Many of the names were unreadable, but some she recognized. Charcoal, cyanide, Dettol, glycerine, greasepaint, horse manure, nicotine, nitrate of soda, paraffin, pyrethrum, soot, talc, Vaseline, washing-soda, wood-ash . . . Marie dropped the list on to the passenger seat and turned on the ignition.

One or more of those substances could have been brought into the shed by the murderer. But which one? And even if it was possible to isolate one of them, and say, yes, this is it, this is what he brought with him, what then? Where would it lead, say, if the murderer had left behind a quantity of tincture of opium?

They were waiting for her in the sitting room in Sam and Dora's house. Sam had gone upstairs to talk with Dora, but Geordie and Celia were sitting there, drinking Sam's coffee which was the best coffee in the world. And Geordie introduced her to the other guy, J.D. Pears, the writer. I suppose you have to call it chemistry, she thought. It was there right from the first moment they clapped eyes on each other. He couldn't hide it, he was really interested in her. And she was so taken with him she didn't hear a word Geordie said. Only J.D. Everything else was a blur.

'What?' she said, taking her eyes off the guy before everyone got embarrassed.

'J.D. Pears,' said Geordie. 'Sam says it's OK for him to follow us around. He's doing research.'

'For a book,' J.D. explained. 'I write crime novels. Need some info on how you gumshoes work.'

Marie nodded her head. She wanted to take his glasses off, ruffle his hair a little. But then again she wanted to leave him exactly as he was. Not spoil the picture one little bit. Except maybe for the beard.

'So,' he continued, 'would you mind if I join you for a few days? I'll only be hovering around in the background.'

Marie was still nodding her head.

Celia, Sam's elderly secretary, said, 'Marie, sweetheart, why don't you sit down, have some coffee. You look like you've had a busy day.'

By the time Sam came down and Marie had got halfway through her second cup of coffee, she'd begun to be coherent.

She told them what the doctor had said about the body, and gave her impressions of Edward Blake.

'Did he do it?' asked Geordie. 'You think he killed her?'

'He's decidedly iffy,' Marie said. 'But that doesn't make him a murderer.'

'So I missed something today,' J.D. said. 'You've been grilling the main suspect, and I wasn't there.'

Marie turned towards him to tell him he could be with her tomorrow, the next day, he could be with her whenever he wanted. But in the turn she forgot what she was going to say. Instead, she said, 'Are you married?'

She looked at him, her mouth open.

J.D.'s eyes surveyed the room. 'Used to be,' he said. 'But she lammed off with another woman.'

'They don't make them like they used to,' Marie told him.

7

Sam's footsteps on the stairs. He opens the door quietly, expecting you to be sleeping. You never sleep, though, only close your eyes. Barney raises his head. He keeps you company; sits upright, ears cocked like an ornament.

Sam comes to the chair and takes your hand. What does he want, this strange young man? Well, young for you. What does he want with your thin and pale hand, your diseased and decaying body? Why does he care?

'Penny for them,' he says.

You shrug your shoulders. You don't need a penny.

'A kiss, then,' he says, bringing his face forward. You feel his lips on your nose, the aroma of digested coffee and peppermint toothpaste.

You shake your head. He makes you feel like a girl, and you don't like that. You are not a girl. You are a living corpse.

He kisses your cheek. He is better looking than Dylan Thomas. There are no tickly bristles, no smell of figs, nothing moralistic or priest-like about him. He has no expectations. Is it possible? He leaves you free.

His face is all smiles. His eyes are wide. He is playing a game. You push him away, not too roughly, telling him he must guess. Your voice croaks, and something moves in your throat. Something that should not be there. Something that is growing.

'The past,' he says, going straight to the mark. He has found you out. He knows your mind. He would like to protect you against the past, drag you out of it into the light of the present. But it is your life, Dora, you can't leave it behind. Not even for Sam.

'The children?'

You shake your head.

'Arthur?'

'Yes.' For a moment you feel as though you will weep. A tear comes to your eye and hovers behind the lid. But it dissolves there and slips back inside you.

Sam squeezes your hand and places his head on your lap. He wants to reach back through the years for you, wishes he could pluck you out of the horror and hold you close to him in the here and now.

You stroke his head. You run your white fingers through his hair. Your life is overshadowed by a pear tree, but grace has been sent to you, late and lovely.

'Arthur's dead,' he says. 'He's dead and gone, Dora.'

Dead? Arthur?

What a cruel thing it was.

Money was the problem. Money was the barrier. You could not leave, not with two children and no money.

Money? Surely not? But it *was* a barrier then. You had to think of the children. If it had been now it would not have mattered. Now you would have taken the chance, starved if necessary.

You earned a little. Private tuition, coaching the children of the rich. Arthur did not take it into account. You were supposed to use it on clothes for the children. You put half of it in a biscuit tin, high up in the larder behind the Kilner jars. Only mice moved up there.

When enough pennies and twenty pence pieces and pounds had accumulated in the tin you changed them for five pound notes, ten pound notes, and eventually a twenty pound note. You remember the twenty pound note, you remember the first large, twenty pound note, bringing it home and standing on the chair in the larder to reach the tin. It crackled as you folded it neatly into four and hid it away out of reach. The tin was as light as the dream it represented.

Was it you, Dora? Was it really you? The woman is tall and thin, already the fine skin around her eyes is beginning to crease. Her three-year-old daughter is playing in the garden, her baby son is sleeping in his cot, her husband out at work. The sun is in the living room, and the back of the house is in shadow. She stands in the doorway, moving from one foot to another. She rattles a few coins in the pocket of her apron, her head cocked to one side. She is listening. All her senses are alive.

She takes a chair from the kitchen and stands it inside the larder door. In a moment she is on the chair and reaching up into the dark of the topmost shelf. She glances at the three ten pence pieces in the palm of her hand and drops them into the biscuit tin. A moment later she is back at the door, moving from foot to foot, her listening head cocked.

That was the first time you put money in the tin which you had not earned yourself, Dora. Those three ten pence pieces were saved from the housekeeping money. You bought bones instead of meat. You were learning to survive.

Dora Greenhills. Guilty.

If anyone else had done it, Dora, you would have been the first to forgive them. But you could not forgive yourself. You were a thief. You were faithless. Your self-respect, your dignity, they ebbed away like the murky waters of the Ouse. You submitted to Arthur's beatings with something approaching the joy of a penitent. When his white and hairy forearms took you from behind, cutting your lungs off from the world, and the fist of his free hand pummelled your kidneys, then, and for a time afterwards, you were released from guilt. You were a Catholic during those years, Dora. You were a Catholic and Arthur was your priest.

But your will was not broken. Every week something went into the tin. You changed your coins to notes, and the notes into higher denominations, until finally you had

57

enough to buy a broken-down house on the banks of the River Foss. A house surrounded by factories and shaken by lorries, a house with no garden and only poky, grimed windows. A house of your own. Paradise.

The switchboard operator put you through. Arthur had that note of impatience, something approaching anger in his voice. He didn't like you to ring him at work.

'Dora? What is it? I'm busy at the moment.'

'I've left you.' The line buzzed into silence.

'What are you talking about, Dora? Can't we speak about this later?'

'No, Arthur. I mean it. I've left the house. It's no good trying to find me. I've only taken what's mine, or what the children will need. Goodbye.'

'Dora—'

You have taken little. Your small collection of records by Lady Day. 'Let's Call The Whole Thing Off'.

'Dora—'

You put the telephone down. Guilt is tangled with relief and another, wilder, emotion. Irresponsibility? You do not stop to analyse your feelings. You are liberated. Free. You have released yourself. You walk along the narrow, grey streets of your new neighbourhood, Diana and Billy at your side. There is a smell of cement and foam rubber in the air. Diana has something in her eye and wants to go home, but to her proper home, where she lives with Daddy. Billy wants to look at the boats on the river. You take in great gulps of air and sand, and you swallow them down.

8

William wondered if he was going off. A large black bruise had formed itself on his inner right thigh and it was the middle of the night and he was in the street where Dora lived. It was dry but there was the ghost of a storm lingering in the air.

Going off. It was a phrase he'd come across in a magazine called *Harpers & Queen*, which he'd found abandoned in the launderette. An article about serial killers. They killed to a pattern, but all the time there was a psychosis growing inside their minds, and eventually the psychosis took over the pattern and they lost it. They *went off*. Killed randomly, indiscriminately.

William had read the magazine from cover to cover. He'd started with the article about serial killers, then he'd read an article about the best schools for posh people's children. There were so many articles he couldn't remember them all. One about Rolex watches, how the cases were made out of a single piece of metal. Another about how at Christmas a bottle of Chanel No. 5 is sold every five seconds. He'd read all the adverts for skin clinics and cosmetic surgery, for introduction agencies and body-management clinics, home gyms and health farms. In this magazine you could find everything you'd never need, from clowns to stretch limousines.

But he'd come back to the article on serial killers and read it again. He'd torn those pages out of the magazine and taken them home with him. The other articles held you for a moment, but this one was compulsive.

Going off.

A strange expression. Not like going off on holiday. Not like that at all.

William only came here in the middle of the night. For the last weeks – was it months? – there had been a light in her room. It was as if she didn't sleep. As if she sat up all night waiting for someone to release her.

He went around the back of the house and climbed over the wall into the garden. The shed was still there, on his right. The fruit bushes in the centre of the garden, and the climbing rose on the trellis. Up near the house was the pear tree, and William walked underneath it and leaned against its sturdy trunk.

He was shaking, but soon regained control of his body, forced it to become still. His will-power dominated flesh and blood, extinguished emotion. An owl began to hoot but shut down in mid call. William ruled the night. The natural world quivered.

He stood in silence. Thoughts of Dora welled up, the sense of her proximity turned his mind. His head was a cauldron of rage. He fabricated an image in which he waded knee-deep in her blood.

He waited for the ghosts.

9

Dora was awake upstairs and Sam was down in the kitchen making a pot of tea. He wanted to go to an AA meeting. *Now.* But it wasn't possible. There were no midnight meetings in York. And even if there had been one, he wouldn't have gone. He couldn't leave Dora alone.

Still, when the feeling came on it was difficult to shake.

He'd go to the meeting tomorrow. There was nothing to drink in the house. All the pubs were closed. All the supermarkets. Booze was out of the question.

Except he knew maybe a dozen places he could get something to drink right now. A dozen places? At least fifty.

He rang Max, his sponsor. 'You're not in bed?' Sam asked.

'Yes, I'm in bed. I've got the light on, and I'm reading a book about Edward Hopper and watching the midnight movie and talking to an alcoholic on the telephone.'

'Just so long as you're not under pressure, Max.'

'Pressure? Hell, I'm looking for a priest, here.' He laughed. 'You want to come over, Sam? Or shall I come over there?'

'No need. I just wanted to talk to someone who was winning.'

'That's me. *And* you. How's Dora?'

'She's great right now. Marie was with her for half an hour tonight. We're gonna have some tea and a chat.'

'Make hers how she likes it, but put sugar in yours. And use a big mug. Tell her I asked about her. Give her my love.'

'Thanks, Max. You're a lifeline.'

'Hey, Sam, we sponsor each other, remember. How many times do I ring you?'

'Plenty, I guess. You can go to sleep now. I'm not gonna drink tonight. One drink'll be too much, and a hundred won't be enough.'

He heard Max laughing as he put the phone down.

Sam made the tea like Max said, and took it upstairs to Dora. Tea with sugar was something he'd never get used to. But it was medicine. Something you had to take to remind yourself not to drink Scotch.

Barney got to his feet when Sam entered the room.

Dora was propped up with pillows. Her eyes were shining with anticipation. No pain for the time being, just Dora feeling good and looking forward to spending time with Sam. She stretched out a hand to him as he sat by the bed, and he took it in his. The thinnest hand in the known universe.

'Tell me about the day,' she said. 'About the world and what's happening.'

'We've got a guy working with us, a writer. J.D. Pears. Everyone calls him J.D.'

'Everyone except Marie,' Dora said, laughing. 'She calls him Mister Right Now.'

'Yeah, she's taken with him. The temperature goes up every time they look at each other.'

'That's nice for her. She's usually so down on men. Expects more of them than they can give.'

'Yeah, but that's healthy,' said Sam. 'Keeps her out of trouble. J.D., on the other hand, appears kind of green. Like he's got no idea what a woman in love will do.'

'Well, he's going to find out. She's itching to get her hands on him.'

'Christ,' said Sam, shaking his head. 'I promised Jill Sheridan she'd get a thorough investigation into Edward Blake. I hope Marie's gonna concentrate on it.'

Dora stroked the back of his hand. 'She will, Sam. She

might be counting the hours until knocking-off time, but she won't shirk the job. You know that.'

'Yeah, I know. And I'm glad for Marie. She's had a tough time since Gus was killed. And J.D. seems to like her all right. But he's a gambler.'

'What does that mean?'

'Means what it says. The guy's a gambler.'

'Horses?'

Sam shook his head. 'Five card draw. Plays in some heavy games around town. Including one patronized by Edward Blake.'

'How do you know all this, Sam?'

'It came out in our talk. I had to tell him about Blake, because he's gonna be with Marie and Geordie, inquiring about the guy. And he said he knew him. Then he had to tell me where he knew him from. The two of them play in a Tuesday game in Patrick Pool.'

'Isn't there some conflict of interest there?'

'I wondered about that,' said Sam. 'But J.D.'s not particularly friendly with Blake. And, anyway, he's only tagging along as an observer.'

'He'll be OK, Sam. Marie's not looking for a husband, you know. She's just found someone irresistible.'

'And he plays in a band. Drums. Band called Fried and the Behaviourists.'

'Freud, surely?'

'No, that's what I said. Freud and the Behaviourists. But it isn't, it's *fried*.'

'As in egg?'

Sam nodded. 'He's a real character. Talks like someone who's just walked out of an American crime novel, sometimes like a man in a western.'

Dora squeezed his hand and closed her eyes. She smiled, and Sam knew she would be asleep in a moment. 'J.D.?' she said, opening her eyes. 'Is *he* fried?'

Sam left a long gap there, so she'd have to go back, look

at that last sentence all over again. He said, 'Can I get back to you on that one?'

She closed her eyes and Sam watched her. She shook gently with laughter; she was radiant like an overblown plant at the end of a glorious summer. A rose with heavy, lush petals, in those final hours before they begin to fall.

When her breathing eased into a regular pattern, he let go of her hand and left the room.

J.D. was probably OK, but you could never take coincidences for granted. If J.D. owed Edward Blake money, and if Blake wanted to know how the investigation was proceeding, this would be an easy way of finding out. Sam didn't think that was what was happening, but he couldn't discount it either. Not at this stage of the game. J.D. Pears would have to be watched, and by a more critical eye than Marie's.

He slipped *Bringing It All Back Home* into the CD player and selected track eleven. Didn't know why, but he listened to the words until the beginning of the second verse. Then he smiled. He'd tell Marie tomorrow, or the next day. Maybe the day after that. Whenever there was an opening so it didn't sound like he was preaching. The highway is for gamblers.

Marie thought things through, anyway. She didn't need Sam to tell her to use her sense. And if passion had the upper hand at the moment, she wouldn't appreciate Sam getting in her face. He knew better than to do that. Catch Sam Turner standing in the way of a tenacious hormone? No way, he'd heard the music himself from time to time; it'd be easier to stop a bull.

Something else he'd learned from J.D.: Blake was on the Millennium Committee. The guy moved in exalted circles. He was perfect for the villain of the piece. As a lobbyist he paid MPs to put pressure on ministers, so that his big-money clients could screw the electorate. He was a moral scumbag. But would someone like him go the extra yard and kill his wife?

Sam shook his head. He didn't know the answer. But he did know that you can't rule anyone out. And when someone was killed with violence, statistically the perpetrator was the person they were married to.

Sam took the CD out of the player and put it back in its case. He went quietly up the stairs and stood by Dora's bed. Her eyes flickered for a moment, then opened. She said: 'Sam, I'd like to see Billy again.'

Her son, Billy. She hadn't seen him or heard from him for years. Sam had never met him. 'I'll try,' he said. 'Maybe Diana'll have an address? But if he doesn't want to be found, I won't be able to do much about it.'

Dora had gone back to sleep. Maybe she hadn't been awake. She knew too much to argue.

An hour later Sam was sitting in a chair downstairs, the television with the sound switched down to drooling level, wondering if he should go to bed. He pressed the buttons on the telephone without lifting the receiver. Practising.

10

She was white, looking thinner than normal, especially her face, her eyes wide and dark. 'I feel sick,' Janet said. Geordie panicked momentarily, a quick flutter at his breast, a tightening around his hairline. Then he breathed again. Something she'd eaten, or too much work.

'Why don't you go back to bed?' he asked. 'I'll give Marie and J.D. a bell. They can manage without me for a day.'

'No.' Janet shook her head. 'I'm going to work. We're expecting deliveries. It'll be chaos if I'm not there.'

'But if you're being sick—'

'I'm not being sick, Geordie. I feel queasy. It'll pass.'

Geordie was standing in the doorway to the bathroom, Janet with her back to the wash basin. She went over to him and touched his face, and he leaned forward to kiss her forehead.

'You sure?' he said.

'Yeah. I'll be all right.'

'I should go in, as well. I said J.D. could come with me today. I'm gonna see the woman who used to be Edward Blake's secretary.' He looked at his watch. 'Time to go.'

'I'm ready,' Janet said. She followed him outside, grabbing a coat from a hook and putting it on while she waited for Geordie to lock the door. Barney looked up at her, his head cocked to one side. Banks of dark cloud had stacked themselves up over the playing field – shadowy, heavy. But to the south the clouds were grey, blue, fluffy. Over the ditch at the bottom of the garden there was a huge tree. Geordie didn't know what kind of tree it was. He made another mental note to look it up in a book.

66

When Geordie looked back a couple of years, to the time Sam had picked him out of the gutter, he sometimes thought it was a dream. But it wasn't. He had been a homeless down-and-out, and for some reason Sam Turner had pulled him out of it. Geordie would never understand why. And he'd never stop being grateful.

Look at him now – not only Janet, and a house with real radiators for the winter, but all this nature as well: trees, and birds, horses in fields.

They hadn't switched on the heating yet, because it would cost money and it wasn't really cold enough. But when they'd moved in during the summer they'd run it one day, just to make sure it worked. The whole house had been unbearably hot. They'd had to open all the windows and take off their clothes.

At the end of the track they waited a couple of minutes for the bus, and sat together on the back seat, looking out at the other commuters making their way into York.

In the city, Geordie left Janet outside the remainder bookshop where she worked, and walked on to the office.

J.D. and Marie were already there, standing close to each other by the window. They turned towards him as he came in, both of them with a sheepish smile. Marie looked like Janet sometimes looked on a Sunday morning after a late Saturday night and a bit of a sleep in. J.D. just looked rough. His beard was pointing in a dozen different directions. But he jerked into life when he saw Geordie.

'Ready when you are, partner,' he said. 'I just have to shake the dew from my lily.' He made his way to the door, and along the corridor to the lavatory.

Geordie looked at Marie, and she hit him with a quick smile and a shrug of the shoulders. 'Yeah, he's a bit naff,' she said. 'But he knows how to treat a girl.'

'I like him,' Geordie told her. 'And I'm glad for you.'

'Yeah, yeah,' said Marie, embarrassed. 'I've shelved all

plans to join a convent for the time being. Jesus's got enough brides to be going on with. I don't think he'll miss this one.'

'I could do without him for today. J.D., I mean. If you'd rather he went with you?'

'No, Geordie. You take him. I want space. I mean, I really like him, but I need to breathe as well.'

J.D. returned and went to Marie. He put his arm around her waist and looked at Geordie. 'Son,' he said, 'I've been stabbed with a white wench's black eye, and shot through the ear with a love song.'

Marie pushed him away, clasped her hand to her breast. 'Be still, my beating heart.' She turned to Geordie. 'Mercy,' she said. 'Get him out of here.'

'Where we goin'?' J.D. asked.

Geordie waited for the car in front to peel off into Lord Mayor's Walk, then accelerated along Clarence Street. 'Wiggington,' he said.

'It's not going to be dangerous, is it? I'm not a coward, but dead men sell no tales.'

It took a while for Geordie to get the joke. And when he got it he didn't think it was funny. Still laughed though, to be polite.

J.D. turned his head towards Geordie, as if expecting more. But Geordie concentrated on the driving. It was true what he'd told Marie, he did like J.D. Or at least he had liked him when they first met. But now that the guy was having a steamy affair with Marie, Geordie was having to reorganize all his preconceptions. And that took time.

Geordie didn't have any claims on Marie. He didn't like her like that, anyway. She was thirteen years older than him, and even if they'd been the same age it wouldn't have made any difference. She wasn't his type, and he was sure that he wasn't her type either. They were friends. And that was the problem.

Marie lived alone, and had done since her husband, Gus,

had been blown away by a particularly nasty psychopath. After that episode Geordie didn't think she'd ever have anything to do with another man. But over the past months she'd had a couple of dates. Nothing serious. The odd night on the town. She might've gone to bed with one of the guys. The soft one, whatever he was called. Stuart? Yeah, Stuart.

All of that Geordie had taken in his stride. Marie deserved a few breaks. A woman living alone, not out of choice, but because she'd been made a widow far too early. That was not something you'd wish on anyone.

'I like her,' J.D. said, as if he'd been reading Geordie's thoughts. 'I like her, and she likes me. Neither of us have got anybody else. We both want this, for Christ's sake. What's wrong with that?'

'Nothing,' said Geordie. 'It's great.'

'So what's with all the downcast looks and the long silences? Shit, as soon as you saw us together you brought out the morgue atmosphere. I'm telling you, friend, something's bothering you, and if it isn't me and Marie, what is it?'

'Yeah, OK,' Geordie admitted. 'I don't know how to explain it, though. It's like Marie's been a friend of mine for ages. And I knew Gus as well, her husband. She tell you about that?'

'How he bought it? Yes.'

'Well, what it is, I don't want her to get hurt.'

'Why should I hurt her?'

'I don't know.'

'D'you think everybody's gonna hurt her? I mean guys. You think her other boyfriends are gonna hurt her?'

'No.' Geordie took his eyes off the road and looked over at J.D. 'I'm sorry. I can't explain it.'

'OK, I'll tell you, Geordie. What you saw between us this morning was passion. And it's passion that you're afraid of. Passion that you think might hurt her.'

'You think so? I didn't think that.'

'OK, maybe you weren't aware of it, but that's what sent you looking for a nervous breakdown. And you might be right. Passion is a powerful force. Marie might get mauled by it. And me. All of us. But if that happens, you won't be able to stop it. Marie and me are thinking about each other all the time. We've been waiting years for this, and now it's come. It's like toothache. You can't get away from it.'

Geordie was quiet for several minutes. 'I'm sorry,' he said eventually. 'It was a gut reaction. I'm glad for her. Glad for both of you. Me and Janet was like that at first.' He laughed. 'We still are sometimes.'

They entered a large estate in which the houses were of different sizes, but looked alike. The roads were designed with a gentle curve to them. Geordie stopped at the edge of a perfectly trimmed lawn, and he and J.D. walked along the path to the house.

The woman who opened the door was under forty. She had blond hair cut short, and wore a lumberjack checked shirt and baggy jeans. She smiled and raised her eyebrows in the most wholesome way imaginable.

'I'm Geordie Black, and this is my associate, J.D. Pears. We have an appointment to see Ms Marsh.'

'I'm Polly Marsh,' she said. 'Sorry, I think I was expecting someone a little older.'

'I get a little older every day,' Geordie told her. He was pleased with that. It came to him naturally, out of the air. And it was the kind of thing Sam would've said. A bit of spontaneous funny to put everyone at their ease.

They followed her through a small reception area into a long living room. She turned to face them, and waved in the direction of a plush-looking sofa. 'Just one thing,' she said. 'It's Miss, not Ms. I'm still in the market for a husband, and they tend to get scared off easily when there's an element of confusion.' The bright wholesome smile again. 'Now, tea or coffee?'

She got them settled, brought up a long, low coffee table with a glass top. Served tea and coffee and biscuits, and those long Italian breadsticks in a flower vase. On a separate plate lay a broken-open chocolate orange, with some of the sections stuck together.

Geordie felt it would be wrong to dive in with questions right away in front of such a spread. It would be more natural to sip the coffee and make small talk for a while, nibble a biscuit, wait at least until J.D. had finished up the chocolate orange. But Polly Marsh didn't want to wait.

'You're private detectives?' she said.

Geordie didn't want to explain who J.D. was, so he nodded and let her assume whatever she wanted.

'I did have a visit from the police,' she said, 'when Mr Blake was "helping them with their inquiries", and they said they'd be back. But I never heard from them again. I thought it was all over.'

'We're working for the insurance company,' Geordie told her. 'You were Edward Blake's secretary for how long?'

'Fourteen months. He head-hunted me. I was his solicitor's secretary before that. One day he asked me how much I was earning, and when I told him he offered me another thousand a year and a car.'

'What were your duties?'

'General Girl Friday. Everything was filtered through me. I arranged his appointments, got him off the hook when he couldn't make them. Fixed his travel arrangements, hotel accommodation, made sure he was met at airports, railway stations.' She sighed lightly. 'I organized his life. His professional life.'

'Did you travel with him?'

'Sometimes. Not often. When he was away, I looked after the office. Maybe once every couple of months I would go with him. Once to Paris, and to Antwerp, several times to London. There was never anything improper about it. If there was any spare time we went our different ways.'

'What about his wife?'

'India? Poor girl, it was a terrible shock.'

'You knew her?'

'Yes, I met her from time to time. When she came into the office. She was always friendly. Younger than him, of course, and very beautiful.'

'Did she accompany him on his trips?'

'Once, when he went to Washington. That's the only time I remember. I was hoping he'd take me along on that one. But it wasn't to be.'

'What were they like together?' Geordie asked. 'Would you say they had a good relationship?'

Polly Marsh hesitated. 'They didn't argue. He'd kiss her on the cheek when she arrived, and again when they parted. They were – conventional – I think is how it's described. They didn't have arguments, or appear to disagree in public.'

Geordie leaned forward and picked up a clump of chocolate orange. He teased one section free, and replaced the remainder on the plate. 'I'd prefer it if you'd be open with us, Miss Marsh. Whatever you have to say will go no further.'

She touched her nose. 'They were rich, and they were different ages. Mr Blake is a businessman, he's involved in everyday hassles, and that's what he likes. He rolls his sleeves up and sweats about money. But India was something else. She was into culture. She'd never had to worry about money. Her life was music and theatre. Books. I never saw her without a book.'

'You're still expecting me to read between the lines.'

'It wasn't a love match. Their marriage was a social convention. A front.' Geordie watched her clench her fists. She looked into his eyes. 'But half a love is better than none.'

Geordie thumbed through his thoughts. 'Did he kill her, d'you think?'

Polly Marsh drew in her breath. 'No, I don't think he's capable of that.'

'Then who do you think was responsible?'

'Oh, Edward Blake,' she said. 'He didn't do it himself. He probably paid someone else to do it.'

Geordie glanced over at J.D., then turned to face Polly Marsh again. He licked his lips. 'But why, Miss Marsh? What possible motive could he have had?'

Polly Marsh had her legs crossed. Now she uncrossed them and looked into Geordie's eyes. 'India Blake was a good woman,' she said. 'She was young and healthy and full of life. And I think she would have continued to stand by her husband for as long as he wanted her. But Edward Blake is a cold fish emotionally. All her needs couldn't possibly have been met by a man like him.'

'You think she may have had an affair?'

'Oh, yes,' said the wholesome Miss Marsh. 'No doubt about it at all. She was seeing someone else.'

'Do you have a name?'

She shook her head. 'Not even a description, I'm afraid. I didn't actually see her with anyone else. But I overheard a telephone conversation. A couple of weeks before she disappeared, she made an appointment to see a man. Mr Blake was away, and she came into the office one lunchtime. That wasn't odd in itself. She'd often slip in if she was in town. But she asked me to give her an outside line, and—'

'You overheard her conversation?' said Geordie.

Geordie noted Miss Marsh's composure vanish as quickly as hot pee in a cold ocean. 'It wasn't deliberate. I was doing something else, and the conversation got taped.'

'That's OK. Relax, Miss Marsh, I'm not going to judge you. Do you have the tape?'

'No, of course not. When I heard it later I wiped it immediately.'

'But you're sure she didn't mention a name? Anything at all that might give us a clue to who he was?'

'No. I've thought about it, of course. Lots of times, especially since they found the body. All I can be sure of is that they were lovers. It was embarrassing to listen to. They mentioned, well, body parts.'

Geordie sat back in the sofa. 'So you think Edward Blake found out about the affair and paid a hit man to get rid of his wife?'

'Something like that, yes.'

'You don't think the lover could have done it?'

'Yes, he could have, of course. But I was there when India Blake disappeared, and Edward Blake certainly wasn't himself. I mean, before he went to the police. He was absolutely calm about the whole affair. I could see he was going through the motions. His wife had disappeared, and he wasn't worried about it. Not really. He knew what had happened. Or he thought he did. He thought she was dead. He didn't know she was still alive, slowly starving to death under that shed.'

'And that's when you left the company? When he went to the police?'

'Yes. I couldn't stay there. I couldn't stand to be in the same building with him, let alone the same room.'

'The plot thickens,' said J.D. when he got into the passenger seat of the Montego and pulled the door closed behind him.

'Yeah,' said Geordie. 'It's already thicker than we thought it would be when we first unwrapped it.'

'If this was a novel,' J.D. told him, 'Polly Marsh would be about fifteen years younger, and she'd be really hot for the PI. She'd have the evidence to put Edward Blake behind bars, and old mad Eddy, there, would be concocting some foolproof plan to put her in her grave.'

'You think he did it, then?'

'He's the only suspect we've got,' said J.D. 'And the more I hear about him, the more suspicious he becomes.'

Geordie turned the key in the ignition and the Montego roared into life.

'Jesus,' said J.D. 'I never expect it to start. This must be the oldest crate in the universe.'

'Don't let Sam hear you say that,' Geordie told him. 'He's very fond of it. Put him back nearly three hundred notes.'

11

You miscalculated, Dora. You forgot about the children. Diana and Billy miss Arthur. They don't like living in this new house with the grimy windows. Diana wants to go back to her old school, and both of them want to play in the avenue with their friends. Billy does not sleep at night. He creeps into your bed and talks about his father. 'Where's Daddy? Why doesn't Daddy come to see us? When are we going home again? Why, Mammy, why?'

Arthur's ghost hovers over the bed. *Well, Dora. The boy asked a question. Tell him why.*

'Shhhhhhhh.' You hold Billy tightly, pulling the covers over your head. 'Hush, Billy. You must try to sleep.'

Arthur had been reading *The Pied Piper of Hamelin* to him before you moved. Billy cries for the lame boy who was left behind when the door in the mountain-side shut fast.

> It's dull in our town since my playmates left!
> I can't forget that I'm bereft . . .

He is quiet for a while, but never still. He cannot rest. His legs move all the time. You try to hold them down, but he struggles against you. His legs are like snakes in the bed.

'Billy. Be still.' You whip back the covers and slap him. You feel his eyes in the darkness, they are pinned to his face with staring pupils. He holds his breath until you think he is dead.

'Billy.'

Silence.

'Billy.'

Then he speaks with his father's voice. 'I want to go home.'

Diana sits by the window. Her new teacher is not the same as Miss Carson. 'She's horrible. She's older than *you*.'

'Shall we go for a walk?' You force a note of gaiety into your voice.

Diana grunts by the window. Billy lolls, half on and half off his chair.

'We could walk by the river. There might be some boats.'

In the distance a longboat's siren seems to echo your words. The children are paralysed.

Billy slowly brings his eyes in line with yours. He stares you down. He is eight years old and he crushes you with his eyes. You step back, until the wall is behind you, feeling the crumbling plaster with the tips of your fingers.

'I just thought . . .' Your words won't come any more.

'I want to see Daddy.' Billy's eyes are still gripping you.

'So do I.' Diana has turned to you as well.

After a week you capitulate. On the Friday you telephone Arthur at work. He is not there. You are ready for anything. You will prostrate yourself in front of him, let him trample on you.

There will never be a way out after this. This was your final fling, Dora. It cost five years of your life. It smashed your self-image. There is nothing left now. You will have to beg. You will take whatever comes.

Billy climbs over the seats on the top of the bus. Diana sits by the window bouncing up and down in anticipation. The bus shunts from stop to stop, taking you home, back to Arthur. The children are overjoyed, but inside of you doors are closing. You look at Diana's profile, and you think, She's my daughter, and I'm going to hate her for this.

The children run ahead along the avenue. Then they run

back again, complaining that they cannot get into the house. The door is locked.

'I've got a key,' you tell them. 'Don't worry.' You stumble over a mound of post. Diana and Billy push you aside, running through the house.

'Daddy. Daddy. Where are you? We're home.' They climb the stairs.

You recognize Arthur's handwriting and pick up the note on the kitchen table. It is like a joke. You read it twice but it does not make sense: *If anyone is interested, I'm in the garden.*

You open the back door, Dora, and step outside. The garden is deserted. Arthur is not there. You walk along the path and try the door of the shed, but it is locked.

A sense of relief floods your body. Arthur must be out somewhere. It is better like that, somehow more acceptable that he comes back and finds you returned. You leave the path to collect a few fallen pears, stuffing them into your pockets, ducking under the low boughs of the huge tree. Something catches your shoulder and swings. You raise your hand to your face, expecting a branch to fall, but it is Arthur's foot which comes towards you. You step back, and again you step back, raising your eyes to take in the full picture. Your hands are in your mouth.

Arthur is hanging by his neck. His clothes are dripping wet. His head is dragged to one side, and he is swinging, ever so gently, swinging backwards and forwards, backwards and forwards.

Involuntarily you take a step towards him, but freeze to the spot as the full horror of it hits you. *If anyone is interested, I'm in the garden.* The words of his note jangle in your head like a mantra. *In the garden. In the garden. If anyone is interested.*

You can see the flies around his eyes. The sockets where his eyes used to be. Their quick movement gives animation to his features. They crawl in and out of his nose and run

78

along the ridge of his teeth. It is as if he were laughing. Laughing at you, Dora, laughing and swinging, backwards and forwards, backwards and forwards.

He has used the washing line. You recognize it, and glance at the posts to confirm it. But your eyes do not wander for long. Arthur is a hypnotist. He demands attention.

Even when you feel the movement behind you, you cannot tear your eyes away from him. You stand there transfixed until Billy's scream sends the birds clapping away over the rooftops. Then you turn and pull him into the house, collecting Diana with her saucer eyes on the way.

'Is it Daddy?' she says, as you push her into the kitchen.

12

J.D. went for the sandwiches and Marie stayed behind the wheel of the Montego watching the entrance to Edward Blake's office. With J.D. out of the car, she snapped into a different mode. Work mode. Surveillance.

In the few days since he'd arrived on her horizon she'd drawn J.D. deep into her life. He hadn't needed a lot of coaxing, either. He'd been a willing victim. But his presence certainly undermined the job.

Marie wanted to hear all about him, and to tell him about herself. His insights into her and into life in general were off-beat and fascinating. Last night she'd been to see his band in the Bonding Warehouse. Almost unbearably loud country blues and electric feedback. J.D. beating out the rhythms like the march of a chain gang or the chattering howl of a strike in the night. He staggered off the stage at the end of the set and put his arms around her. His face slick with sweat, his eyes hollow with dope. 'Take me to bed,' he said. 'Get me out of here.'

The sex was disappointing. Probably, Marie thought, because their bodies had not yet grown accustomed to each other. The closeness was good, but the act itself seemed somehow mechanical, leaving her with a sense closer to division than to consummation.

This morning Marie had wanted to be on the job by eight, but J.D. couldn't get out of bed. He wasn't a morning person. 'Why such a rush?' he said. 'We're only going to be sitting outside the guy's office.'

'This is how we work,' Marie told him. 'The early bird gets the worm.'

'Mornings. Christ,' he muttered. 'Fucking mornings. The early worm gets eaten alive.'

They'd arrived at eight-thirty, and hadn't seen Edward Blake. J.D. took a walk round the car park and found the guy's car, so they assumed he was in the office. And they'd spent the whole morning talking about five card draw.

J.D. had slowly woken up. 'What you have to know,' he said. 'You have to know the odds. Be able to calculate them. There are over two and a half million possible hands every time you deal the cards.'

'So you have to be a mathematician?'

'No. The game's exciting because, although there's all those possible hands, you're only going to end up with one of them. And to win the pot your hand doesn't have to be the best one. It wins if all the others round the table *think* it's better than theirs.'

'So it's a confidence trick?'

'Yeah. Everyone in the game is a con-man. You can't be sure of anything. Nothing is what it appears to be.'

'Sounds like hell,' she told him.

But he laughed. 'No. It's like life.'

It was good to be with him. Except when she was working. Marie loved the feeling she got from the job, the buzz. Even on a long surveillance it was always there, the anticipation, the expectation of a pay-off. Geordie and Sam complained about surveillance jobs; they couldn't stand the hanging around, the boredom. But Marie didn't mind the negatives. She loved every aspect of the job.

Edward Blake came through the front entrance and walked to his Beemer. Pin-striped suit, incongruous looking sky-blue satin tie. He used a remote to deactivate the alarm and open the driver's door, and he was inside and heading out of the car park within a couple of minutes of his appearance.

Marie looked around, but there was no sign of J.D. Her heart seemed to slip sideways at the thought of leaving him behind, but it didn't stop her. She moved into first and joined the stream of traffic a couple of vehicles behind Blake's car. They crawled forward, pedestrians passing them and disappearing into the distance.

She glanced at her watch as they joined the inner ring road, and spoke into her small Sanyo voice-activated system. 'Twelve thirty-eight. Blake left his office ten minutes back and is travelling from Museum Street along St Leonard's Place. Traffic bloody slow as usual.' She put the recorder down, then picked it up, and spoke again: 'Lost J.D. along the way. Which means he's got twice as many sandwiches as he needs, and I haven't got any.'

The Beemer indicated left in Gillygate and turned into Portland Street. Marie followed it into the cul-de-sac, reckoning that if she stayed with the traffic in Gillygate she might be in the Montego for several weeks. Not a pleasant prospect. Next time she came this way she'd remember to pack a camp stove and a chemical toilet.

Blake took the only parking space in the street. Marie drove down to the end and watched through her mirror while he found a key and opened the door of a house which appeared to be rented out as flats.

While she was backing out of the cul-de-sac, she saw Blake standing at an upstairs window. He was alone, framed by shabby curtains, and obviously at odds with the environment. He consulted his watch and looked out along the street. Then he had another go at the watch, but must have got the same time again, unless he was counting the seconds.

Marie reversed up to the junction and was attempting an illegal three point turn, when she was stopped in the middle of the road by a girl running in front of her. The girl could not yet have seen her twentieth birthday, she was loaded down with three supermarket carrier bags, and in a hurry. Blond hair with dark roots to match her black eye, a V-necked white woollen sweater, and tight jeans cut off just below the knee. An expanse of gooseflesh calf, then black plastic high-heeled sandals. When she got to the house she looked up and attempted a wave at the window where Blake had consulted his watch. Then she put her bags down on the step, opened the door with a key, collected the bags and stepped inside.

Marie reached for her tape recorder.

J.D. got to the Pancho Villa Sundance sandwich bar and joined the queue. He was awake now, and less grumpy than he'd been with Marie that morning. It was nothing to do with Marie. He was like that in the morning. That's how the day started, grumpily, and then as it wore on it got better. By the evening there was not a trace of grump left.

In normal life, where there was no relationship to worry about, he wouldn't let himself be seen in the morning. He would work. He would stay in his room in front of his computer and write. Two thousand words, minimum, before he'd inflict himself on the world.

He glanced up at the menu board and decided what to order if he ever got to the front of the queue. One chicken and paprika, one giant turkeyburger with trimmings, and an apple pie with cream. Oh, yes, and Marie's tuna salad in pitta bread without mayo, though God knows how anyone could exist on that for the whole day.

One of the guys behind the counter kept sizing him up. It's like, you know you've seen him before somewhere, but you don't know where that was. There's something familiar about him, he could be a relation. But it might be he's just someone you pass in the street, you've never actually been introduced. If it was a woman you'd smile at her, take a chance. But as it's a guy, sexual orientation unknown, you content yourself with sneaking the odd glance, hoping you'll remember where you met.

It doesn't come, though. J.D. was second in the queue now, hoping the little guy wasn't planning to inject salmonella into his turkey burger.

The woman at the head of the queue finished paying for a shipping order, packed into seven, yes, J.D. counted them twice, *seven* Pancho Villa Sundance thermal carrier bags, collected them together and struggled out of the shop. He looked down at the little guy with the raised eyebrows and said, 'One chicken and paprika, one giant turkey burger with trimmings, an apple pie with cream, and a tuna salad in pitta bread without mayo.'

The little guy blinked twice.

'Please?' J.D. said. Hoping he'd got it right.

'It's the beard,' the little guy said. 'Without the beard, you'd be J.D. Pears.' Then he smiled.

'Wimp?' J.D. said. And he knew who the guy was. They'd been to school together back in the time of Ted Heath. J.D. looked at Wimp and was swamped by a host of images that had not entered his consciousness for a quarter of a century. Simon and Garfunkel's 'Bridge Over Troubled Waters', men on the moon, Lee Marvin's 'Wanderin' Star', Decimal day, and Jimi Hendrix. '*Voodoo Chile*,' he said. 'Remember that?'

Wimp did an imitation of Hendrix, picking with his teeth at the strings of an imaginary guitar, and the thin man behind J.D. in the queue sighed heavily and shuffled his feet.

'Yeah,' said Wimp. 'And Ned Kelly. Jagger playing dressing-up games.'

'I knew your face,' J.D. told him. 'I was in the queue here, getting closer and closer, saying who is this guy? But I couldn't put the face in the right place. I'd've got home tonight, maybe even in bed just dropping off and I'd've remembered it then. Jumping out of bed, man, screaming round the bedroom in me jimjams, "Wimp, hell it was *Wimp* sold me a fucking turkey burger and I didn't recognize him."'

'Took me about ten seconds,' said Wimp. 'I saw you looking through the window, and it was like a face I knew, couldn't quite place it, but when you came through the door I'd already clocked you.'

The thin man behind J.D. coughed and looked round at the people behind him for support. 'Christ,' he said, glancing upward at a ceiling in the advanced stages of flaking.

'So, what're you up to?' J.D. asked.

Wimp turned round in a complete circle. He held his hands out. 'Sandwiches,' he said. 'Temporarily.' He looked over J.D.'s shoulder at the queue. 'Look, I'll get your order, then I'd like to talk. You got time?'

'What? Now?'

'Yeah. Just a few minutes. I've got a break coming.'

'Where?'

'Outside, there's a bench over by the green. It won't take long.'

'OK,' J.D. told him.

'What was it you wanted? Lemon chicken.'

'One chicken and paprika, one giant turkey burger with trimmings, an apple pie with cream, and a tuna salad in pitta bread without mayo.'

'You been rehearsing that?'

'Jesus,' the thin man said.

J.D. turned round. 'He's not coming, man, uses a place round the corner, the service is better.'

He'd taken the first bite out of the turkey burger when Wimp arrived and sat on the bench next to him. 'I've read your books,' he said. 'They're good. Specially *Fungal Fatigue*, that was my favourite.'

'You want to talk about my books? Wimp, my ego's as big as the next man's. When people want to talk about my books I forgive them everything and join in. Only just now I'm with somebody else, like a woman, and this is her sandwich in the bag, and she's waiting for it.'

Wimp put a hand on his shoulder to hold him down. 'No,

it's something else. Christ, J.D., you're just the same as you was at school. You haven't changed a bit. Apart from the beard, you're exactly the same. Fuckin' weird.'

J.D. sighed. 'Can we just get to it?'

'What I do,' Wimp explained. 'I work in the travel business.'

'A travel agency?'

'Yeah. I was with the big one for ten years. Last year some of us went to Nepal. Just checking it out. We were thinking of doing some more tours. There's a lot of money to be made out of that area.'

'Let me get this straight,' said J.D. 'Sandwiches aren't your main thing?'

'I told you. Sandwiches is temporary. I got hold of this dope while we were in Nepal. Temple balls. It blew my brains out.'

J.D. laughed.

'S'not funny, man. The stuff took me apart. It was more like acid, something like that. I don't do heavy dope, never have. Grass, yes. Even used to grow my own, when we had a conservatory, when I was married. And this stuff, this temple balls stuff was too much. Wasted me. I had a nervous breakdown.'

'In Nepal?'

'No, in York. I was in the hospital, shuffling round a mental ward in carpet slippers and a dressing gown. I thought I'd never get out. I was terrified.'

'Jesus,' said J.D. 'I never heard of dope that could do that. You sure you wasn't on anything else?'

Wimp shook his head. 'It's me, man. I can't take it, that's all. The other guys I was with, they smoke it all the time, they bake it in cakes, slip the odd shavings in their mother-in-laws' coffee. You know, the usual stuff. I wanna get rid of it.'

'You brought me to this bench to unload dope on me?'

'That was the first thing I thought, when I saw your face

86

through the shop window. J.D. Pears sent from Jesus to take this fuckin' dope off my hands. Was I right?'

'Maybe,' said J.D. cagily. 'I'm only a poor writer. What's the deal?'

'I'm not on the make here, J.D. All I want is what I wanted in the first place, some good old-fashioned, *mild*, dope. A straight exchange.'

'How much have you got?'

'A weight.'

'All right. So if I come up with a weight of something *gentle*, you'll take it away and give me a weight of Nepalese temple balls that's guaranteed to blow my mind, and the minds of all my friends, and make me the most popular guy in town?'

Wimp nodded. 'That's the deal.'

'No catch?'

'No catch, J.D. D'you wanna do it?'

'Let me think a minute.'

'Think all you want.' Wimp was quiet for two seconds. He looked back at the sandwich shop. 'So, have we got a deal? You gonna go for this dope?'

J.D. pursed his lips and slipped the remains of his turkey burger back into the bag. He gave Wimp his right hand, said, 'Press the flesh, my man.'

J.D. got back to the place he'd left Marie in a B-registered Montego. And neither of them were there. A Montego is not a small car, and Marie was not a small woman. He scanned the street and the car park where Edward Blake's Beemer had been. No one was hiding. They'd all skipped.

All right, so he'd been longer than planned, but he was back now, and he'd remembered the tuna salad in pitta bread. 'Fuck,' he said to the spot where the car had been, 'if I'd've known this was gonna happen I'd've put mayonnaise on it.'

*

87

The Montego, with Marie at the wheel, edged its way along the main street of the village of Osbaldwick. The houses to the left were fronted by a beck, and access to each of them was over a series of individual bridges. She crossed one of the bridges, the Montego passing under a canopy of mature pear trees, before emerging at the gothic arch and weathered door of a stone-built cottage. There was a garage attached, housing a cool white Rover. The Montego shuddered to a wheezing halt as Marie switched off the engine.

As she approached the house the door was opened by a slender vision dressed in a silk purple body with matching jogging pants. A petite, wraith-like face, perfectly made-up, gave her a wide-eyed smile, and said, 'You must be Marie Dickens. Did you find us OK?'

Marie put on the best face she had, and shook the woman's tiny hand. How did they do it? These women? Didn't they eat? Weren't they haunted day and night by fantasies in chocolate and cream? Or was the pain of denial sweeter than sugar?

'And you must be Naiomi,' she said. 'Naiomi Leaver.'

They were eventually settled in the leaded bay window. Antique Royal Doulton tea service, probably made by the original Sir Henry. One of those tiered cake stands with scones, tiny silver knives and forks, and cherry jam in an earthenware pot. Marie sipped the tea and swore she wouldn't touch the scones.

'Did you know India a long time?' Marie asked.

'I knew her for ever,' Naiomi Leaver told her. 'We were at school in Cheltenham, we learned to ski together in Switzerland. Our families were connected, I don't know how, some dealings between my father and India's. You know how these things are? Wheels within wheels.' She leaned forward and swung the tiered cake stand towards Marie. 'Do eat these scones, won't you?'

'Yeah, thanks.' Marie took one of them, sliced it in two and reached for the cherry jam. What the fuck.

'And you kept in touch?' she said.

'Very much so,' Naiomi Leaver confirmed. 'I saw her the day before she disappeared. We had lunch together, here.'

'And her husband, Edward? You knew him as well?'

Naiomi smiled. 'Knew,' she said. 'Past tense? I still do know Edward Blake. I'm sure India has gone on to better things.'

'You don't approve of him?'

'I don't like him, if that's what you mean. I didn't like the way he treated India. His women.'

'You knew about that?'

'Yes,' said Naiomi. 'I knew about that. And India knew as well.'

Marie finished off the scone and looked at another one.

'Please eat them,' said Naiomi.

Marie took the one from the middle tier; looked a little fatter than the one at the bottom. 'You said "women" – plural.'

'Yes. There are currently two. In the past there have been others.'

'And if India knew about these women, I can take it that their marriage was not particularly happy?'

'Surprisingly,' said Naiomi, 'it wasn't a particularly unhappy marriage. Edward likes to keep a couple of scrubbers on the go. He gets off on that kind of thing. Lower-class women, young ones, easy to exploit. I suppose they'll do anything for a fiver or a pack of cigarettes. India would have minded more if he'd had one woman, a love affair.'

'Are you seriously telling me that India didn't mind?'

Naiomi smiled. 'Yes. She didn't know that Edward paid the rent for their flats. She would have drawn the line at that. She was keen on counting pennies, was India. Always used to quote that thing about counting the pennies and the pounds looking after themselves. Got it from her father. But as long as she thought it was just sex she didn't mind. Took the pressure off her.'

89

'And India,' said Marie. 'Did *she* have any extra-marital affairs?'

'I wondered that during the last few weeks. Before she disappeared. But when I asked her about it, she denied it. I think she'd have told me if she was. We talked about men, about sex, about other girlfriends. If something like that had happened, if she'd met someone, she'd have told me.'

'You're sure about that?'

Naiomi shook her head. 'I'm *fairly* sure.'

Marie didn't remember it happening, but when she looked at the cake stand it was bare. The cherry jam was gone, too, the pot which had held it was as if it had been licked clean. She dabbed at the crumbs on her plate.

'Have you any idea who killed India Blake?' she asked her hostess.

Naiomi shook her head. 'I honestly don't know,' she said. 'But I can tell you that India was worried about the amount of insurance Edward took out on her. She said, and this was last year, when he took it out, and she was joking, of course, but she said she thought he might be planning to kill her.'

13

Sam shifts his head and takes your hand. He is kneeling on the floor, in front of your chair by the window. He has left the door open so you can hear Lady Day singing, 'I'll Get By As Long As I Have You'. Johnny Hodges' alto saxophone oozing a warm, refined balm. When the song is finished Sam looks up into your eyes. 'It isn't worth worrying about, Dora,' he says. 'It's all in the past.'

You stick a smile on your face and ruffle his hair. The past, the present, it is all the same to you. The future, too. Your life is not going to continue for long. The past and the present, they are the only realities, and they are impossible to separate.

'Are you here?' he asks.

'Yes.'

'With me?'

'Yes, Sam. I'm here with you.' The past is not a forbidden country. It is familiar territory. It is not a landscape you love, Dora, but it is a landscape you know. The present is unknown. It is the land in which Sam is king, and in which you feel yourself a guest. He loves you, this Sam. You have no doubt about that, and you are happy to be his guest. Only, only . . . you cannot help feeling that happiness has come too late. If he had arrived ten years earlier you would not have been a guest, you would have been a queen.

He twists the ring on your finger. 'You remember Diana's coming today?' he says.

'Oh.' You don't remember, Dora. You don't know what day it is. You who knew everything. Now you think about it, there is a vague memory. Sam will be going to work;

and Diana will come to make sure you don't fall out of bed.

'It's Geordie's birthday.' You bite your tongue as the words leave your lips. It is not Geordie's birthday.

Sam smiles and shakes his head. 'No,' he says. 'I'll be seeing Geordie, but it's not his birthday.'

'Yes, of course.' You remember now. Geordie's birthday was a long time ago. It was in the spring. You went for a walk with him and Janet and Sam in the park. Now it is autumn, soon to be winter. Saturday. Something always happens on Saturday.

You close your eyes and put one foot into the world of sleep. This is as close as you get these days. In the real world (if it is real) Sam releases your hand and gets to his feet. You are aware of him standing over you, and though your eyes are closed you can see the expression on his face. It is an expression of tenderness. It is an expression that streams out of him and into you, that settles on the surfaces of your body and seeps through the pores and into the bloodstream, your bones, into every crevice of your body, and warms you.

He stands still while part of you drinks in his life forces, and the other half of you walks in dreams. Large limpets cling to your body, beneath the skin. As you take strength from Sam, they appropriate it, using it for themselves. They suck you dry, becoming fatter and firmer while you become thinner, frailer; they light up like beacons, illuminating the desert of your body. They have no purpose, Dora. They are insane.

Sam moves towards the door. He stands for a few minutes, looking back at you before going downstairs. You can read his mind. He is happy that you sleep. He hopes you will gain strength and live for ever. But that is not how it will be.

You slip into darkness and the events of your life unfold themselves in reverse order. As time regresses you become

92

lighter and younger. Everything is reversed. You are hanging from the pear tree while Arthur brushes the flies from your eaten eyes. You are a girl in the countryside leaping a stile; you leave the ground and fly, you do not come down on the other side, your movement is arrested in the air. You leap the stile for ever and ever. You never come down. You hover in a rush of leaping skirts and legs, your head thrown back and the wind in your hair, completely free of the earth. And down below there is everyone you ever knew, alive or dead, and they look up with amazement, waiting. Waiting.

This is your private land, Dora. Yours alone. A land you share with no one. Not even Sam. Because you have beaten the limpets and the eggs. They might eat you alive now, they might suck the life out of you, but it will do them no good, because they cannot live without you. When they take the last ounce of strength, you will be released. Then there will be Arthur again, quiet and repentant; your mother writing the history of the stars, your father with his yellow skin, and Dylan Thomas, too, sucking figs. You will be separated no longer, not even from Sam. He will remain behind, but you will wait for him beyond time.

You open your eyes when the large disc under your arm goes into spasm. It passes quickly and you stare at the avenue. The old trees beginning to lose their golden leaves. You strain your ears for the sound of Sam downstairs, but there is nothing. The house is silent. You wait and watch the avenue.

Diana trips along the opposite pavement. She has developed a strange, quirky walk, swinging both arms in the same direction at once, not forwards and backwards, but from side to side like a sailor. She's been walking like that for years now, since she was eighteen. It started as a nonsense and has developed into a facet of character. You wish she wouldn't do it, but you don't say so. She would take no notice, anyway. She does what she wants to do. She is independent, thank God.

Diana does not look up at your window. She thinks you might be there, and then she would have to wave. Or perhaps she does not even think of looking up? Which is it, Dora? Is Diana avoiding you or not? You do not know. You cannot make up your mind. Questions like these make you tired.

She passes out of sight, below the house, and you hear Sam's voice in the hall.

'Diana. You're early.'

'How is she?' Diana's voice is bland, but with something elastic in it. A masculine voice.

'Sleeping at the moment,' says Sam. 'A bad night, but she's better now.'

'And you?'

'I'm fine,' he says.

'Don't let me stop you. I'll check she's all right.'

You count her footsteps on the stairs. Nine, ten, eleven, and the handle turns on the door. It is your daughter, Dora. She comes over to you, her hair in an uncombed afro style. Maybe it's not called that any more. You don't know, and you're not going to ask. She wears no make-up, and the hem of her skirt dips and rises in all the wrong places. Her shoes are like boats. She puts her face close to yours and pretends to kiss you. Fifty-odd years too late you feel a pang of pity for your father.

'I hear you had a bad night.'

'Not too bad. Sam was with me.'

Diana flings an old doctors' bag she uses as a handbag on to the bed, and Barney lifts his head from the quilt to see who is disturbing his rest. 'You're a lucky woman,' Diana says. 'To have a man like that.' She smiles and sits on the floor at your feet. She pulls her skirt over her knees and crosses her legs. You catch a glimpse of her knickers, and your memory goes spinning back in time.

She was twelve when you began the affair with Smiley Thompson. You had started work again, lecturing in History at the University of York. Smiley was a senior lecturer, ten years older than you, a small man with glasses and a shining cranium. He was married, of course. Everyone after Arthur was either married or passing through. Smiley was married, and between girlfriends.

A few days after the Iron Lady sank the *General Belgrano* Smiley stopped you on the steps of the library. 'Dora, I'm getting a petition together over this fiasco in the Falklands. Would you like to help?'

Help? He is asking you to help, Dora. Would you like to help Smiley Thompson? Help the children who were blown up on their training ship? You, Dora, who cannot help your daughter, Diana? You, who cannot stop your own son from screaming the night away. Do you want to help?

'Yes, of course. What do you want me to do?'

Not much really. He wants to talk. He wants you to listen. There are signatures to collect from members of staff, petition forms to draft and duplicate. It is straightforward work, leg work; but if other universities can be pulled in, the weight of an academic statement could push the government towards a negotiated settlement.

And listen, Dora, to that voice inside. That voice that has murmured away since they cut Arthur down from the pear tree. It is raving away inside your head as you accost your colleagues with the petition. You are useful, Dora. You have a function. Listen to that voice. You are needed. If your children reject you (and they do reject you, Dora), if you can be of no further use to them, at least you can function for the world.

You enter into a week of change. You wear your head high. After how many years? Smiley is waiting outside the lecture hall for you, he leaves messages, he telephones you in the evening. You are busy, too busy to think or to worry. The past recedes into a dim bundle of events, and as it does so the future unfolds. The days shorten in relation to the vast amount of life you pack into them.

And though Billy kicks and screams through the night, and Diana prowls like a sullen ghost through the house, you are infected by a germ of happiness. Well, that is what you call it during the day. At night you know it is something else. It is an escape. But an animal in a trap tries to escape. It is its nature. You were not the first, Dora. And you will not be the last.

'People are allowed to be happy, Dora,' Smiley tells you as his hand moves over your knee. You watch his fingers playing with the hem of your skirt, three of them disappear under it, then emerge again and come to a hesitant rest.

The week has brought you to a small private hotel on the edge of the park. You have passed it hundreds of times, and never given it a second glance. It is where the more athletic staff of the University bring their particularly ambitious female students. Smiley has used the place before, he is known here. He calls the proprietress Julie.

'It's a place I would not take my wife,' Smiley explained earlier. 'A place where two adults can be alone. Where they can relax. Where they can get to know each other.'

The prude in you was outraged, Dora. But not enough to say so. The lonely woman in you was so much stronger, so much more present, that the other was cast into shadow.

He was talking about sex. For some time you failed to understand that. How could you have been so dumb? Whose fault was it that you were so dumb? Arthur's? Your mother's? You were a widow, the mother of two children.

But sex had never entered your life. It was an occasional Saturday night occurrence with Arthur. Something else he did *to* you, something else you had to submit to. It never occurred to you that it might be a pleasure. You never thought about it seriously. Dylan Thomas enjoyed it, apparently, but he was a man.

And Smiley was a man. He chased you around for a week, every time you turned a corner he was there. He enthused about the number of signatures you had collected. He took

96

you by the shoulders and laughed, kissed you on both cheeks when the University of Durham asked for a supply of the petition forms. He sent a bunch of daffodils to your door with a note: *Thanks for all your help. Love, Smiley.*

And then it was sex. It had not occurred to you, Dora, but you were quick enough to respond. He was not another Arthur, after all. He was Smiley. He was a compassionate and concerned human being, and he had lifted a veil for you, shown you a glimpse of another life, an involved and busy life which would release you from the guilt of your marriage, your children, and your conscience.

Poor Dora. Arthur's ghost is never far away. Living, he was ever present, and now he's dead you feel his silent gaze every time you look at Smiley Thompson.

And look at Smiley, Dora. Just look at him with his baggy-knit crew-neck sweater and his paisley-patterned cravat. Look at the shining dome of his head and his huge, almond-shaped eyes: the eyes of a thoroughbred horse. He has dressed for the occasion. He is presenting himself to you, a neatly packaged gift. You notice the broad check of his cotton shirt protruding from the neck of his sweater, his manicured nails, and the stiff whiff of aftershave.

'A girl like you shouldn't be alone.' You sip at the gin and tonic and listen to the resonance of his voice. You are not a girl, Dora. He is wrong about that, but you concentrate on the sound, on the deep timbre of his voice, letting it enter you and then recede again to its origin deep within his chest. What he has to say comes back into you again, warm, obliterating the frozen loneliness of your life. Now he swims away again, separate, paisley-patterned, silent and predatory.

He reaches for your glass and removes it from your hand. The pink flesh beneath his nails pulses bright. He brings his face to yours, his breath beneath your ear. His lips lightly pressing your cheeks, eyes, forehead. His arms enfold you. He whispers hungry words into your hair.

Your fingers are entangled in the wool of his sweater, and you let your head fall backwards and feel his mouth on your neck, first on one side, then the other. His hand cups your breast and in spite of yourself you hear a long, ancient growl escape from your throat. A growl you never knew you possessed. Smiley cups the other breast and emulates the sound. You laugh nervously, a quiet, conscious laugh that is a counterpoint to the harmony and the rhythm of these two physical bodies. Your laugh is an agony. A quick agony that inserts itself into the ecstasy of the moment.

Smiley laughs as well, he laughs and growls again from the back of his throat. He pulls apart the folds of your dress and moves down your body. You groan and sigh in response to his movements. You quickly brush unwanted tears from your face and lift his sweater over his head, unknot the cravat, and pick at the buttons on his shirt.

It is a game, Dora, and you enter into it like a child, like a pup in spring sunlight. Smiley's body is smooth, and brown, and warm. The texture of his skin ripples beneath your fingers and you discover the spastic quickness of your movements as the heart in your breast heaves and throbs with an ever faster beat.

Smiley tantalizes. He shows you where he will go, and then recedes, only to advance more slowly on his target. You play the same game, quick to notice every shade, every nuance of pain or pleasure in a stream of breath or half arrested movement. His finger catches the elastic at your waist and releases it. He moves over your thighs and takes your foot in his hands, holding it close to his cheek, brushing the surface of your skin with the tip of his tongue. In a moment he is traversing your thighs again, the heel of his hand grazing the mons Veneris, and then onwards to circle your erect nipples, your lips, your ears, your eyes.

It is a game, Dora. A crazy merry-go-round in which your clothes and your emotions are flung away. The chaos of your consciousness is streamed, strained to a thin red line on which you are shunted and chuffed along, relentlessly, inevitably, to orgasm.

Your teeth ring. Your eyes spin inside your head. Your arms thresh the pillows. A furred, animal rattle leaks from the folds of your throat. Below, somewhere deep below in you, a quake turns everything placid and still into tumultuous falls, which gush relentlessly downwards. You are a river, Dora. A river rushing, a river roaring towards oblivion.

Subsiding now, quickly, into trickles. A rushing upwards, back into your head. Smiley, smiling. His tongue hanging out like a dog. Sunlight, pale, slanting into the room. Somewhere, far, far away, a car's horn. Liquidation. The word, liquidation, like a mantra in your brain.

Smiley says it was 'Super', and you laugh a laugh you have not heard yourself laugh ever. A laugh so earthly, so erotic, that the falls begin again and you avert your face and watch your knuckles turn white gripping the whiteness of the sheets.

Has anyone ever been so grateful? In the history of human copulation, Dora, has anyone ever been so grateful as you were that day? Dressing, you move over to Smiley and nuzzle into his neck. You tell him how wonderful it has been, that it has never been as wonderful before. That you never dreamed it could be like that. Smiley smiles in his deferential way, a smile that disclaims all responsibility for your happiness, your gratitude. He has a tutorial which begins in precisely twenty-seven minutes.

'I think it would be politic to leave separately,' he says, standing by the door. 'We don't want to draw attention to ourselves.'

After he leaves, you sit on the edge of the bed and count to two hundred and fifty, then you walk down the plushly carpeted staircase and out through the swing doors. It is getting late. You will have to rush to prepare food for Billy and Diana.

14

Diana asked him: 'Is she OK?'

'She is today,' Sam said, his face creased into a smile. 'When she's like this I think she could live for ever.'

'Really?'

There was an edge to Diana's voice. Incredulity.

Sam turned to her and let his smile drift away. 'Look at me,' he said. 'Do I look like a dreamer to you?'

'Well, yes, Sam, you do. You look like a guy who's been raging against reality all his life.'

'All right. Point taken. But I know what's happening here, Diana. To me, to Dora, to all of us. She's gonna die. And in some ways it'll be a relief when she does. But at the same time, when she's gone nothing'll ever be the same again. I'm looking for a miracle; and even while I'm looking for it I know it's not going to happen. But in these intervals, when she's not in pain, when her eyes sparkle, I let myself be carried away. I let myself be happy, for myself, and for Dora. I'm not fooling myself. I know reality'll come booling along tomorrow, or the next day, or even five minutes from now. And when it comes I'll deal with it. That's how I've come this far.'

'Whoa, boy.' She held up her hands. 'I was just checking. Reality's a question for me as well. Dora's my mother. She's always been here. I'm not sure how life'll feel when she's not here any more.'

Sam moved towards her and took her hand. They were standing by the window, looking out at the avenue. 'It won't be the same,' he said quietly. 'For either of us. But when it happens I'll still be around, if you want me. We might need each other to get through.' He made eye contact with her. 'But for now she's still alive. Today she's free of pain. I want to enjoy that.'

Diana thought about it briefly. It was as if you could see the thought taking root in her mind. See her accepting it. 'Yeah,' she said. 'I'll tell her a joke when she wakes up. No one appreciates a laugh more than Dora.'

She looked down at her hand, which Sam still held enclosed with his own. 'Can I have it back?' she asked. 'I mean, you do belong to Dora. And, pretty as you are, you're not the right sex for me.'

Sam laughed loudly. 'When you get to my age, Diana, a woman can fool you by saying you're smart, but she can't fool you by saying you're pretty.'

'I dunno that I was trying to fool you,' she said. She cocked her head to one side, the better to see him. 'But it's not a bad face. I like older faces. There's more to go at.'

'Wrinkles?'

'Yeah. And lines. Drama, really. I'm not impressed by the smooth countenance of youth.'

Sam shook his head. 'I know what you mean,' he said. 'But their teeth are better.'

A silver Toyota space wagon crept along the street, the driver leaning out of the window looking at the house numbers.

'What was Dora like when she was young?'

Diana frowned. 'Difficult to say,' she said. 'She was the boss, the one in charge. She was the one who always got us wherever we were going. An organizer. She was a benchmark for me, something I should aspire to. In a way, she still is. If I live to be a hundred I'll still feel inferior to her. I'll never be able to muster the same amount of energy, of will-power.'

'That's because she's your mother,' Sam said. 'She provided all your needs. That's what mothers do.'

'You mean if I was a mother I'd suddenly get more energy?'

'Yeah. You'd have to. It's a tough job, so they say.'

Diana shook her head. 'I don't feel maternal. I look at women with kids, even some of my friends, and I say a prayer, thank God it's not me.'

Sam let her words hang there for a moment, then he said, 'Talking about kids, Dora wants me to find Billy.'

'Yeah, it comes up from time to time. The question is: does Billy want to be found?'

'Do you know where he is?'

'As far as I know he's in York. Or somewhere in the area. But he's disowned us. He doesn't want anything to do with us.'

'Dora gave me the impression he was somewhere else. I thought he might be in London.'

'He was at one time,' Diana said. 'When he first left home he went south. I heard reports every now and then, not from Billy himself, but from people who knew him. He was at RADA, financed himself through the course. He worked at a club in Soho, some kind of bouncer. I couldn't believe it at first. Billy, a bouncer. When people say "bouncer" you imagine some huge bruiser. And Billy was always smart. If you look at him you could imagine him being a jockey, even a dancer, but not a bouncer.

'Could have inherited some of Dora's will-power, I suppose. Maybe he got my share. He was not only a bouncer, he was the one the punters feared more than the big guys. With the big guys you got some kind of warning. You could walk away from them. But with Billy, apparently, if you were causing trouble, or if he thought you were causing trouble, he'd just wade straight in. A girlfriend of mine said she watched Billy put some guy out of action, and he was more worried about his shirt than anything else. His shirt got ruffled in the fight. There was some dirt on his collar, Billy's collar, and the young guy was sat on the bottom step with blood coming from his nose, and Billy was screaming at him for ruining his shirt.'

'Dora didn't say anything about him being a bouncer,' said Sam. 'Does she know?'

'Probably not,' Diana said. 'I never told her. She knew he was at RADA, and she must have wondered how he financed it. She grieved for him when he disappeared. She knew he didn't want anything to do with her, and she blamed herself. I've always taken the line that he's a shit, and we're better off without him.'

'Isn't that simplistic?'

'Maybe,' she said defensively. 'Our father killed himself because Dora took us away. Some people would say Dora did the right thing, and others would say she got it wrong. But when Dad killed himself that was enough of a punishment for her. At least that's what I thought. But Billy wanted to punish her more. He withdrew his love. He disowned her. And he's still doing it now.

'I don't want to rub that in. I didn't want to tell her that he'd thrown out all her values, that he'd become a vicious little thug. That he was living at least on the edge of criminal society, if not up to his neck in it.'

'Have you ever seen him, since he went away?'

'Yes, once. It was on York station. Three years ago. It was summer. I was going to stay with some friends in Birmingham, and I was drinking coffee, waiting for the train. I saw Billy get off a train on the adjoining platform. Don't know where he was coming from. He had a bag. He came in the café, but he didn't notice me. He didn't look around, it was as if he was alone in there. He got a drink and sat at a table.

'Something told me not to approach him. I knew he would reject me. If I'd said something to him he'd have ignored me. He might've got up and walked away. Whatever, it was one of those situations where you have a sense of certainty. So I sat and watched him.

'He was not one of us any more. He wasn't my brother, or Dora's son. He'd set out to reinvent himself, and he'd gone away and done it. He'd changed. It was obvious from the first moment I set eyes on him, when he stepped down from the train. He still had that broad forehead, and his eyebrows met in the middle, but there was only a vestige of the Billy I'd grown up with. Like a ghost that clung to him, something invisible. He'd actually changed physically, filled out and got a couple of inches taller. His features had changed as well, his nose was smaller and broader, and his eyes seemed closer together and darker. His hair was a shade lighter than I remembered.

'He'd gone away to change, and he'd come back changed almost beyond recognition.' She looked at Sam. 'Do you think I'm exaggerating this?'

He shook his head but didn't speak.

'I'm not exaggerating it in the least,' she said. 'He'd transformed himself. I thought about that saying, you know, when people say, "His own mother wouldn't recognize him." And I thought it was true, if he'd passed Dora on the street, she might have walked on by. Not even known he was there.

'Except for the ghost, the aura around him. He'd probably changed the way he thought, but the thing that hadn't changed about him was the core of disappointment. That was still there. Confusion and disappointment. He was steeped in it. He'd been like that as a child, ever since Dad killed himself, maybe even before that. Maybe he'd been born like it. I don't know, I was too young to've noticed things like that. But when I was old enough to notice it, it was already embedded in his soul, and it's not something he'll ever be able to shake off.'

'D'you have a photograph of him?' Sam asked.

'Yes, there'll be some in Dora's album. I'll look one out. But he doesn't look like that any more.'

'And, something else,' Sam said. 'Why d'you think he

came back to York, if he is here? I mean, if you're right about him not wanting anything to do with you. Is there something else here for him? A woman? Some friends? Why did he come back?'

'He was friendly with a girl for a while before he went away. Pam. Pammy. Can't remember her surname, it'll come to me later. She was very keen on him, and he went along with it for a while. But he doesn't make deep attachments. He could've come back for her, but I doubt it. I don't really know why he came back. I've thought about it and I can't come up with a satisfactory answer. But I think he watches us.'

15

The rat had been scraping and tapping at his door all evening. But when William got to his feet and opened the door it had disappeared. It left no droppings, not a single hair. There was no scrambling on the stairs as it scuttled back to its lair. Twice William had opened the door to the landing and discovered nothing. He had stood at the threshold, listening, watching. But there was no rat.

Until he sniffed.

His features were stolid. A keen observer might have detected apathy around the eyes, the line of his mouth. His body language was that of a young man who had encountered disappointment. He turned and closed the door quietly, leaning back against it.

Rats! They were cunning. They were quick, savage and ferocious. Too fast for the eye, but not for the nose. William had smelt a rat.

He tasted bile at the back of his throat.

Rats had spread the bubonic plague.

> Anything like the sound of a rat
> Makes my heart go pit-a-pat!

He turned his breathing down, adopted the listening pose. At first all was silent, but after some moments there was a small thud and the shuffling of its feet as it returned to his door. William couldn't tell from the sounds if the animal was scratching with its front feet or gnawing with its pointed teeth.

The door did not move, but it was easy to imagine that it

was moving. Easier still to imagine the rat was unstoppable, that it would gnaw its way through the door. Then begin on William himself. Gnawing its way into his brain.

He took his knife from the sheath and lightly ran his thumb along the blade. Then he threw the door open again, smashing it back with force against its hinges. He caught a glimpse of the scaly tail as it disappeared down the stairs. With the blade of the knife flashing in his hand, he gave a shriek that strained his lungs and plunged down the stairs after the predatory monster. Leaping five or six steps at a time, yelling at the top of his voice, William strove to narrow the gap between himself and his prey. He followed it through the doorway of the ground-floor front room of the house.

The rat slipped greasily through a blackened hole in the floorboards.

William threw himself full-length on the floor and pushed the knife through the hole, stabbing wildly at the blackness within. When he connected with nothing, he forced his arm deeper into the hole, until he had it in up to his shoulder. The knife sparked against the foundation wall beneath the floorboards and spun away, out of his grip. William retrieved his arm and pushed his face up close to the hole. He looked and listened. Although he could see nothing, he could hear small cries down there. And his nostrils and lungs were filled with the stench of the rat's domain.

His right hand was cut and bleeding, and he peremptorily wiped it on the leg of his trousers. He could feel adrenalin rushing through his veins. This animal may be crafty and fierce, but it would soon discover that it had met its match. Rats and men had been pitted against each other through the ages, and would continue the fight until the end of the world. But the battle, for this particular rat, was almost over.

In the kitchen William found an old axe with a rusted head and brought it back to the front room. Working close to the black hole into which the rodent had vanished, William smashed his way through the floorboards. The timbers fractured and split as he pulled them away from the cross-beams. The cut on his hand widened and deepened and beads of blood splashed along the floor. William sucked at the wound and sprayed the blood and dirt in an arc behind him.

He collected the splintered floorboards and threw them to the side of the room. Now he could step down into the foundations, among the mess of paper and household rubbish that had accumulated there. He carefully poked amongst it until he retrieved his knife.

The nest was located in a corner, beneath one of the cross-beams. It was a loose construction of chewed crisp packet, what appeared to be a shredded newspaper, and some dried vegetable matter – grass? leaves? – perhaps a mixture of the two. The litter consisted of ten blind and naked young, each intent on fulfilling its genetic destiny, crawling over each other in an instinctive panic to escape annihilation.

> Go . . . and get long poles.
> Poke out the nests and block up the holes!

William sensed a movement over to his left, and he gazed in that direction until his eyes adjusted enough to see her. Mother rat. Crouched on a split board, her body, together with the tail, took up a space of almost eighteen inches. Omnivorous. Fecund. Her long snout twitched. Her red eyes processed information, but she did not move. She waited for William to do that.

He deliberately pushed the tip of his knife through the head of one of the litter. He held out the tiny body to mother rat, made sure that she saw what he had done. Then he dropped the carcass to the floor and crushed it under the heel of his boot.

William smiled in the direction of the mother as he skewered another of her offspring, this time through the eye. He took them one at a time, varying the procedure slightly with each kill. The fifth suckling he sliced like a sausage, the sixth he decapitated. The seventh he disembowelled, scraping out the tiny contents with his thumb and throwing them fiercely at the mother. She moved fractionally to one side, so the innards of her nestling flew past, missing her by an inch and a half.

Only when William moved to take the last of the litter did the mother rat attack.

> And folks who put me in a passion
> May find me pipe after another fashion!

It was as if she had grown wings. She rose up from her perch with a shriek that sounded almost human. She hovered briefly on her hind legs and flew forward with a velocity that defied the eye. William realized instinctively that the target of her leap was his throat, and he brought up his hands to ward her away. He was fast, he had anticipated such an attack, and was confident that he would be capable of dealing with it. But mother rat was faster still.

As William brought up his hands, she flew between them and he caught her fetid scent as her jaws closed over the fold of skin below his larynx. He was pushed backwards by the force of her landing, but somehow managed to remain standing. All four of her feet scrabbled for a grip of his shirt and his chest. In a flash William saw his own death approaching like an express train, but his mind remained calm and collected, his will absolutely focused.

The rat needed a couple of seconds, perhaps only a few fractions of a second to consolidate its position. Once it had established a secure base with its feet and tail, it would commence ripping and tearing at William's throat. The soft skin would offer no resistance, and in moments the larynx and trachea would be shredded, cutting off the oxygen supply to his lungs. At that point the battle would be over, William vanquished, and mother rat victorious.

Without a hint of fear or emotion, and in one movement, William took hold of the body of the rat with his left hand. He lifted her clear of his chest. Her teeth were still clamped to his throat. Holding her body horizontally, feeling her long scaly tail winding its way around his forearm, he brought up the knife in his right hand and severed the body from the head.

Mother rat's warm blood spouted like a cloud-burst over his face and chest. He laughed wildly as it flowed between his lips and raced along his tongue, feeling rivulets of plasma running into his eyes and watching while his world turned a scarlet hue.

16

Janet was sitting on the edge of the bed in her nightgown. 'It's happened,' she said. Geordie looked at her and tried to guess what it was that had happened. She wore a pair of scuffed slippers, and the right one was dangling from her foot, looking as though it might fall off. He looked at her face, but couldn't read it. She said, 'I'm pregnant.'

Geordie couldn't respond. It was such a mechanical word. He had to think what it meant. He knew what it meant, of course, but he had to translate those two sharp-sounding syllables into a meaning with a human perspective. He looked at the lamp by the side of the bed, the soft light coming from it. He licked his lips and tasted salt. A dry stickiness inside his mouth. 'A baby?' he said.

Janet allowed herself a smile. 'Not yet, but that'll be the end result, if we let it.'

'Let it?'

'Yeah. If we want it.' She flicked her foot and the slipper fell to the carpet, bounced, rolled over, and was still.

Geordie picked the slipper up and took it over to her. He knelt in front of her and put it back on her foot. He looked up at her. 'If we want it?'

'You're like a parrot,' Janet said. 'You repeat everything I say.'

'Because I can't believe you're saying it. "If we let it . . . if we want it . . ." What d'you think? Don't you want to have it?'

Janet was beautiful. Most of the time Geordie thought she was beautiful. But sometimes her face turned to stone. It was at times like this. When she wasn't sure about something. When she felt insecure. Geordie walked forward on his knees and got up on the bed with her. He put his arms around her and pulled her to him. He tried to turn her face towards him, so he could kiss her, but she pulled away.

'No, Geordie, don't.' She kept her face away from him, but didn't move his arm from around her shoulders. He could feel the stiffening of her body beneath the flimsy material of the nightgown. 'Before I did the test I was fairly sure I'd caught. And then when it was positive, I was glad about it. I'd never thought it would happen, and it was like a confirmation of something. It felt like an achievement, that it was something I'd gone out and done. Like pass a driving test or getting a raise at Christmas. I was going to ring you at work and tell you over the phone.

'But then I thought you wouldn't like the idea, and the next thing I knew I was crying my eyes out. And everything I'd thought before was swamped. Instead of passing a driving test it seemed more like a biological accident. Something that happens to women whether they want it or not.

'And it's the kind of thing, you tell the guy, the father, and he waves goodbye and heads for the horizon very bloody quick.'

Geordie tightened his grip of her. 'So why am I still here?'

'Because you're stupid,' she said. 'You're not a real man.'

He turned her towards him and kissed her wet face. She didn't resist this time. She laughed between the tears.

'I know it's your decision,' he said. 'But if it was up to me there'd be no question about it. A baby, Christ, Janet, that'd make us into a real family. What're we gonna call her?'

Marie had the car so Geordie walked to Portland Street. He was twenty minutes early and called in at Cassady's second-hand record shop to see if he could find some Irish music for Sam. There was a Bonnie Raitt CD playing. A song about an Angel from Montgomery. Geordie knew it wasn't

Irish and knew that Sam'd love it, so he told the guy behind the counter he'd take it.

The guy smiled. 'Sorry, it's mine. Not for sale.'

'You got any more like it?'

'Not here. I've got them all at home.'

'What about Christy Moore? Irish singer, you got anything by him?'

'Not on CD. There's a couple of tapes on the shelf over there.'

'I wanted it on CD,' Geordie said. 'Sam's got a cassette player in the office, but at home he's only got CDs.'

The guy shrugged. 'They'd brighten up the office.'

Geordie held his hands up and backed away from the counter. 'Hey,' he said. 'You giving me the hard sell, now.'

The guy laughed. 'D'you want 'em or not?'

'How much?'

'Three-fifty each.'

'All I've got,' Geordie told him, 'is this valuable gift voucher bearing an engraved portrait of Queen Elizabeth II and personally signed by the Governor of the Bank of England.' He handed it over the counter. 'I'm completely at your mercy.'

The guy put the two cassettes into a brown paper bag and handed Geordie three pounds change. He winked. 'All the time I spent in salesmen's school's beginning to pay off.'

Geordie pocketed the change and left the shop. He took in a lungful of exhaust fumes and followed a zigzag path through the stationary traffic in Gillygate.

Portland Street was quiet. The house with the shabby curtains at the upstairs window was not particularly inviting, and looked as though it might be unoccupied. He walked down the short path and glanced around. There was no one else in the street.

He pressed the bell and listened for the ring inside the house, but heard nothing.

After a moment, though, there were footsteps on the stairs, and the door was opened by a girl with blond hair and a black eye. 'Doesn't work,' she said. 'The bell. It's never worked, not as long as I've been here.' She looked past Geordie, up and down the street. 'D'you wanna come up?'

'I've got an appointment to see Miss Prine,' Geordie said. 'Joni Prine.'

'Yeah, yeah. That's me. You're Geordie Black. I've been waiting for you, saw you come down the street. There's nobody else in, anyway, apart from old crusty knickers at the front.'

Geordie followed her up the stairs. Her legs were blotchy, but she wore a short skirt so she could share them with the world. She turned to face him on the first landing. 'Got an eyeful, did you?'

Geordie blinked and nodded. There was no point in denying it. It was an eyeful he could have done without, but he wasn't about to tell her that.

A baby was crying in the room. Not a full-scale yell, a half-hearted attempt to bring the world to its cradle. It wasn't a breathless cry, and Joni Prine wasn't fazed by it. While Geordie was still reeling from the pungent odour of unwashed nappies and ammonia, she plucked a dummy from the cot, dumped it into a huge jar of raspberry jam, and stuck it into the child's face. The crying stopped.

'Come and sit down,' Joni said, collecting a mound of clothing from a worn sofa and plonking it on the threadbare carpet.

Geordie placed himself in the space thus vacated, and Joni Prine placed herself right next to him, seemingly oblivious of her skirt riding up to the rim of her pants.

'And?' she said, turning to face him.

'Sorry,' said Geordie. 'And what?'

'And what you here for, love? It's not a café, is it? How'm I supposed to help you?'

114

What Geordie was really grateful for, was that she hadn't offered him a drink. Tea or coffee. He knew she was trying to confuse him with sex and legs and the way she'd handled the baby, and now sitting so close to him that their thighs were touching. And she could do all that, and think she was getting away with it – Geordie didn't mind what she thought. 'What I said on the telephone,' he said. 'We're investigating a claim by Edward Blake, and we understand that you are acquainted with him.'

'How'd you know that?'

'Is it true?'

'Yes, it's true. Acquainted isn't how most people'd put it, but even they'd understand what you mean. Are you from the police?'

'No.'

'And Eddy. Mr Blake, well, I call him Eddy. Will he find out I've talked to you?'

'Not from us. Anything you tell me is in strict confidence.'

'Did you bring the money?'

'Fifty pounds. I've got it here.' He tapped his jacket pocket.

'Hand it over, then.'

'After the interview. First, I ask the questions, then, when you've answered them, you get the money.'

'I already told you everything on the phone. Fuck, that walk up the stairs was worth fifty quid. I showed you everything but the Post Office tower. How do I know you won't get the answers you want and then just leave me here, take the money away with you?'

Geordie looked at her. 'You don't, Joni. All right to call you that?'

She didn't smile. She looked him right in the eye. 'I don't give a fuck what you call me, Geordie, so long as I get that fifty pound note.'

The baby began to cry, and Joni repeated the dummy and raspberry jam trick.

'How long've you known Edward Blake?'

''Bout eighteen months.'

'What is your relationship?'

'He's a sugar daddy. I service his fantasies. Sometimes I'm his princess, and sometimes I'm a slut.' She giggled. 'Actually, I'm a slut all the time.'

'D'you dress up?' Geordie asked, hearing an element of fascination in his tone that he'd hoped to suppress.

Joni smiled. 'Sometimes. I'll show you if you like.'

He shook his head. 'Not really necessary. What I was getting at—'

'—I think it's fairly obvious what you're getting at. Yes, he comes round and fucks me once or twice a week.'

'Is that all?'

She put her hand up to her face. 'He's rough from time to time. Last week he gave me this black eye. Knocked me over a chair, and hurt my ribs.' She pulled up her V-necked, off-white sweater to reveal bruising under her left breast.

'Was that an unprovoked attack?'

'What?'

'Did you give him any reason to hurt you?'

She nodded her head. 'Yeah. He pays the rent, gives me money. Jacqui was crying all the time. He doesn't like that. But he never touches her, he takes it out on me.'

'Did you report it to the police?'

Joni laughed. She laughed so loud the baby started crying again. Geordie didn't laugh, but he couldn't stop himself smiling when he remembered what he'd asked her. When she stopped laughing he asked her, 'Do you think he killed his wife?'

'No,' she said. 'If he killed her, he could kill me. I don't get that kind of vibe off him. Also, the way she died, his wife, I mean, she starved to death, didn't she? He's more physical than that. He likes a bit of rough and tumble. If she'd been beaten to death, strangled, something like that. If she'd been stabbed, I might've thought he could've done it.

But not starving someone to death. He wouldn't do that. Not Eddy.' She shivered. 'Starving someone to death? That's Creep City. I've met some weird fuckers in my life, but I've never met anyone who'd do a thing like that. Jesus and Mary, that's worse'n Hitler.'

There were lots of things Geordie could have said about Joni Prine, but he contented himself with one. As he walked along the street after leaving her house he glanced back once and shook his head. 'She's piss-poor,' he said.

The register office was around the corner in Bootham. Geordie walked up the steps and followed a short corridor round to the right. Behind the glass partition was a receptionist with a face like a vampire, about the same age as him. Peroxide hair, blue and cerise eye shadow, and freshly applied cerise lipstick to match. She gave enough of a smile to encourage Geordie to state his business, but not nearly enough to crack the stark white porcelain foundation which caked her face.

'How do you go about getting married?' Geordie asked.

She glanced behind her quickly, then looked him in the eye. 'First you get a girlfriend,' she said conspiratorially. 'And you take her out dancing, and buy her jewellery, and take her to fancy restaurants, and you tell her you're earning about twice as much as you're really earning, and that your boss is going to die soon and leave you the business.' She smiled again and took a deep breath, obviously prepared to go on if no one stopped her.

'Yeah,' Geordie said. 'Am I the first customer today?'

She shook her head. 'Let me put it like this – you're the first customer today who looked like he could take a bit of fun.'

'Only I've heard that more people live together, don't bother getting married at all, even when they have kids. So I thought maybe you was bored. Not getting enough customers.'

'It's not true,' she told him, leaning forward on her elbows. 'The people who come in here, they nearly all want to get married, or register a birth or a death. This morning I've had five people registering deaths, six births, and you're my first marriage. Who's the lucky girl?'

'Janet,' Geordie told her. 'We've been living together, but now we're gonna have a baby, so we want to get married.'

'Romantic.'

'We wanna do it as soon as possible.'

'*Very* romantic.' She consulted a calendar. 'This year?'

Geordie shook his head. 'This week.'

'Oooh, la la.' She clasped a hand to her breast. Silver nail polish. 'I've gone all of a flutter.' A door opened behind her and an older woman in a sober suit walked into the office. The vampire girl shuffled on her seat, then looked back at Geordie and came with an altogether different tone of voice. 'The minimum notice is three days, sir. This is Wednesday, so the earliest we can do you is Friday. And it's £72.50 for the special licence.'

'Friday'll be fine,' he told her. 'What time?'

'You have to fill in this form,' she said, passing it over to him. 'And read the accompanying notes, which explain the procedure.'

'Thanks.' He picked up the form and walked away to a small table. He took his pen out of his inside pocket and began reading the questions, scratching his head from time to time in an effort to recall a date or the correct spelling of a word.

When he'd finished the older woman had disappeared, and the vampire girl was alone again. Geordie handed her the completed form and leaned over the counter towards her. 'What I've heard,' he said, in little more than a whisper, 'in the old days they used to have wives and concubines.'

17

Diana is cross-legged on the carpet. She teases a lock of hair from the mass and pulls it forward, inspecting it myopically. She should wear glasses, but is too vain. You wonder if you should suggest contact lenses, but it would be of no use. She does what she wants to do.

'I dreamt I got a letter from Billy,' she tells you. 'He sent his love.' She continues to inspect her hair. She is not kind, Dora. Your daughter is not kind to you. If she says Billy sent his love in a letter in a dream, then Billy must have done so. Diana would not make it up. Diana would not say she'd dreamt that Billy sent his love if Billy had not sent his love. It is something you can rely on, this scrap of information. Something incontrovertible. Billy sends his love to you in a letter in a dream. He sends it from London, where he practised to become a bouncer, or Bradford where he lived in an Asian community. The land of the purdah. The land he ran to in an unconscious flight from the image of his mother. The land from which he will never return, except, possibly, for your funeral.

'No, he didn't say much,' Diana tells you. 'He's not in Bradford any more, I can't remember where he is. Closer to home.' She shrugs her shoulders. 'D'you remember Dotty?'

'Yes.' You have a vision of a small spotty girl, aged twelve or thereabouts.

'Was at school with me,' Diana reminds you. 'She's gone into a convent. She's a bride of Christ.' Diana shrieks with laughter. She is like you, Dora. She does not waste her time on God. You do not know what she does waste it on. You cannot ask her. She will only go through her Ms routine:

Men, marijuana, music, menstruation, masturbation, mac-robiotics, madness, magazines, monotony, money, magic, myopia, mutilation, moussaka, and madeira. She will mor-tify you with her Ms.

You wonder if Billy writes often. In dreams.

'Not a lot,' Diana tells you. 'Twice, maybe three times a year.' She looks at you and a shadow passes over her face, an internal shadow, such as you have not seen from her since she was a child. 'It doesn't seem as though you'll get well again, Dora?'

You shake your head. There is a discernible tremor in Diana's voice. Something inside her is trembling. You are unnerved. You are always unnerved when she is like this. It is not a common occurrence. Even as a child she was sure of herself, certain that her own perceptions were reality, and that reality was something to overcome. Whenever her voice wobbled you could take her in your arms, crush her into your body. Only when her voice wobbled. At no other time.

You hold out your arms and she scrambles towards you on her knees. Your frail arms pass around her back and you press them against her until they ache. She is trembling, Dora, your daughter. This big girl of yours. This woman.

You tell her you might live for ever, but there is no conviction in your voice. You know that you are dying. And Diana knows as well. And she knows that you know. It is not possible to play games with Diana. She lives in the hard kernel of the truth.

She is convulsed by sobs, speaking only in the small intervals between them. 'I don't want you to die, Dora.'

She does not need a reply. You stroke her body, you make sounds of encouragement. You coo like a bird. Like a silly old bird.

'You're all I've got, Dora. You and Billy. I can't face it if you die, and Billy is only there in dreams. I don't know what'll happen to me.'

You tell her it will be all right. A woman's life is like that.

No one can see into the future. Sometimes it is bad, sometimes it is very bad. But the good times come round again, often when you least expect them. You cannot afford to be weak. Not too weak, anyway; and certainly not all the time. Life is good. In the end life is good. Whatever they take away from you, there is always so much left. She will probably marry a rich old man, have children of her own. You laugh, Dora, hoping she will laugh with you. Yes, why not? Children of her own. She is only twenty-seven. Stranger things have happened.

'I wish we were a normal family,' she says. 'I wish Father was still alive.'

You have not been a good mother. You never approached perfection.

'But that's not what I mean,' Diana tells you. 'I wouldn't want you to change, Dora. You're my mother, and I love you. Only I don't know what drives me. I don't know why I'm like I am. I don't know why I'm different, Dora. Do you understand? I don't know why I'm not normal.'

She loves you, Dora. That is what she said. It is another incontrovertible fact. Your Diana has never been one to mince words. If she says love, she means love. You pull her to your face and feel the warmth of her entering your body.

Her life has not yet begun, you tell her. You had exactly the same fears at her age. It is not hopeless. It is never hopeless. You will always be with her. You will live inside of her. Long after you are dead you will still live inside her. She will never be able to shake you off. And there will come a time for her when she turns a corner, when the past, when everything that has hampered her will fade away. The physical past will no longer be there, it will be spiritualized, and she will be able to take from it whatever she finds useful. That is how it is in life. It is like the sea. It comes and goes in waves, now turbulent, crushing, frightening, exciting, full of passion, and then it is calm, peaceful, empty, boring, slow, and silent. You only have to remember that the waves come and go, come and go. There is constant change. Life and death. Life and death. It is the rhythm of the universe.

She kisses you, Dora. She really kisses you. She reaches up her face to yours, and you feel her lips on your cheek. She gets to her feet and stands back, hands on her hips.

You tell her there is a song by Lady Day, 'I'll Never Be The Same', and she goes off to find it. Buck Clayton and Lester Young together for the intro, then Billie holding back, intentionally lagging behind the beat all the way. Recorded in 1937, one of the happiest years of her life, and you can hear it in her phrasing, in her harmony. How she takes hold of banality by the throat and coaxes from it a kind of nectar.

'You were always a bloody philosopher,' Diana says. But she is smiling. She used to smile like that during your time with Smiley. At least at the beginning. During the first few weeks.

You were both in love with Smiley. For you he was a man, a man who had pulled you out of yourself, given you the key to your sexuality. But for Diana he was a dream. For Diana he was a reincarnation of Arthur. He was exactly what you and she were looking for. Nothing. A heaven-sent nothing. A spaceman filling up the spaces in your lives.

Smiley was comparatively fresh in those days. He had died an existential death the day the Russians moved into Czechoslovakia, but as yet the smell of death had not consumed him. He had removed his body from the Party, but there was no way he could recover his soul. And it was his body that came to you and Diana, a cadaver, an empty projectile wrapped in a paisley-patterned cravat.

You cannot be hard on Smiley, Dora. The dead are forgiven everything.

18

Sam was out of bed at six. It was still dark. He pulled on his clothes and checked Dora. She was sleeping. Barney followed him out of the room and he took the dog to the park. Donna, his first wife, had come back in the night, in a dream. He hadn't recognized her at first. He'd thought she was Dora in disguise. She kept trying to tell him something, but he couldn't make out what it was, couldn't hear her. There was a mist, in which she was half dissolved. And an over-amplified chorus of 'Visions Of Johanna', the man at the Isle of Wight in a white suit wishing he was somewhere else. Sam sweating in the dream, a yellow bandanna tied around his head, a Californian sun squeezing him like a sponge.

'Visions Of Johanna' was punctuated regularly by the piercing scream of a child, and Sam held his fists to the sides of his head wishing for a drink, knowing that wasn't the answer, but wishing for a drink anyway. A drink in a glass as long as a dream.

Donna came crashing through it all. She didn't look anything like Dora. She burst through the mist and the amplified music. She was wringing wet, dripping a river, dressed in those tight black jeans and her T-shirt, like always, her skinny arms hanging by her side. 'You've forgotten us, Sam.'

Sam hauled in the dog's lead, patted Barney's head and let him loose. He took the pebbled path behind the tennis courts, then veered left under the trees and along the edge of the water. Donna, and their daughter Bronte, had been his life before they were swept away by a hit-and-run driver. The twenty-five years between then and now sometimes seemed like hours. It was a lie about time being a great healer. Time was nothing.

Sam smiled as he lengthened his stride to keep pace with the dog. There were no ghosts apart from the inventions of the human mind. There was memory and fear and guilt, and the three of them had somehow conspired in the night to bring his long dead wife to the forefront of his mind. But the vision that spoke to him was wrong. He hadn't forgotten her. She was as fresh in his memory as the breeze that skipped over the lake. 'I've changed,' he said to himself. 'I'm not the same man I was then. But I haven't lost my memory. God knows, sometimes I wish I had . . .'

Celia arrived at the house a few minutes before nine. She had been Sam's secretary for four years, after retiring from a career as a schoolteacher. For the greater part of her life she had paid lip service to middle-class good taste, but since getting involved in the PI business she had let all that go. This morning she wore a wide-brimmed hat, shades, and a bright red T-shirt under a black velvet trouser suit. She'd clipped a thin gold rope around her neck, and she had rings on seven of her fingers. Her lips were outlined with peachy pink lipstick, which somehow contrived to highlight the slight gap between her two front teeth.

'You look stunning,' Sam told her.

'I know, and it took a long time,' she said, ducking under his arm and heading for the stairs. 'How's Dora?' It was a rhetorical question, which Sam didn't attempt to answer. Celia was sixty-nine years old, she drove an ancient black MG with no heating, and she only listened when she wanted to.

At the top of the stairs she stopped and turned around. 'I know where everything is,' she said. 'I don't have anything else planned today, so take your time.' She flashed him a smile designed to melt an iceberg.

*

Geordie was using the Montego, so Sam got his bike out of the shed. Diana had found the address for Pammy Shelton, the girl who had been keen on Billy before he did his disappearing act. Although it was seven years ago, the telephone directory still had Pammy's parents listed at the same address. Sam had resisted the temptation to telephone, knowing from long experience that a face-to-face was the best route to information.

He took the cycle track along the river, leaving it at Water End and carrying his bike up the stone steps. The house was large, five bedrooms at a guess, built of custom bricks with a slight sheen to their surface. Carefully tended roses were blooming in the garden, on both sides of the path. The net curtain in the ground-floor window moved slightly as he approached the front door.

He hit the bell and listened to an old-fashioned chime, like the prelude to Big Ben's gong. Kind of thing would drive you crazy if you lived with it. Unless you didn't get any visitors.

There was a scratching sound on the other side of the door, then it was opened wide by a handsome woman in her forties. Dark hair with the occasional grey wisp. What looked like dried mud on her jeans, and behind her a chemical smell, some kind of air freshener.

'Mrs Shelton?'

'Yes.'

'My name's Sam Turner. I'm looking for Pammy Shelton. Your daughter?'

The woman's face changed. It was as if the blood had been sucked out of her in front of his eyes. She reached forward and put her hand on the door-frame to support herself. But it wasn't enough. Her knees buckled, and Sam took a step forward and offered his arm, fearing she would faint. There was a chair in the hallway, beside a telephone table, and he lowered her into it. 'Can I get you something?' he asked. 'A glass of water?'

He left her in the chair and went through to the kitchen. He found a breakfast mug with a picture of a cherry on it, rinsed it under the tap and half filled it with water.

'I'm going to need something stronger than that,' said Mrs Shelton. She had left the hallway, closed the front door, and followed him into the kitchen. Now she walked through an alcove to a sitting room and took a bottle of vodka from a glass cabinet. She waved the bottle at Sam. 'You'll join me?'

'No, thanks. Are you OK?'

'Give me a second.' She poured a double and a half into a leaded glass, took a good swallow and let herself sink into a deeply upholstered black leather chair. 'Sit down,' she said to Sam, waving with the bottle in the direction of a low settee.

There were eight bottles on the floor, beneath the cabinet. A group of three, then a gap and a group of two, then another gap and a single bottle. After that there was a flute case and two more bottles. Sam had a look-see what they were. The first group were Côtes de Luberon, a Navarra, and Bulgarian Russe, all from Sainsbury's.

Then there was a Santa Ema 1990, and a Beaujolais Villages. The Santa Ema wasn't from Sainsbury's. The single bottle was La Mancha. After the flute case was a bottle of Campari with only two inches in the bottom, and two thirds of a bottle of Ginger Wine. We weren't talking serious drinking here.

Sam settled himself into the low settee, watching a shoal of brightly coloured tropical fish travel the length of an aquarium that spanned the wall behind Mrs Shelton. She took another sip of the vodka and appeared to have regained her composure. She looked Sam in the eye. 'Pammy.' She hesitated, flicked her eyes away from him for a moment, then continued. 'She doesn't live here any more.'

Sam shook his head and looked at the fish. Some were ultramarine, tiny, as if they had been squeezed from a tube of pigment. There was another one, much larger, light orange in colour, which seemed to consist of two huge eyes and a mouth equipped with fins and a tail.

Mrs Shelton caught his gaze and glanced behind her. Her tone was sharpened when she spoke again. 'I said Pammy doesn't live here any more.'

'I heard what you said. Trouble is I'm having a hard time putting that together with your reaction when I asked for her at the door. Something's gnawing at you, and if you don't want to tell me what it is, I won't push you. But it seems like the fish are making more sense at the moment.'

She put the remainder of her glass of vodka away in one swallow. Must have been two centimetres there and she didn't even blink. 'What's your business? Why're you looking for my daughter?'

'Mrs Shelton, I'm looking for my wife's son. Billy Greenhills. I understand he was friendly with Pammy some years ago. There is a possibility she could help me trace him. She might even know where he is.'

Sam watched as Mrs Shelton's body exhaled. The glass slipped from her grip and lay on her lap. A tic on her lower right cheek staggered once or twice then went into a flamenco. 'Pammy's dead,' she said. 'She was murdered three years ago.'

Sam let his breath go. He began to speak, searching for some formula of words that would not be patronizing, that would express his regret, his intrusion.

She held a hand up to wave away his apology. 'People don't ask for Pammy any more. Most of the time they avoid speaking her name.'

'If you'd rather not talk about it, or if it would be better some other time, I don't mind.'

The woman picked up her glass and splashed vodka into the bottom of it. 'You've started me off now,' she said, a smile without joy moving round her eyes. 'Once I start talking about Pammy I can't stop.' She sipped from the glass. 'Billy Greenhills. Yes, I remember him. Nice boy. Polite. They were the same age. He was round here a couple of times, just after they left school. Pammy was keen on him, always talking about him, but he went away.'

'You don't know where?'

'London, wasn't it? I don't remember. I'd forgotten all about him.'

'You never saw him again? When he came back to York?'

She shook her head, slowly, from side to side. 'I didn't even know he'd come back. When was that?'

'Three years ago, we think. During the summer.'

Mrs Shelton wasn't listening. She spoke with a quiet, dream-like voice. 'Pammy died in the autumn. September. She'd been married for eighteen months. Sandy, her daughter, was six months old. They thought it was her husband, Russell, but he was devoted to her. He'd never have harmed her.'

'Did they arrest him?'

'No, but they wasted a lot of time with him. By the time they'd finished with Russell the real murderer had covered his tracks.'

'So he was never caught?'

She shook her head. Her mouth fell open.

'Mrs Shelton, is your daughter's husband still in the area?'

'Russell? Yes, he and Sandy live in Clifton. Not far away.'

'Could you give me his address? There's a possibility he might know where Billy is.'

She left the chair and found a small address book. Sam took it from her and copied Russell Wright's address and telephone number into his own notebook.

When he left, Mrs Shelton didn't see him to the door. She was tucked in between the bottle and the glass, framed by the relentless voyage of the multi-coloured fish in the aquarium.

*

He had intended to ride round to Russell Wright's address, but once he got on the bike, Mrs Shelton's grief got to him. He followed the cycle track along the river, back into town. The woman's sorrow over the death of her daughter brought back Sam's earlier thoughts about Donna, his first wife, and Dora who would soon return to him his widower's mantle. He fully intended to speak with Russell Wright later, but after facing the grief of Mrs Shelton, the breeze and the boats on the water were too good to miss.

He bought a chicken tikka sandwich and watched the river flow.

In the Walmgate offices of the *Evening Press* he read through the newspaper reports of the murder of Pammy Wright. Three years earlier, during the first days of September, she had been found by her husband when he returned from work. She was stretched out on the kitchen floor, strangled with a rope. Their infant daughter, Sandy, was upstairs in a high-sided cot, her nappy heavily soiled. She was distressed because she had missed a couple of her feeds, but otherwise unharmed.

The killing was puzzling, as there appeared to be no motive. Pammy had not been sexually assaulted, and there was nothing missing from the house. The woman's purse, containing nearly fifty pounds, was left by the kettle in the kitchen, in open view. There were signs that there had been a short struggle before she was overpowered.

The press called the killer the Surgeon – because he was meticulously clean, having left behind no fingerprints, nothing to indicate who he was.

And because, before he left to fade away into the anonymity of the city, he had taken a knife from the cutlery drawer and stabbed deeply into both of the dead woman's eyes.

Sam asked the receptionist to ring the crime-desk and see if Sly Beaumont was available. In the age-old tradition of favour-for-favour Sam had a couple of points in hand with the old reporter. But Sly was looking for even more. He stuck a cigarette in his mouth and lit it as he walked over the plush carpeting. 'Sam. You've come to offer me a scoop. Am I right?'

'If I had one I'd give it to no one else, Sly. But I don't have anything. I'm looking for enlightenment.'

The old guy laughed, his face creased up like a crumpled paper bag. He took a long draw on the cigarette and coughed. 'Enlightenment? Sorry, old son, you've got the wrong department. You want my wife.'

'The Surgeon,' Sam said.

'You know something about the Surgeon, Sam?' Sly's tone changed abruptly, he reached for the notebook sticking out of his hip pocket.

'I only know what's been in the press, Sly. What I've heard and seen on the news. I'm here to find out what *you* know.'

'Let's walk.' Sam followed Sly out of the office and joined him on the pavement outside. They walked towards Walmgate Bar, the Elizabethan house on top a perfect silhouette in the afternoon sun.

'He's a nutter,' Sly continued. 'Strangled three women in the last three years. Leaves no evidence, no clues. Doesn't steal anything, has no sexual intentions, doesn't even ruffle their clothes.'

'I know about Pammy Wright,' Sam said. 'I talked with her mother, and I read up your articles. What about the others?'

'Pammy was the first. The following year he killed Amy Munroe, thirty-five-year-old, mother of three. Lived out at Escrick. Then last year Lynn Camish, a widow. Her daughter found her in the kitchen, like the others. House on the Haxby Road.'

'No connection between the women?'

'Nothing at all. Amy Munroe was Afro-Caribbean, Lynn

Camish was from the coast, she'd only been in York for two years, and Pammy Wright was born in the city. They'd never met, didn't belong to any of the same clubs, their children went to different schools.' They reached the Bar and walked through it, passing the wooden doors and portcullis.

'What's your interest, Sam? I know you, once you get your teeth into something.'

'I'd tell you if I had anything,' Sam said. 'But I don't. A completely different case threw up a connection with Pammy Wright. But my man only knew her when they were at school together, when she was a girl called Pammy Shelton. I don't know anything new about the Surgeon.'

'Then, why the questions?'

'I got waylaid. After I talked with Pammy's mother I wanted to know more.'

'So you came to the oracle.'

'Yeah, Sly. For enlightenment.' They turned around on the pavement and walked back the way they had come. 'Is there forensic evidence connecting the three murders?'

'Yeah, the guy's got a roll of washing line. When he's ready for the next kill he cuts a piece off specially for the job.'

'Anything else?'

'Not hard evidence. But the MO is almost identical. They're all women. Nothing is ever stolen. They're not raped or sexually assaulted. They're all strangled in their kitchens. And after they're dead he gouges their eyes out.'

'Sounds like someone with a mission.'

'Too fucking true, Sammy boy,' said Sly turning into the Press offices. 'If you hang on for a minute I'll get you photocopies of the file. Then you'll know as little as the rest of us.'

19

Billy is asleep when Smiley comes. Diana is ready for bed, she has washed and brushed her hair. The hem of her white nightie is showing beneath her dressing-gown. She takes him by the hand and shows him the table which she has helped you to set. She points to the candles and explains that they are not to be lit until the meal is served.

They sit on either side of the fireplace, their faces lit by the flames as you baste the lamb one last time. Diana has discovered a face of utter serenity. She sits with her hands clasped together in her lap, her wondering eyes drinking in the potent sweetness of this god who has descended on her house.

'Billy's in bed,' she tells him. 'He's too young to stay up.'

Smiley shrugs his shoulders, shifts uncomfortably in the chair. He has nothing to say to her. He tugs at his cravat and looks at the pictures on the wall.

'We don't usually have a fire,' Diana continues. 'It's specially for you.' Her wide eyes follow the movements of his fingers as he scratches his nose.

'Mmm,' he says, making a superhuman effort. 'Mmm.' And a little later, 'Mmm. Hmm.'

'It's lamb,' says Diana, leaning forward in her chair, gaining confidence from his obvious encouragement. 'In the oven? Lamb with mint sauce and potatoes. Are you hungry?'

Smiley opens his mouth, but then closes it again, contenting himself with a nod of the head. Diana sits back in the chair, satisfied. She lets the serenity seep back into her face, and speaks again, her voice steady. 'Do you know my name? It's Diana Miriam Greenhills.'

'Mmm. Hmm.'

'And you're called Smiley,' she says. 'Smiley Thompson. Is it true? Are you really called Smiley?'

He clears his throat and finds a word. 'Yes.'

'Oh.' Diana leaps from her chair and jumps up and down on the carpet. 'Wonderful. It's the most wonderful name in the world. Smiley. It's so, so happy.' She claps her hands together and rushes through to the kitchen. 'It's true, Dora,' she says. 'He is called Smiley. He is. He really is.'

When you have put her to bed you light the candles and serve the lamb. Smiley comes alive in his memories. He talks of the campaigns and the personalities of the Party before '56 and the later betrayals, Czechoslovakia, Poland. He was born in the year that Ramsay MacDonald's Labour government resigned, and was visiting the seventy-year-old Ernest Bevin the day that China invaded Tibet. The old man talked him out of a career in politics, something that Smiley has regretted for the rest of his life.

You were ten then, Dora. Dylan Thomas was wandering *Under Milk Wood* between orgies of alcoholism, but the memory of his lips had already faded. You knew nothing about the Chinese invasion of Tibet. You were in love with King George VI and his beautiful daughters Elizabeth and Margaret. You cried when he died. It seemed so unfair.

Smiley tells you he has been dreaming about your body, and you push the fat of the lamb to the side of your plate and stand. You are already forty-one. Your body has a lot of lost time to make up.

Lady Day is singing 'Carelessly' on the turntable but neither of you is listening.

Afterwards, when Smiley has gone home to his wife, you go to the children's rooms to tuck them in. Billy is a sleeping angel spilling out of the quilt. Diana is clutching a photograph of Smiley, stolen from your dressing-table. It is wet with her kisses.

20

Russell Wright told Sam where Billy lived. Wright didn't know Billy personally, but his name was entered in an old address book which had belonged to Pammy. The house was in St Mary's, a bleak edifice, badly in need of paint and general maintenance. It was dusk when he arrived, and Sam found himself walking past the front door. He had intended to knock on the door and confront Billy, tell him that Dora was ill, that she wanted to see him. But he didn't do it. Instead, he walked beyond the house, then crossed over to the other side of St Mary's and slowly retraced his steps.

Some kind of instinct at work? Sam didn't know what it was. There was an unconscious process going on which had kept him from knocking on Billy's door, and he needed to sort out what it was. Alcoholics learn to distrust the unconscious, knowing better than most that it plans disasters for them, and for everyone around them. He glanced at the house as he passed, noted that all was in darkness apart from a single attic light which was so dim it could have been a candle. Then he negotiated the small pedestrian passage and steps which led him on to Marygate Lane. He made his way towards the Museum Gardens, but when he got there the gate was locked. He took the river path instead, and eventually sat on the same bench he had used earlier to eat his sandwich. There it was again, that old river rolling along.

The moon came up and Sam shook his head slowly from side to side. He hadn't knocked on the door because he'd put Billy in the frame for the murders of three women. Yeah, there it was, summary justice. He'd never met the guy, had no evidence against him apart from a flimsy possible connection with Pammy Wright, and he'd already convinced himself that Billy, the son of Dora, the brother of Diana, was a serial killer.

And it's always the way that as soon as you do that, as soon as you make that kind of judgement, then everything else, every event and coincidence just goes to prove that you were right in the first place. So the fact that the building Billy lives in hasn't been painted, and the dim light in the guy's bedroom, all conspire to augment his guilt.

Sam smiled to himself. That was one of the great drawbacks to being a detective. You had to think everyone was guilty. Oh, sure, Billy Greenhills was the Surgeon, he probably killed India Blake as well. Different MO, but what the hell, she was a woman, and Billy killed women. At least three we know about, probably a whole lot more we don't know about, yet, in different parts of the country.

Look at this. The guy lives alone. He has no contact with his family. Probably masturbates and lives off the state. Never changes his socks.

Blow the fucker away.

Sam Turner, radical, liberal thinker and social reformer. Move over, Mother Teresa, there's a rival on the scene.

He walked back to St Mary's, and this time he would have knocked on Billy's door, except that Billy left the house and made his way towards Bootham, while Sam was still seventy metres away. Sam followed, telling himself that's what detectives do. Getting into that old familiar argument with himself: I don't wanna shout out the guy's name in the street in the dark, then go through all that business of introducing myself, making sure he's who I think he is. And I know I don't *have* to follow him, but why not? I'm here. He's here. I might learn something. OK, so I'm a bloodhound. That's how I got into this kind of work.

Billy walked to High Petergate and went into the York Arms. He bought himself a pint and took it through into the back room. Sam got an orange juice and stood at the bar, close to the entrance, so he'd see when Billy left.

After twenty minutes Sam walked through the back to the Gents. Billy was sitting alone at a small round table, about a third of a pint of beer in front of him. The other tables in the room were occupied by couples and groups. A hen party had put two tables together and commandeered all the unused chairs and stools in the room, so that Billy's table had no spare seats at it. He was swarthy. Thick, well-shaped lips. He had Dora's chin. His hair was styled like Elvis Presley's, but without the sideburns. It rose in a quiff at the front, and then sailed backwards over his head, held in place with enough gel to get a trifle started. His eyes were deep set and dark, hidden beneath pronounced brows, just a glitter there, a flash of white. A large elastoplast was sticking to the front of his throat.

When he got back to the bar, Sam was disappointed. The glance he'd had of Billy had not been enough. It was as if he hadn't seen him at all. He'd seen what Billy had wanted to project. But that projection contained no essence of the man behind it. It was a mask.

Was he wearing make-up?

Sam listened to a monologue from the table behind him. A middle-aged man's voice said: 'We're all up for grabs as far as he's concerned. The guy's got the morals of an alley cat. What do you think, Sugar?'

Sam half turned his body so that he could get a picture of the face behind the voice. Middle-aged, as he'd guessed, rotund and fresh-faced, going bald. Sugar was a tall guy with a moustache, reminiscent of Freddie Mercury in the old days, long ago.

In this town there was no such thing as a bar without a poet or a philosopher. Does anybody know what we are living for?

Sam struggled through another orange juice before Billy

136

left the pub. Counted to twenty-five and hit the pavement behind him. There were still several people about, flitting among the pubs and restaurants, gazing in the lighted windows of the shops. Billy took a slow, sauntering walk towards Stonegate, where he mingled with groups of tourists, and parties of drinkers outside Ye Olde Starre Inn and the Punch Bowl. A busker playing a battered guitar was insistent that he was the piano man, and, sure, he could be a movie star if he once got away from this place. Sam watched him for a full minute, then dropped a coin into his cup. The guy was really shook.

A saxophone some place far off played.

A table was overturned and a couple erupted into a spitting, scratching battle on the pavement. The chaos came out of nowhere. Suddenly they faced each other, talons drawn. She went for his eyes, and he brushed her aside and pushed with both hands on her chest. She staggered back, her arms flailing to maintain balance, but she was always going down. A couple of latter day knights decided to bruise her assailant's kidneys, and a running fight developed.

'A pretty piece of business,' someone said. The crowd quickly divided into those who wanted to stay, perhaps join in the fun, and others who favoured a change of scenery. The girl who had gone down was back on her feet. She screamed something unintelligible at her boyfriend and stalked off towards Coney Street.

Billy followed.

Sam was not far behind.

Maybe he wasn't following her, just travelling in the same direction. Except he was close to her, dogging her footsteps. Not so close that she felt threatened, though she'd obviously drunk a lot, and might not have noticed him. Billy kept ten metres behind, and followed her on the same side of the street. After Coney Street she went past the fire station and eventually stood with her finger on a bell of a flat in

Fishergate. Billy crossed over the road then, and stood inside a bus shelter, watching until a man answered the door and pulled her inside.

Sam watched the watcher.

Billy stayed inside the bus shelter for a further ten minutes. Then he made his way back across town to St Mary's. Sam followed. They passed hopeful whores and despairing ones. Billy let himself into the house and Sam heard him locking out the world, a mortise lock, and a couple of bolts at top and bottom.

Later, at home, Sam looked at a couple of photographs. Both black and white. The first showed Billy as a boy, fifteen years old. Dark eyes staring out of a white face. There was a trace of Dora there, around the mouth, but the broad forehead and the setting for those eyes were a direct gift from Arthur, the subject of the second photograph.

Arthur was not posing. He appeared to be staring into space, unconscious, and the photographer, probably Dora, had caught him in profile. Someone else might have made something of the photograph, taken hints from the way Arthur was holding his body, diagnosed character and personality. Sam couldn't do that. He saw a guy who'd been dead for seventeen years. Someone who'd made a final decision, decided not to pass on any more replicas of his forehead and his eyes.

He let both photographs lie where they fell on the desk. He felt in his inside pocket for another one, and looked at that for several minutes. It was a copy of a photograph Marie had given him of India Blake. She was a truly beautiful woman. A stylish coat over a black lace blouse and a knee-length skirt. She was gazing past the photographer, at the future, wondering what it might hold, and not guessing the truth. His eyes were always drawn back to her face. The symmetry of her features. Flawless. Completely beautiful and completely dead.

21

William threw off the covers and stretched himself out on the bed. He slept with the window open and the morning air was sharp. Glancing down along his pale body he watched the goose pimples raising themselves up to defend his borders. Mindless, the struggle for survival, cellular, molecular.

As the dawn took its course and light slowly filtered through the curtains he felt his body temperature dropping. He didn't move, that would be cheating. If he moved his heart would respond and send a warm rush of blood to all those peripheral regions. What William wanted was the opposite; he wanted his heart to slow down, his blood to run cold.

There were people in the world who could slow their heart rate to a fraction of its normal activity. Some of the Brahmin holy men could wind it right down to a few beats a minute. William's heart, at rest, was normally sixty-four beats a minute, but in his morning sessions he could get it down to under forty. He could control it.

He could begin to feel how his father had felt.

William had first experienced the cold, real cold, when he had touched his father that day they took him down from the tree. His mother had taken them upstairs, William and his big sister, left them in the large front bedroom while she went to a neighbour's house for help. His sister had said they must stay there, but William wanted to be with his father. 'You can't make me stay,' he'd told her. 'You're only ten, and you're a girl.'

'Daddy's dead,' his sister had said. 'We'll never see him again.'

William shook her off and went down to the garden. Daddy was there, swinging on the tree, gently, back and forth, swaying. He didn't answer when William spoke to him. Daddy didn't say anything, but he knew William was there, and he was glad they'd come back. He was much fatter than William remembered. It was as if he was full of air, like a huge tyre that had been blown up too much. He was still William's father, but a person with all that air inside them might burst.

What it was, he was stuck up there in the tree. The rope around his neck was keeping him from speaking. A person with a rope around their neck, they wouldn't be able to speak, even if they wanted to. And the rope was what was keeping all the air inside. Like with a balloon, you tied string around it to keep the air in, didn't you? Yes, or you tied a knot in it.

And if the rope was very tight, then a person wouldn't be able to undo it all by themself. Of course they wouldn't. They'd need help.

William knew if it was him up in the tree, William up there with a rope around his neck so tight he couldn't speak, then Daddy would get a ladder or a chair or something and climb up and help him get the rope off his neck. There was a chair on the grass. One of the new chairs out of the kitchen, which wasn't supposed to be outside. And it certainly wasn't supposed to be kicked over in the grass. William righted it and climbed up on to the seat, but even when he stood on tiptoe he couldn't reach higher than his father's knees.

He ran down to the garden shed and pushed at the door. Locked. He went back to the house and got his mother's stepladder from the laundry, set it up under the swaying feet of his father. The stepladder wasn't firm on the lawn under the pear tree, it wobbled as he got higher. The top step of the ladder brought William's head level with his father's waist. Even if he stretched to his full height he couldn't

140

reach the rope. He would have to climb the tree itself, crawl out on the branch above his father's head. Or, and a new thought came into his mind, he could climb up his father's body. Sit on his shoulders like he used to before they went away. That was one of the things he missed when his mother took them away. Sitting on his daddy's shoulders while his daddy pranced around on the grass. It felt like you could fall off any minute and really hurt yourself, but you knew that Daddy would never let you fall. So it was dangerous and safe all at the same time, made you squeal and laugh at the top of your voice.

William grasped hold of Daddy's belt and kicked off. The stepladder clattered over on to the grass. The two of them swung from side to side together, and William wrapped his legs around Daddy's waist. He pulled himself higher by grasping his father's lapel, and eventually he got his foot onto the buckle of Daddy's belt, and from there it was easy enough to get up to his shoulders. And easy to sit there as well, because he could hold the rope as well as his father's head.

But he couldn't loosen the rope. He couldn't unpick the knots. Once William had managed to unpick a knot in his shoelaces, and that had been difficult, had taken him nearly an hour. But the knots on the rope around Daddy's neck were much tighter than shoelace knots. It was going to be terribly difficult to untie knots like these. If shoelace knots took a whole hour, then knots like the ones around Daddy's neck might take years and years and years.

It was then that he felt the cold. His father's forehead was sticky and cold. Squashy on the surface and slabby like rubber underneath, and much colder than anyone William had ever touched before. And there was something else, that he'd noticed earlier, but that now he was sat on his father's shoulders was nearly unbearable. And that was the smell.

William had never smelled something before that got

inside your mouth as well as your nose. It was a vile and rank odour that clung to his tongue, crept down inside his throat so that he thought he might suffocate. He retched, and his stomach moved inside him, his mouth filled with bile, and he spat it out, over his father's head. The stench remained. The nearest he could get to it, it was like the time the freezer broke down and all the ice cream and meat melted, and when they came back from holiday the floor was covered in blood and maggots.

He was sitting on Daddy's shoulder, hanging on to the rope, smelling the smell and trying to work it out in his mind when the men arrived in their uniforms. At first there was just one of them. He came through the house and out of the back door. He was dressed in black, with boots and a leather jacket, an enormous crash helmet, so you couldn't see his face. He looked up at William, his hands on his hips, and he said, 'Jesus fucking Christ,' and he shook his head and walked back towards the house.

Then there was another man, and another two with a stretcher. And the new man came over and took hold of Daddy's legs to stop them swinging, and he reached up towards William and said, 'Come down, son. It'll be all right. I'll catch you.'

And William might have come down then, only the original man came back, the one in black with the crash helmet, and he said it again, 'Jesus fucking Christ, d'you believe this?' He picked up the stepladder and set it up, stood on the bottom rung. William was suddenly frightened and he stood on Daddy's shoulders and caught hold of the upper branch of the tree and climbed up on to it.

'No, not that way,' the crash helmet said. Then to the other man: 'For fuck sake, it's bad enough without the kid. Stink's worse than the wife's breath.'

William kept climbing. He climbed to the very top of the tree, where the branches became thin, so that if he'd gone further they wouldn't hold his weight. They tried to coax him down for a long time, but he wasn't going to move, not as long as the one with the crash helmet was there. You couldn't see his eyes under that thing.

William watched as the photographer arrived, and while he took photographs of Daddy. And then there was a much older man with a white beard and a briefcase who had one of those things they stick in their ears so they can listen to your heart. Crash helmet held the stepladder for him and the bearded man climbed up and listened to Daddy's heart. 'This is ludicrous,' he said as he was climbing back down.

Eventually they concentrated on getting his father down. But they didn't undo the knot, like William expected. They cut him down. One of them did the cutting and the other one tried to catch Daddy. He had him by the legs, and the first one said, 'You right?'

'Yeah. I've got him.'

So the first one cut the rope and William's father plunged down on top of the second one. The stepladder slid away and it ended with Daddy and both of the policemen in a heap on the grass. The other two men with the stretcher laughed, but William didn't think it was funny.

After they'd loaded Daddy on to the stretcher and taken him away, the policeman with the crash helmet left and the nice one asked William to come down from the tree. When he got down the policeman said he'd been very brave and he could cry now if he wanted to.

But he didn't feel like crying.

Later, when he pushed his plate away, his mother said he should eat something. But he didn't feel like eating.

And the next day, when Diana said she was going to the shop for some sweets and he could go with her, he didn't feel like moving.

*

Seventeen years later, he remained inert, naked on the bed for an hour and a half, his mind working, his other bodily systems flickering uncertainly. He didn't shiver once, though he gritted his teeth for the last twenty minutes as the morning air chilled him to the bone.

22

You gag with pain as an iron bar leaps through your body.
Diana spins from the window and comes forward, fear in
her eyes, and in her shaking hands. 'Dora. What is it?'

'Aghhhhh.' The bar is cold and hot, with all the compassion of the industrial revolution. It drags your eyes from
their sockets; sends a line of spittle dribbling along your
jaw. It sticks, lodges in a thick crevice of muscle and nerve
from the pit of your left arm to the dead inside of your right
hip. It is an old axle, rusted and heavy, as taut as Arthur's
rope.

'Hang on, Dora. I'll get Sam.'

'Dear God.' Outside, a squall of wind whips the leaves
along the avenue. A car speeds past, too fast. Ignore the
pain. Try to ignore it. Short breaths. That's better. Short,
fast, tiny breaths. In out, in out, in out. There are still leaves
on the tree.

Sam crosses the room in two strides, wiping his hands on
the front of his T-shirt. His face is drawn. Your eyes leap
towards him. 'I'm going to carry you over to the bed,' he
says.

In out, in out, in out. 'No. Don't touch me.' Keep the
breathing going. 'It's an iron bar, Sam. Right through me.'

He puts his arms under you. 'You'll rest better in the bed,'
he says. 'Don't worry. I'll be gentle.'

You are flying, Dora. Flying through the air. You look
back at the window, the leaves in the street, the solitary
trees. A quick, last glimpse before you are lowered to the
bed. The bar shifts inside you, settles, pushes your jaw and
neck to the left, hard against the pillow.

'How's that?'

'No.' You shake your head.

Sam moves you over on your side and the bar passes out of focus. The bar does not go away, it lies with a degree of acceptable discomfort inside you.

In out, in out, in out. 'OK.' It's OK if you don't move. Keep up the breathing. 'Get her out of here.' Diana is hovering in the doorway. She shouldn't see this. Sam should get her out of here.

'No, Dora. I'm staying.' She comes forward, places a hand on the quilt. 'I'm not a baby. I *want* to be here.'

You try a deeper breath and let it whistle out through your teeth. There's no point arguing with Diana. She's going to stay.

Dear God, Dora. You have no strength now. Your eyes close. The room is silent. Sam and Diana recede. Smiling Smiley scowls down at you from the past. He has found another woman.

A woman? He has found a girl, one of his students, twenty years old. You are forty-one. No contest. Experience counts for nothing. Smiley is on a quest for innocence. He discards his cravats; buys a pair of suede shoes, slip-ons, without laces.

His girl is called Sally Bowles. She has never heard of Isherwood. She is a kid. She watches you with sharpened teeth. She smiles every minute of the day, maliciously. She has caught a big fat Smiley fly in her silken web. She is the happiest, the hungriest, the most popular girl on campus. A witch-woman, sick with her own power. Smiley tells you she carries contraceptives in her saddle bag. And you, Dora? You don't even have a bike.

Smiley lasted for ever. He was always there. Part of the fixtures, until he was gone. And then there was you, Dora. You and Diana and Billy. And no one else.

Diana rampaged through the house like a wild thing. It

was your fault, Dora. It was all your fault. You had lost him. Lost him for yourself, and lost him for Diana. It was the Arthur story all over again. You were not grasping enough. You should have pinned him down when you had the chance. Now it is too late. He has gone to Sally Bowles.

He has gone to Sally Bowles and you indulge yourself in a year or more of enforced domesticity. You spend time with your children, you take them out at the weekends, you read to them, you buy them new clothes and alter the old ones. You make dresses for Diana, sprawling over the carpet with paper patterns, cutting, sewing, rainbow silks and satins. The three of you toddle off down the avenue to the theatre, a box of Cadbury's Bourneville Selection passing to and fro in the dark. You try everything to make it feel like an ordinary family, a normal family. But there is no man there, only the ghost of one. The father of your children strung himself from the pear tree. You cannot alter it, Dora. You are different. Billy and Diana are different. They know what people say. They take the jibes from the other kids at school. Billy screams out in his sleep. Diana never speaks about it in words of more than one syllable.

You were all born a generation too early. What was acceptable in 1990, and what will be commonplace at the turn of the century (far too late for you), is still barely thinkable in 1980. You are a victim of history. You nudged too far ahead of your time, on to the spearhead ledge where saints and martyrs stand. The ledge where all personal magic is anachronistic; where the only possible redemption is grace.

You dared to think that Philip was grace, and that Philip's world might hold a nook for you. You had courage, Dora, in those days. Or was it something else? Bravado? Madness?

The doorbell rings. You are reading a first-year essay, poised above it with your red pen. It is an essay you have read a million times before, penned by different hands; it

147

has no originality, no resonance, no life. It is Wednesday evening, the last time you looked at your watch it was after ten. You glance at it again. It is still after ten.

You open the door to a slim young man. Very young. You guess he is not much more than twenty. He is dark with quick, penetrating eyes. When he speaks you catch the rough edge in his voice, intimations of Arthur and an origin in the working class.

'Are you Dora?' he asks. 'My name's Philip. Smiley sent me.'

'Smiley? Is something wrong?'

'No. He gave me your name and address. I'm starting a campaign to free Rachel Lloyd. Smiley thought you might be interested in helping.'

You know about Rachel Lloyd, Dora. She has been arrested in Argentina. What does he mean, a campaign? Why should Smiley give your name to him?

Philip shivers on the doorstep. 'Is it too late to come in?' he asks.

You show him into the kitchen, offering coffee, still not sure if you want to be involved in this scheme.

'Milk,' he says.

'Milk?'

'Yeah, just a glass of cold milk. If that's all right?'

You go to the refrigerator, asking him how he thinks you can help. When you turn back he has seated himself at the table and is unbuttoning his coat. He looks even younger in the artificial light. Perhaps he is not yet twenty. His eyes flash around the room.

He places a sheaf of papers on the table. 'I've got together as many facts as I can,' he says. 'There's something about her history in there, previous research, et cetera. It's obvious they've got her on a trumped-up charge. They must need a scapegoat.' He pauses to drink milk from his glass, leaving a white film on his upper lip. 'Christ, that's really good.

Smiley wants to help, but he's tied up at the moment. We thought you could handle the university end of things. I'm working on the trade unions and trying to push it through my Labour Party branch, but it would be good if the university was involved.'

'Do you have a petition?'

'Yeah.' He points to the sheaf of papers. 'It's all in there. We need to get some bread together to start a campaign fund. Smiley thought you could help with that.'

'Money?'

He nods his head. 'Bread, yeah. If you want to help you could have a party or something. Charge admission. The petition form has a section for donations to the campaign fund. We don't need a lot. Something to cover expenses, and if we get more we can send it to Rachel. She's probably being starved in prison.'

A party, Dora. Why not? It would bring people to the house. New contacts. As well as providing money, er, bread?, for the campaign fund.

'You invite the university crowd,' he says. 'I'll bring a group from the Labour Party, well, Young Socialists. We'll ask everyone who comes to sign the petition and give a donation to the fund.'

'OK.' You laugh, and realize that you have not laughed like that for a long time. Not a real laugh.

Philip looks around the room as he prepares to leave. 'It's a nice place,' he says. 'A really nice place.'

And a fortnight later he is there again, together with his friends from the Young Socialists. Smiley is there with Sally Bowles. The University Socialist and Labour Societies, and the trappings of the party, wine, bottles and kegs of beer, and for you, Dora, a special treat and indulgence: a bottle of gin.

You drink far too much of the gin. Smiley's fault, of course. You would not have drunk so much if he had stayed

149

away, or at least left his Sally Bowles at home. But she is there, looking ravishing, and young, and clinging to Smiley's arm, her eyes flashing.

The party works anyway, despite you, Dora. Someone takes over the record player and plays silly pop songs, which seem to be exactly what everyone wants. They drink, they mix, they dance, they talk and laugh together, and no one leaves until well after midnight. Then they come to you, singly, and in couples. They have to leave, but it has been wonderful. Really enjoyable. Their faces are shining, their eyes sparkling. They are not putting on an act, being merely polite. The best party for a long time. You must do it again, Dora. People should mix more. There is not enough social life in this town. It really has been wonderful. Everyone is pleased.

When they have gone there is only you and Philip. He makes coffee for you in the kitchen and brings it through to the living room. He drinks milk. He rubs his stomach thoughtfully, nursing his ulcer. You don't believe in his ulcer. He is far too young to have an ulcer. But maybe you are wrong. Your head is difficult to hold. The coffee seems to help, but you have drunk a lot of gin.

You never get to know Philip. He reveals himself all the time. He is naive, even endearing, but there is no substance to him. He is a leader. People follow his lead because he is open-ended, vacant. It is possible to make of him whatever you will, to project on to him qualities that you wish were there. But there is nothing. In reality he is a simple soul: he fucks (will you ever be completely comfortable with that word?), he coins platitudes, he takes. You can never resist him.

You could talk to him all night and still not find his core, because he has never found it himself. When he leaves your bed he leaves nothing behind, not even a memory. The sheet is cold next to you. It is as if he has never been there. He is an escapologist like Houdini and Dylan Thomas. His kisses fade on contact. You make him real by discussions about him with a third person; everyone wants to talk about him. But when everything has been said he has slipped away into the mists of Argentina, or Rachel Lloyd, or marriage, or, finally, he has disappeared, gone, vanished.

For some weeks (was it months?) he used your bed like a urinal. He comes to it on impulse, relieves himself, and goes away. Eventually he comes no longer, marries his Jude, and leaves an epitaph tacked to your soul: *Christ, Dora, I like old women. They're so grateful.*

But the parties go on. The parties go on for ever. And the gin bottle becomes a fixture. It leads you from one Saturday night to the next. You experiment with marijuana, taking small drags and aping the reactions of the rest of the group. It does not do anything for you. The young men hover around like flies, and you do not brush them away.

They are all Philips in different shapes and sizes, young bucks eager to flex their new-found sexual muscle. They bring a kind of warmth with them, even a kind of meaning. But they do not stay. They never stay for long. You do not have what it is they seek. You only have the semblance of it, the remains of it. You are a teacher, a practice ramp. They always take their proficiency elsewhere.

Even Cecil did not stay for long. And you could have loved her, Dora; she was different enough, odd, even ugly enough. You could have loved her if she had not been jealous of your past.

You slept through the eighties, Dora. You slept with everyone. You were unconscious, dreaming. Life was a nightmare, a succession of unfulfilled promises.

That day.

Diana comes home from school early, refusing to return, ever. The other kids say her mother is a cow. She stands and screams until you slap her face. There is a fire in the York Minster and an abducted Nigerian exile is found in a crate at Stansted. You need a drink.

Remember. An ex-sailor draping a black cape on the carpet. His friend called Scottie. You lie naked on the bed. The sailor and Scottie sit on either side of you. Scottie has a full day's growth of beard, and earlier in the evening you fed him figs and asked him to kiss you on the cheek. Things have progressed since then. Terry Waite has been kidnapped in Beirut. The sailor watches you and Scottie undress each other; he sits like Buddha at the end of your bed, waiting for his turn. Now they are both saying thank you. They have to go. They have never met anyone like you.

When was it? A stuttering revolutionary called David. What the hell, Dora, you might be able to cure him. Of stuttering? Of spots? Of impotence? He's got everything. He curses you, having read somewhere that language turns women on. His cock lies in the palm of your hand like a dead mouse. You are the ugliest woman he has ever slept with. He cannot believe you are that old. He must have been out of his mind to come here, to your room. You are a filthy wrinkled cow. He couldn't; he just couldn't. If you are desperate he will help you out with the neck of the gin bottle. The Internationale unites the human race. In the morning. The *Guardian* tells you: *All-day opening in English and Welsh pubs.*

Television pictures. The Berlin wall is pulled down. You return home to find a long black cape on the living-room floor. Diana is in bed with the sailor. You scream. You pull him out of bed by his leg, drag him across the carpet, along the corridor, down the stairs. You scream and tear your hair. You stand and scream until Diana slaps your face. She is only having fun. 'You don't have a monopoly on it, Dora. You have no right to interfere.' She stands at her bedroom window and watches the sailor limp along the avenue. She is naked apart from a T-shirt. She turns adult eyes on you. Eyes you have never seen her wear before. 'You . . . you . . . God.' She stamps her foot in frustration. 'We hadn't even finished.'

You go to your first AA meeting. You stop drinking. There are no more parties. Just you and Lady Day.

Diana goes to Czechoslovakia to fight for democracy. You watch the demonstrations on the television. She does not return when she said she would. One hundred and seventeen Czech policemen have been injured. She is not among those arrested. You wait for three and a half black weeks before she writes to Billy from Prague. 'Having fun. Tell Dora not to worry.' Alexander Dubček has become chairman of the Federal Assembly. Vaclav Havel is President.

23

J.D. had been playing poker last night. Might be playing still. Marie had slept fitfully. Alone. She thought she would never get used to having a man in her bed again, but it had only taken a couple of nights. Now, when he wasn't there, she found it hard to adjust. She dragged herself to the bathroom and stood under the shower. J.D. must have altered the settings because it was hotter than usual and the water velocity swifter, drumming her flesh.

Gus, her late husband, had installed the shower. From time to time Marie thought of leaving this house, moving somewhere else, somewhere new, where Gus hadn't fitted the shower, or painted the ceiling, where he hadn't built a corner unit. Somewhere he hadn't left a print.

But she didn't move, because it would be pointless. The man had left his mark on *her*. There was never a gap of more than a few days when she didn't think about him. After the initial shock of his death, a kind of dazed withdrawal, she had pulled herself together for the funeral. Everyone had gathered around, Sam and Geordie, and especially Celia, and walked her through it. Literally. Held her up by the elbows.

That had been the easy part.

Later she had gone on a quest for Gus, a tense period of restless behaviour, a kind of madness. She would see him in the street. She would see someone, some *thing* in the street, which wasn't Gus, which could not possibly have been Gus, but which, in her madness, she thought was him. There was a day when she followed a man she believed was her dead husband. She saw him in Parliament Street and tracked him through Marks and Spencer and along the Stonebow, and caught hold of him outside Sainsbury's, touched his shoulder, and sucked in her breath as he turned towards her a face which belonged to a stranger.

In her desire for a miracle she would hallucinate him. Reading a book at the small table in the living room, lost in the plot or the syrupy lives of the characters, unaware of real life, real events, she'd look up and watch Gus materialize opposite her. It was as if he were real. As if she could reach out and touch him. He'd be wearing the green sweater, the one that had lost a thread near the collar, and she'd want to reach out and take it from him, mend it before it got worse.

And at night, in deep sleep, he'd lead her through a dreamscape of fantasy and contradiction. She dreamed that he had died in her dream, that in reality he was still alive. She simply had to wake up and everything would be all right. Morning after morning she'd awake with incomprehension, total disbelief, that he wasn't there beside her. In those moments before waking she could feel him next to her, hear his breathing. She'd say, 'Gus.' And then a little louder, trying it out, hoping to hear him reply from the bathroom or the stairs.

But he couldn't.

She'd explode then, tell him to get himself back here. And the anger would consume her, because who the hell did he think he was getting himself shot like that? How could he, how *dare* he take that kind of risk with her life, her future. She was abandoned. A woman deserted. He'd gone out and got himself killed rather than face up to his responsibilities. He'd died rather than love her. He couldn't love, not really. Because love doesn't die, not ever. Love goes on and on for ever. And he'd died, and taken all the love away, and it wasn't bloody fair.

Guilt.

Guilt because of the anger. Gus hadn't wanted to die,

hadn't committed suicide. He was killed by a psychopath. Without warning. He hadn't wanted that. No one volunteers to be shot in the face.

Only . . .

Sitting alone in that house it felt as though she'd been deserted.

Ambivalence, then. Give guilt another name.

Because that's what it is. The thought was always fleeting. She didn't see it coming, but suddenly it'd got her. It was a feeling of triumph. Triumph because she'd survived, and he was dead.

She didn't want that thought. That feeling. But it kept coming back. She didn't want to be the survivor.

Whichever way she turned there was guilt.

Or there used to be. That didn't happen any longer. Marie grinned in the shower, threw up her head and laughed. What had happened in the end was that she had identified herself with Gus. She'd become a PI herself. Taken his place. Contracted the disease that had killed him.

She hadn't idealized or denied him. What she'd done was something in between. When they'd lived together she'd allowed Gus to take over parts of her personality. And when he'd died she'd lost those parts of herself. To have lost Gus would have been a disaster difficult to cope with, but to have lost him and at the same time be unable to recognize her own self, that was unbearable.

But through grieving, through mourning she'd learnt something. The fundamental crisis of that whole period, that whole episode in her life had not been the loss of her husband, the loss of Gus. No matter how much she missed him, and sometimes still she did miss him terribly, the fundamental crisis for Marie had been the loss of self, and in identifying with Gus now, she had regained that self.

'Why revisit all that?' she asked herself as she switched on her hair dryer. But she knew why. Meeting J.D. was one of the reasons, having him in her bed invited all those images

156

back. And then Geordie and Janet getting married was bound to remind her of her own marriage.

But thoughts of Gus would always return. Not obsessionally, not now, and not particularly often. They would return from time to time, and she would live with them, because her time with him had been a formative time, and something she thought would last for ever.

Marie got a window table in Betty's and told the waitress she didn't want to order yet. She'd arranged to meet Janet there, and after coffee she'd help her choose a dress for the wedding tomorrow. The investigation of Edward Blake had been shunted into the background for the duration. Real life had taken over.

Janet arrived looking as cool and collected as always. She had let her hair grow over the last months and had it worked up in a girlish style from the fifties. Marie thought she looked like Catherine Deneuve in *Les Parapluies de Cherbourg*. Geordie was getting a real peach of a woman. And then some, because Janet wasn't just a pretty face.

'Sorry I'm late,' she said, placing several packages down by her chair. 'We were buying the ring. Geordie wanted me to get white gold, and it took me ages to talk him out of it.' She sat down and looked round for the waitress. 'I hate that kind of thing, don't you? Then, when I'd convinced him it wouldn't suit me, he wanted me to get something studded with little stones. He said conventional wedding rings looked like curtain rings, and I said, "Yes, that's what I want. I don't want something that's gonna stand out. Look at my fingers, they're really long and thin, I don't want to draw attention to them." '

'They look like pretty good fingers to me,' Marie said.

Janet made a face. 'That's what Geordie said. But I've got to wear this ring, with a bit of luck for the rest of my life, and I want to be happy with it.'

'So what did you get?'

'Looks like a curtain ring,' Janet said. 'A thin band. Geordie said all his friends will think he's a cheapskate. He's gone to buy a suit with Sam. Wants something with wide lapels and a metallic fleck in it. I told him if he finds anything like that I won't marry him. But you know what he's like, he'll spend a teenage fortune. By the time the wedding's over we'll be broke.'

Marie sipped her coffee. 'What about the dress? What kind of thing are we looking for?'

'If there was time I'd have had it made. The idea I've got in my head is something in silk, dark blue, not too dark, full skirt, gathered at the waist. I saw one once, ages ago, in French Connection, I think. And I called in there on the way here, but they haven't got anything like it.'

'Sounds easy enough,' said Marie, ironically. 'How far are you willing to compromise?'

'We've got about three hours. If I haven't found anything by then I'll call the wedding off.'

'What happens in three hours?'

'I meet my mother. She arrived last night. She thinks Geordie's the pits. She thought he was scum before she set eyes on him, and as far as she's concerned he's already lived up to her expectations.' Her lips quivered and a tear darted down her cheek, but she brushed it aside.

Marie reached out and covered her hand. 'Oh, Jesus, Janet. That's not fair.'

'She doesn't give him a chance. For hours before she arrived he was cleaning the house. He bought flowers to put in her room, made the bed up himself. I told him not to bother, that she was an ungrateful woman, and that she didn't really like anybody in the world. But he wouldn't listen. "This is gonna be my mother-in-law you're talking about," he said. "And I don't wanna get off on the wrong foot with her." He probably expected somebody like Celia, you know, someone who was interested in people. Or at least somebody who was interested in something outside of

158

herself. But my mother's never been like that. She's interested in herself and her own thoughts, and she doesn't have many thoughts. Not nice ones anyway. Basically she thinks everyone in the world is out to screw her, and she sets out to immobilize them before they can get near her.

'Geordie went out an hour before she arrived and bought magazines at Smiths, *Cosmopolitan* and *Vanity Fair*. He went to Fenwick's and got a new eiderdown for her bed because he thought the old one looked as though it had been washed. White, with little yellow flowers on. And he bought a picture, reproduction of some Matisse flowers, and hung it on the wall. We met her at the station, and when I introduced them she wouldn't even shake hands with him. She wanted to rest, so I showed her the room, and five minutes later she was back downstairs with the magazines and the flowers, saying she didn't read magazines, and flowers gave her a wheezy chest.

'That was just the beginning. When we were eating last night Geordie tried again, thinking he'd just got off to a bad start. He turned up at the table with a collar and tie, and he'd been polishing his shoes for, well, must've been more than an hour. They were shining like they had batteries inside. My mother just pushed the food around on her plate. Geordie asked her what it was like back home, if she'd had a good trip on the train, what she thought about the royal family, if she'd read any good books lately. I could see he'd really thought about it. He'd lined up a whole gamut of topics to try out on her. If one of them didn't work, he'd have another one ready to tempt her with. But she wasn't having any of it. Whatever he said she'd grunt and look at her plate or out the window.

'Finally she said, "The only thing I'm interested in is Janet's welfare, and as she's already pregnant before she's even married, I can't see very much future for her, can you? In my experience the kind of man who gets a girl pregnant before the marriage is not the kind of man who is going to be able to provide for a family, and will most likely desert the ship as soon as something goes wrong."

' "I wouldn't do that," Geordie said. "Janet's the most important person in the world. I'd never desert her, no matter what happened. And the baby's gonna be a blessing. It's gonna have everything in the world."

'Mother turned on him. "And how're you going to provide for them? That's what I'd like to know. You don't have a proper job. You've got no education. As far as I can see you don't have any ambition."

'Geordie got up from the table and went to our room. I gave her what for, but she knew she'd drawn blood with him, and it didn't matter what I said, she was happy because she'd made him miserable. I don't see how she can say she's interested in my welfare. She's never been interested in anything I've done. We only invited her because I thought the silence had gone on long enough. She's old and lonely now, and I thought she would've responded to us including her in the wedding, and with the baby coming.'

Marie squeezed her hand over the table. 'That sounds terrible,' she said. 'How can you stand it?'

'I know her. I spent my childhood with her. I can phase her out, forget about her, even when she's in front of me. But it's harder for Geordie. At breakfast this morning he was trying to be polite.'

Marie shook her head. 'Geordie won't put up with it for long, though. Specially if he talks it over with Sam. Sam'll tell him to poke her in the eye, and he's liable to do it.'

'I know,' said Janet. 'He was burning *Vanity Fair* this morning, a page at a time.' She laughed. 'What gets me is the hypocrisy of it. All that nonsense about Geordie's prospects. Mother doesn't give a damn about that. She hates him because I'm in love with him. Anybody I liked she'd find fault with. When I was at home she hated *anything* I liked. Music, films, books, clothes. You name it, if I liked it she'd think it was the work of the Devil.' Janet stopped talking. She shook her head from side to side for a moment, then she said: 'But I don't want to think about all that. What about you? How're you getting on with J.D.?'

Marie turned up her nose. 'So-so,' she said. 'Oh, I like his company well enough, when he's there. It's good to have a man around for a change, though I can't help comparing him to Gus. But I find myself getting irritated with him. He'd changed the shower settings this morning. I know it's trivial, but if I'd done that in somebody else's house I'd have changed them back again when I'd finished.'

Janet smiled.

'And he gambles,' Marie continued. 'Gambles everything he's got. Comes away from the table without a bean. Needs to borrow money to get a sandwich or buy a newspaper.'

'What about the sex?'

Marie eyed her. 'First indications seem promising. But it's so long since I did it, I'm not the best judge.'

'So what you're saying,' said Janet. 'There's a guy in your life, you've invited him in and asked him to take his coat off, but for the time being he shouldn't remove his shoes.'

'Yeah,' said Marie. 'And there's something else beginning to put me off. You know those tight little balls of fluff you get on a jumper when it's been washed too many times?'

Janet nodded.

Marie shook her head. 'All his jumpers are like that.'

The waitress arrived and asked if they wanted more coffee. Janet glanced at her watch. 'We'd better get going. There's not just the dress. I need shoes, tights, order some flowers. Oh, and don't let me forget make-up. I need pink eye-shadow, blusher, some white highlighter, and a black pencil. Going for the Bo-peep look.'

When she got to the office the door was locked. Inside there was a note from Celia saying she'd be back in half an hour. Marie sat quietly at her desk, glad of the break after the lunch-hour shopping.

161

She was beginning to unwind when she heard the footfall on the stairs. It wasn't a sound she recognized. Sam took two steps at a time when he arrived. Geordie scurried up the stairs, something like a hungry mouse after discovering a grain-store. Celia placed her feet crisply on each tread, advertising the organizational flair and precision which enabled her to run the office.

But the steps on the stair now were none of these. Whoever was coming up was having some difficulty with the climb. Probably someone for one of the other offices. Except the sound was ominous, creepy, setting an echo in the stairwell, and, finally, in the passage leading to the office.

The figure that presented itself on the other side of the frosted glass was much smaller than Marie had expected. There was a quick tap on the door, which was immediately pushed open to reveal a woman who Marie felt she should know, but didn't quite recognize.

She'd obviously been beaten. Her right eye was at the centre of an angry bruise, the flesh around it ranging in hue from yellow to black. Her nose had stopped bleeding, but it was swollen and there were tell-tale traces of dried blood around her nostrils. She stumbled forward with a limp and each step creased her face with pain.

'Geordie Black,' she said. 'Is he here?'

Marie swivelled her chair around to face the woman. She shook her head. 'No, I'm sorry, he isn't in at the moment. Can I help?' She saw that the woman behind the bruises was only a girl. Blond hair with dark roots, tight jeans cut off just below the knee and black plastic high-heeled sandals.

She was Edward Blake's girlfriend, Joni Prine, the one Marie had seen at the house in Portland Street. She'd had a black eye when Marie had first seen her, maybe walked into a door that time, but the way she looked now, the door had come back and walked all over her.

Marie helped her to a chair, but Joni wasn't looking to

make herself comfortable. 'Give him this,' she said, taking a brown envelope from the pocket of her jacket. 'It's all there, fifty quid. I told him lies about Eddy, everything I said I made it up.' Her lips trembled as she watched Marie take the envelope from her hand. 'I don't know any Eddy, never even heard of him.'

She turned her back on Marie and limped towards the door.

'That's not true, Joni,' Marie said. 'I saw Edward Blake in your room. The guy's got his own key.'

Joni turned her head. She said, 'Leave me out of it, OK?' She turned completely around and took a step back into the room. She said, 'Look at my face. How much more of this d'you think I can take?'

Marie took her arm, and led her back to the chair, made her sit in it. 'Listen to me, Joni, that's all I'm asking you. Listen to me for ten minutes, then if you still want to be left out of it I'll let you go. What if you could walk away with five hundred, instead of fifty pounds?'

'And be beaten black-and-blue, probably killed? The cash'd be no good to me if I was dead.'

'No,' Marie said. 'I think there's a way you could end up with five hundred and a guarantee that you get no more aggro from Edward Blake.'

Joni took a deep breath, squinted up at Marie. 'Ten minutes?' she asked.

'That's all I want.'

'Well, you've got five,' said Joni. 'Then I'm gonna find somewhere to lay down.'

It was shopping for the make-up that jogged Marie's memory. The black pencil, watching Janet buy the black pencil, she suddenly felt herself tremble. *Make-up*. There was a connection. She couldn't remember what it was, but somewhere the investigation had thrown up that connection.

Back at the office she dug out Simon Cod's list of substances found in or around the allotment shed. *Cyanide, Dettol, glycerine, greasepaint, hops, horse manure, lead . . . greasepaint!* That was it. Greasepaint in a garden shed. The other substances, yes. She could think of a reason for all of them being there. But not greasepaint. Not specifically greasepaint. Unless some mad gardener used it to paint the base of his shrubs, keep the slugs away. She mentioned it to Celia, when she arrived at the office.

'I'm not the keenest gardener in town,' Celia assured her. 'But I never heard of anyone using greasepaint in a garden. The only people who use it, as far as I'm aware, are those connected to the art of acting. Try the theatre, the local amateur dramatic groups.'

'I think I'll do just that,' said Marie. 'See if we can turn up someone who might have access to greasepaint and who also had some connection to India Blake.'

24

There is a flat in Notting Hill Gate. No one answers the door so you walk in. Diana is sitting cross-legged in the centre of the floor; she is wan, undernourished, black rings around her eyes. She looks through you. Behind her at the window is a tall, bare-chested youth. His hair is long and unwashed. He gives you a broad smile and places a large cowboy hat on his head.

'Diana.'

She looks up at you. ''Lo, Dora.'

You move towards her but she scrambles to her feet and links arms with the cowboy. 'Friend of yours, Di?' he says in a hopeless imitation of a southern twang.

'A relative,' says Diana.

And you agree, Dora. You imitate her. 'Yes, a relative.'

The cowboy extends his hand. 'Well, Dora, come right on in,' he says. 'It ain't often as we git kinsfolk calling in.'

You take his hand. It is wet, wet and cold. Diana has got herself behind him. She tries to keep him between you, whenever he moves, she moves with him.

'Ahm Capt'n America,' he tells you. 'Me an' Di wuz just goin' out.' You can go along with them if you want, Dora. It is nothing special, a visit to some friends along the road.

'No,' says Diana.

'OK. I wanted to see you. To see that you're alive. To say that you can come home whenever you want.'

She nods her head, but still hides behind the cowboy.

He grins at you. 'That's real nice, Dora,' he says. 'But if you really want to help Di, you could lay some bread on us before you fly away.'

You leave fifty pounds and promise to send more before you stumble blindly out of the flat into the street outside. You leave the tube at Bayswater to vomit. You cannot stomach it, Dora. You cannot stomach life, and circumstances, motherhood and rejection, guilt and history. You spew it up on the tiles of the Bayswater underground.

Back in York Billy has packed his case. He has two things to say to you. Nelson Mandela has been released from prison. Billy has got himself a room on the other side of town.

When he closes the door they have all gone. Arthur, Diana, and Billy. Lady Day sings 'Where Is The Sun?' You watch the pear tree putting forth its bright green leaves. It is the same every year. A mindless celebration of the coming spring.

25

At first light William was up and about. He finished setting up the candles in the first-floor front room. Using two fingers as a measure he spaced them out on every surface in the room. The pelmets, the desk, and the rest of the furniture were festooned with candles. He didn't light them, but he checked in the right drawer of the desk to make sure the box of matches and tapers were there. He sat on the chair and felt the quiet and peace his father must have felt when he was in his study alone, a study that was identical to this one in every detail.

He left the room and entered the stark contrast of the rest of the house as he walked down the uncarpeted staircase to the ground-floor kitchen. It was cold and grimy in there, but William didn't mind, he spent only a little time in the room twice a day. He melted butter in the pan and fried a couple of eggs. When they were almost ready he pushed them to one side and fried a thick slice of bread in the remains of the butter. He put the fried bread on a plate and arranged the eggs on top of the bread. Then he carried the plate up to his attic room and ate the food while sitting on a cushion on the floor.

It was a ritual. William had the same breakfast in the same way every day. If a person ate food like that, regularly, arranged in the same way, in the same surroundings, the food was more nourishing. A person's body digested it properly, because a person's body didn't have to adjust. It knew what was coming and what it would have to do to deal with it.

Next a cup of coffee. Then a shit. Ritual completed.

Now the day could begin.

After breakfast William changed the sheets on his bed and put them in a black holdall with his underwear and shirts and set off for the launderette. Fridays he used the launderette on Bootham. Wednesdays he went to the one on Clarence Street, and Mondays he walked to Clifton Green. He'd learned to use different launderettes when he was in London. If you used the same one every time people started talking to you. Being familiar. They wanted to know things: where you live, what you do for a living. William didn't like that kind of thing. You couldn't be too careful. Disaster might be waiting around the next corner.

What if it happened to William? That he was destroyed, like his father had been destroyed? Who would be the avenger then? Who would keep his father alive?

When he got back to the house in St Mary's, Charles Hopper was waiting for him. Hopper was secretary of the Fulford Players, one of the local amateur groups which hired William to do their make-up. A busybody.

William discouraged people coming to the house. He never invited anyone in. He had no telephone, and when a professional or amateur group, sometimes a magazine or photographer needed his skills as a make-up artist, they knew to drop him a postcard and he'd contact them the next day. Most of his clients respected his privacy. One or the other might think his behaviour a little eccentric, but he was good at his job, and eccentricity was a trait not unknown in his profession.

Hopper was different. Charles Hopper never sent William a card, he came round to the house. The other people who used William's services sent a cheque in payment through the post. Hopper brought it round by hand. He'd sometimes look over William's shoulder as he stood at the door, really intrigued by William's house, and how William lived.

Charles Hopper would love to be invited inside, but William would never give him the satisfaction.

As he approached along St Mary's, William reflected that the Fulford Players didn't owe him money, and they also, as far as he was aware, were not ready to begin a new production. So what could Hopper want?

'William.' Hopper extended his hand. He had a flattened nose. William thought that was funny, that a busybody, a nosey-parker, should have a flattened nose. Perhaps someone had given it to him. He'd stuck it in somewhere it shouldn't have been, and got it flattened. But if that was the case he hadn't learned anything from the experience. And you had to, or you were destroyed. You had to look long and hard at every single experience in life, find out what it meant, learn a lesson from it.

William put his holdall on the step and gave Hopper his hand. The last few metres along the street he'd moved into sociable mode. He had a smile on his face, and he'd relaxed his shoulders, shortened his stride. 'Charles,' he said. 'You were lucky to catch me. I've been to the launderette, and I've got to go out again, I'm afraid. Hope it isn't something that won't keep.'

'It'll only take a couple of minutes,' Hopper said. 'You might be able to help solve a murder.'

William kept the smile on his face. The pace of his heart moved up a notch, and he increased the depth of his breathing to get it down again. 'Murder,' he said. 'Sounds rather dramatic, Charles.'

'Yes, doesn't it. I had a call from a private detective last evening. A woman, would you believe? Working for an insurance company. About India Blake.'

'What's this got to do with me?'

'Hang on,' said Charles. 'I'm getting there. You remember India Blake, the woman who was killed in the allotment. They found her—'

'Yes,' William told him. 'It was in the papers, back in July.'

'Good memory. I thought it was May, but yes, you're right, it was in July they found the body.'

'Charles, I don't have a lot of time.' William glanced at his watch. 'Can you get to the point.'

'Sorry, I'm rambling again. This woman, the private detective, was looking for someone who knew India Blake and had a connection with the theatre. Would that description fit any of our members? I said I'd enquire, but I'm sure if any of our members knew her we'd have heard about it.'

William took his key out of his pocket and picked up the holdall. 'I'm sorry, Charles, I've got to get on. I don't know why you're telling me all this.'

'I'm telling you in case you knew the woman, or you know anyone else who might have known her.'

'But why should I, Charles? Why did you choose to come to my house instead of any of your members? You said the detective was enquiring about your members.'

'Yes, she was. But when I asked her what she meant by a connection with the theatre, she said she was looking for someone who knew India Blake who might have access to greasepaint.'

William let his breath go. 'And you told her that I did all the make-up for the group.'

Charles shook his head. 'No, I didn't. I didn't even think about you at the time. It was only later, when I got to thinking about it. That's why I came round. I didn't think you'd know her, India Blake, I mean. But you must know other people, the suppliers you buy greasepaint from, the other make-up artists. What I thought was, I should put you and this detective woman together. Maybe you can help solve the murder.'

William unlocked his front door and pushed it open. 'You haven't told her about me already, Charles?'

'No. Of course not. I wouldn't do that without asking you first.'

William turned towards Charles and gave him the warmest smile he could raise. He felt a trickle of saliva at the corner of his mouth and wiped it away with the side of his hand. 'You'd better come up,' he said. 'This sounds more important than my other appointment.'

26

Alice Trimble came in from next door to sit with Dora. Sam had sat up with her since before dawn. They had talked about Geordie and Janet and how they would begin the day as single people but end it as a married couple.

There was a sense in which Janet wouldn't have minded if they got married or not. As far as she was concerned they were married already. But that would never be enough for Geordie. Sam wondered if anything would ever be enough for Geordie. He'd known complete rejection, by his family and by society at large, and he'd known the horror of that when he was still really a child. It had marked him. If the whole fucking tribe had taken a knife and opened Geordie up from gullet to groin, cleaned him out and sewed him back up again the cut wouldn't have been deeper. If fate had been twisted slightly, this way or that, Geordie could have gone screaming mad from his experiences. He might have turned to the bottle or some other drug, or he might have decided to wreak vengeance with physical violence on himself or others.

The point where that might happen had passed now. Janet was a great slice of redemption in Geordie's fate, because she was able to see beyond his damage, through to the core of him. She was able to drip-feed him tiny doses of confidence and dignity, and he was able to accept them and build on them. More importantly, he was able to return them to her. To love her. The deprived and neglected kid, half starved, who had walked into Sam's life just a few short years before had almost disappeared now. When he stood next to Janet at the civil ceremony today there would be no lack of magic, no lack of absolute spiritual intensity. If there was a god, or anything resembling a guiding hand in the universe, He, She, It, and the whole host of accompanying angels would be belting out a tune to celebrate that small part of Geordie, that tiny piece of all of us, which is big enough to carry us through.

'What are you talking about here,' Dora had said. 'Spirit, the soul, will-power, some primitive instinct of survival?'

Sam had tried to think of an answer for several fractions of a second, but caught himself doing it. 'Gimme a break, Dora. I'm a PI. Ask me about distressed damsels, something I can get my teeth into. Philosophy's for the clever guys. All I know is people usually give themselves to God when the Devil wants nothing more to do with them.'

She'd given him that smile he suspected he couldn't live without. Then, shaking her head she'd said, 'Sam Turner, master of disguise.'

Since no man could show any just cause why they might not lawfully be joined together, the deed was done. Tricky moment there for Sam, though. He was next to Janet's mother, and she did a real good shuffle, like she was going to stand up and tell the whole room that this detective kid just wasn't good enough for her daughter. Fortunately, she didn't do it, so Sam's two and a half year record for not hitting a woman remained intact.

Janet was a dream. She'd concentrated on the outside, the blue silk dress, her hair and make-up, the small bouquet of Sweet Fairy miniature roses, but she was as if lit from inside. There was a real warm glow going on somewhere deep within her, and it showed in her face, her eyes, the way she walked and talked, even the way she sat there, next to Geordie, listening to the registrar.

But if Janet was composed and serene, Geordie was a mumbling wreck. Sam had seen the kid in some pretty tough situations since they'd been working together. But even the time when Geordie had got himself shot he'd not acted up as badly as he did during his wedding ceremony. When he was asked if he wanted this woman, he looked at the registrar with incomprehension for several seconds before blurting out: 'Pie Glue.'

After the ceremony they had a photo session in the garden behind the register office. The photographer was a Norwegian woman Sam had met socially, and he smiled to himself as she tried and failed to squeeze a civilized expression out of Janet's mother. There was one group shot with the whole gang: Geordie and Janet at the centre, and arraigned around them were Sam, Celia, Marie and J.D. 'If that one turns out we'll have a blow-up for the office wall,' Sam told the photographer.

The reception was at George Forester's house. Forester was one of the solicitors who retained Sam's firm for routine jobs, and he and his wife were childless and had a soft spot for Geordie. A couple of their neighbours had prepared a buffet, and J.D. had brought his band along to provide the music. When they first arrived there was a couple in tennis whites on the court in the Foresters' garden. The French windows were thrown open and as people arrived they gravitated towards the buffet and took food and drink outside on the lawn.

J.D. began rolling up joints as soon as he arrived, and before the buffet was half demolished everyone was stoned.

Janet's mother was sitting on a chair by the temporary stage eating a salmon paste sandwich as if it contained anthrax. She wasn't stoned. Celia was standing next to Sam under a sun umbrella by the tennis court. 'I'm not sure this is my kind of scene,' she said.

'You're not stoned?' Sam asked.

Celia smiled and shook her head. 'No more than usual. You?'

'No,' Sam said. 'But you, me and the mother-in-law are the only ones who're not totally out of it.'

The couple in tennis whites were falling around and

giggling on the court. They were both from the university, she a lecturer in the English department and he some kind of technician in physics. 'It gives you a nervous breakdown,' she said, dropping her racket.

The technician hooted. 'It's giving me one. What is it?'

'Dunno. Temple balls something.'

'Balls? Didn't think they allowed them in temples.'

They both thought that was seriously funny.

Sam took Celia's arm. 'Shall we mingle?' he said. 'I can't stand all the hooting.'

As they moved away the couple on the court were prostrate, their rackets abandoned for the day.

The taxi driver who had brought Geordie and Janet from the register office hadn't managed to get away. He'd had a plate of sandwiches and some trifle, refused wine because he was driving, but accepted a couple of tokes from J.D.'s magic stash. Now he was facing the wrong way in his cab. All alone in there. Giggling.

'I'm going to have a try with Janet's mother,' Celia said. 'She looks lonely over there. Coming?'

'No, please,' Sam said. 'She looks as refreshing as a day with the tax man.'

Geordie left Janet with a group of young people and walked over to Sam. His eyes were sparkling. 'This is great,' he said. 'I should get married more often.' He looked at Sam's face. Held out a half-smoked joint.

Sam shook his head. Smiled.

'Come on, Sam, it's a wedding. A little bit of blow won't hurt you. Don't be so serious.'

'Serious. Christ, Geordie, I'm an alcoholic.'

Celia was deep in conversation with Janet's mother, so Sam helped J.D. and the band set up their instruments. Took a long time.

'Tell you what,' J.D. said to the lead guitarist. 'Once we get going we won't be able to stop one song and start another.'

The guitarist thought about it for a while. 'Right,' he said eventually.

'What we could do,' J.D. told him. 'We could run through all the numbers without stopping.'

'Like fade out one and bring up another?'

'No. You're not listening. Don't be a bunny. What we do is, we allow one song to *metamorphose* into the next one.'

'Like Kafka, man?'

J.D. raised his eyebrows. He handed a tambourine to Marie. 'You can play this, pretty woman.'

Marie took it from him and shook it, then she turned it upside down and shook it again. Seemed to play better that way.

J.D. turned to Sam. 'Did I thank you for letting me run with the pack?'

'Forget it,' said Sam.

'I can't forget it. I'm jingle brained with dope and goofy about this woman here, and I still can't forget it.'

They went into the first song, and Sam listened closely for the time it would metamorphose into the next one, but it didn't happen. After twenty-eight minutes, 'With A Little Help From My Friends' showed no signs whatsoever of transforming itself into a second song.

Everybody in the band reckoned it would do, though, eventually.

With a little help.

Sam drifted over to Celia and Janet's mother. Celia had the butt of a joint between the first and second fingers of her right hand. There was a guy in front of them had adopted the fig-leaf position. Both of the women were staring at him. But he was out of it. Didn't even know they were there. Paralysed with paranoia.

'How're you doing?' Sam asked, indicating the cigarette. Celia waved her hand nonchalantly. 'Over-rated, this stuff,' she said. 'I don't feel any different at all.' She got to her feet and headed for the buffet table. 'Hope there's something left to eat. My stomach thinks my throat's been cut.' And she howled with laughter.

Late at night Sam took the newly wedded couple to see Dora. They sat with her for around fifteen minutes. She laughed at their descriptions of the reception, but she quickly tired. 'I'm not sorry about missing the party,' she said. 'But I'd have liked to be at the ceremony.'

'I thought about you, then,' Geordie told her. 'I thought about my mother for a while, then I thought about you.'

Dora reached for his hand, and he gave it to her. 'Thank you, Geordie,' she said. 'I thought about you as well.' She glanced at Janet. 'Both of you.'

A couple of minutes later she was asleep.

Sam took the two of them home in the Montego. They got into the back seat. 'You should have gone away,' he said. 'Even if it was only for a couple of days.'

'Too much responsibility,' Janet said. 'Geordie doesn't want to go away till this case with India Blake is finished.'

'Yeah,' said Geordie. 'And your mother. We can't go away and leave her by herself in the house. When that's all sorted we might go to Amsterdam for a couple of days. I've bought a Dutch phrase book. We read it in bed.'

'Not tonight, though,' said Janet.

'Not likely,' Geordie agreed. 'Whadda you think I am? Reading in bed on our honeymoon?'

27

There was a moment there, when she first opened her eyes, Marie didn't have a clue who it was in bed with her. Her consciousness had wiped J.D. out of the reckoning, totally forgotten about him, so he didn't figure in the equation. She knew Gus was dead, so it couldn't be him. There'd been a wedding and a party long into the night last night, so taking everything on balance, including the alcohol and the Nepalese Temple Balls, it could be just about anybody. She sneaked a look at him.

It was J.D. with his mouth open.

Christ! J.D. How could she have forgotten about him?

She lifted her head from the pillow and swivelled round, swinging her legs over the side of the bed, and a knife, several knives, a canteen of cutlery fell off a shelf inside her head and almost forced her eyes out of their sockets.

'Yuuuuuuuuuk,' she said, gently lowering her head into her hands. 'Yuk, yuk, yuk.' But no one was listening. As she sat there she recognized that her head was only one of the problems. There were so many things wrong with her she couldn't begin to count them. She needed to pee, that was the first thing. Then the sphincter guarding her back passage seemed to have taken on a life of its own, and was currently dividing its energies between a rhythmic spasm, something akin to African tribal drums, and a bubbling intensity like the dance of hot metal being poured into a mould. Her limbs ached, arms and legs, especially the legs, thigh and calf muscles having been forced into exertions of dance never before contemplated. And then there was the inside of her mouth. She knew all the old descriptions from the politically incorrect

Arab's armpit, to the bizarre bottom of a budgie's cage, but the imagery that came to Marie's mind now reminded her of the photograph of the decayed body of India Blake.

She didn't have time to dwell on it, however, as the absolute need to pee forced her mind to organize the reluctant tissue and muscle. The journey to the bathroom was one for the Israelites, or those guys who hauled the big rocks to Salisbury plain, but she made it.

Nepalese Temple Balls. Never. No more.

Everyone would be late in the office. Geordie might not make it at all, with a honeymoon on his hands. She and J.D. had walked Celia home last night, Celia telling jokes she'd heard in the nineteen thirties and not been able to understand. Marie and J.D. still didn't understand them now, but all three of them laughed just the same. Then Celia had gone into a medley of Gracie Fields' greatest hits, 'A Little Dutch Boy And A Little Dutch Girl', 'Little Donkey', 'Sally', and 'Around The World'.

Marie did try to get J.D. out of bed, but decided she'd have more luck raising Lazarus. He had said that he'd come to the office with her last night, but now he was full of reasons why that wasn't possible. He had to go back to George Forester's house to collect his drum kit. He'd arranged to meet up with the guys in the band. He needed to do something quiet, like maybe play some cards.

'Did I tell you I was reliable?' he said.

'No, but you did say we'd spend the day together.'

'I can't get it on. The band's got another gig tonight, somewhere up near Whitby. I need to sleep.'

'Please yourself,' she said. 'It's your life.' When she left the house, J.D. didn't look like he had enough ambition to make the trip to Whitby.

When she got to the office, Joni Prine was sitting at the top of the stairs waiting for her. When she saw Marie, Joni developed a coy smile. There was more than a hint of apology in it, but it would have taken Raphael to disguise the underlying avarice.

Marie waited until Joni got to her feet. She watched as the girl smoothed the wrinkles out of her skirt, and continued watching as the same wrinkles cracked straight back into place. 'Does this mean you want to talk to me about Edward Blake?' said Marie.

'Five hundred quid's a lot of money to somebody like me,' said Joni. 'I've got Jacqui to think of as well, that's my daughter. With that kind of money I could go back to Sunderland, get a place near my mum now the old man's given up the ghost.'

'Sounds like the right decision,' said Marie, leading her into the office and showing her the clients' chair.

'Well, yeah,' said Joni, 'as long as Eddy doesn't find out it was me that grassed him. If something happens to me who's gonna take care of Jacqui?' She became agitated, rubbing the backs of her hands on her thighs, gnawing away at her bottom lip.

'You're still not sure, then?' asked Marie.

'I think it could work,' Joni said. 'It's a good plan, the way you explained it to me. But there's still a risk.'

Marie nodded. 'Small one.'

'What I thought,' said Joni, looking down at her hands. 'I thought I'd feel better about that risk if there was more money involved.'

Marie felt a smile building inside her, but she kept her face straight. 'How much were you thinking, Joni?'

'Six hundred. If that's possible. I'd feel a lot better if the pay-off was gonna be six hundred quid.'

Marie put her hands on the desk and leaned forward. 'Joni,' she said. 'If the story is as good as you say, and provided it's all completely true, you'll end up with six hundred *as a minimum*. If we get the timing right and catch

Edward Blake with his proverbial pants down, you could get a lot more.'

'A lot,' said Joni. 'What we talking here, a grand?'

Marie nodded. 'Maybe. Just tell me the story.'

'He's working for the tobacco industry,' Joni said. 'I don't know how much he's allowed to spend, but it seems like there's no limit on it. What he does, he has to get MPs to vote the way the tobacco companies want. They're frightened that the government'll be pressured into banning cigarettes, you know, by doctors; or they'll have to put out adverts saying that smoking fags gives you heart attacks as well as cancer, and if you're pregnant it makes the kid get born with two heads but no brains. Stuff like that.

'There's a few MPs who keep at it, bring up bills to ban smoking. What Eddy has to do, he has to make all the other MPs vote against the ban. And the way he does it is to make them realize that the tobacco industry is always gonna give them a good time.'

'By paying them?' asked Marie.

Joni nodded. 'Cash and sex,' she said. 'Booze, holidays, anything they want. Tell you the truth, I don't know the half of it. I only really know the bits that've involved me. I've spent weekends with MPs, done more or less whatever they want, then at the end of it I've slipped them a brown envelope bulging with used notes.'

'Can you give me names? Dates?'

'Names, yeah. Dates I can probably work out. But I can do better than that. The last year I've been recruiting girls for Eddy. He's got a couple of cottages in Wheldrake now, and he sets them up with an MP and one or two girls, whatever the guy wants.

'Or if there's two guys he'll put three or four girls in there. Or boys if they're that way. We stock up the bar, make sure there's plenty of mirrors in the bedrooms, dressing-up clothes, everything they might need, and leave them to it.

The girls do whatever the guys want. They're young, they like them younger all the time, so we recruit runaways, homeless kids, whatever. After a bath and a bit of scent and make-up they all look great. Eddy gives them a hundred quid for the weekend.'

'You know where these cottages are?' asked Marie.

'Sure. Eddy doesn't go anywhere near them. I have to get them cleaned up, stock the bars, deliver the girls down there.'

'D'you get much warning?' Marie asked. 'When will the next party be?'

Joni smiled. 'That's why I'm here,' she said. She pulled two fat brown envelopes from her bag. 'Eddy gave me these last night. I'm taking four girls to the cottages today. Then a couple of politicians'll arrive around six o'clock tonight. According to Eddy one of 'em's a top civil servant, but the other's a cabinet minister.'

When Joni left, Marie went through the India Blake file. She read through the transcripts of Geordie's interviews as well as her own. Something was nagging at her. Something they'd missed. But she couldn't work out what it was. She made coffee and drank it looking out of the window. The pain in her head slowly ebbed away. She turned to the file again and read it from beginning to end.

She was putting all the paperwork back into order when Sam arrived. Marie told him about Joni Prine, and what she'd said about Edward Blake.

'It's only a hunch,' he said. 'But if I was on this case I'd have another go at India Blake's old friend, whatever her name was.'

'Naiomi Leaver? You think she knows more?'

'Just reading between the lines,' Sam said. 'There was no love lost between Naiomi and Edward Blake. Naiomi could still be guarding India's secrets in the belief that she was killed by her husband.'

'Slow down, Sam,' Marie said. 'We can't be sure that Edward Blake didn't kill her.'

Sam shrugged. 'The police don't think so. If they did they'd never have let him go.'

'OK,' she said. 'I don't have anything else to go on. I'll drive over to Naiomi's house. Got the car keys?'

Naiomi Leaver was posing in the doorway to her cottage. She was a perfect miniature, composed entirely of fat-repelling enzymes. So small, she's almost a waste of skin, thought Marie. Then checked herself quickly. Women's bodies were a no-go area. Soft targets. Easy meat. She's just small, for Christ's sake. You could be, too, if you lived on pencil make-up and eye-drops.

This morning Naiomi was dressed in white designer jeans and a short-sleeved red top with a plunging neckline. The plunge was extraordinary, almost reaching the woman's navel, yet betraying not a hint of mamilla, not an air bubble, or a blob. Marie reflected that the entire garment would not supply herself with enough material for a headband.

No scones or fine tea service today. Marie was invited into a warm kitchen and provided with a ladder-backed chair next to a red gas-fired Aga. Naiomi Leaver remained standing. She poured coffee from a cafetière into black mugs, handed one to Marie. 'Didn't expect to see you again so soon.'

Marie sipped the coffee. A lot of money had gone into cutting Naiomi's age from a good thirty-five to an excellent twenty-eight. 'I want to ask you again if India was having an affair.'

Naiomi shook her head. 'I thought she was, yes. But when I asked her about it, she told me she wasn't. I told you that last time.'

'Yes, I know. But you said you were *fairly* sure, not absolutely sure. What did you mean by that?'

Naiomi tightened the lines around her mouth. 'Who can

be absolutely sure about another person? People tell you what they want you to know. The rest is guesswork.'

'Did you believe she was killed by her husband?'

'Yes. I still do. Edward is a rotter. He's capable of anything.'

Marie put her mug on top of the Aga. 'He's certainly a womanizer,' she said. 'And his political and business methods aren't exactly whiter than white. But there's no evidence to show he murdered her. On the contrary, it looks as though he didn't.'

Naiomi laughed harshly. 'He's clever, that's all. He fooled the police, and now he's fooling you.'

'But what if he isn't as clever as you think, Naiomi? What if India was killed by someone else? And that someone else was left free to kill again? Because of your vendetta against Edward Blake.'

'It's not a vendetta.' Naiomi Leaver clenched her fists, the tension turning her knuckles white.

'OK, what would you call it?'

'I don't call it anything. India was my friend. Edward fucking Blake left her to starve to death in that shed. I think he should be punished for that.' Her voice had risen to a shout. But she checked herself, and the next words were little more than a whisper. 'I couldn't believe it when the police let him go.'

There was a pine kitchen table behind her, and Marie could see her hands gripping the edge of it. Suddenly Naiomi raised herself up on to the table. Her eyes glazed over and a single tear fell down her cheek. 'He even tried it on with me,' she said. 'He knew we were friends and he'd happily have taken me to bed.'

'The guy's the worst kind of slime,' Marie said. 'He cheats and lies, and he's always on the lookout for the main chance. But that doesn't make him a murderer. If you know something else, something that India mentioned, about another man, then you should tell me.'

'India didn't mention anything.'

'Maybe she wasn't having an affair. Even if it was a friendship, we should know about it.'

Naiomi shook her head. 'I asked India about it, and she told me she wasn't having an affair. She never mentioned another man. Not a lover. Not a friend. Nothing.'

Marie sighed and got up from the chair. 'The police have closed the case against Edward Blake. They've looked at all the possibilities and decided that he didn't have anything to do with her murder. We've also looked at it and come to the same conclusion. I've personally interviewed the guy, and I have all the same reservations about him that you have. But I don't think he murdered his wife.

'And something else. He's not going to be arrested again. Whoever it was murdered India Blake has got away with it up to now because everyone assumed her husband did it, and a lot of time was wasted investigating him. I don't know if you're trying to protect India's reputation, or if you're hoping that Edward Blake'll be arrested again. But whichever it is, the end result is that the man who killed India is still free and liable to murder again.'

Marie walked to the door of the cottage and opened it. Naiomi stayed put on the table. 'Thanks for your help,' Marie said. She walked out of the door and closed it behind her. She got into the Montego and put the key into the ignition. She'd reversed around the white Rover before the door of the cottage opened and Naiomi came over to her. Marie wound the window down.

'Come back,' Naiomi said. 'I don't think it'll help, but I'll tell you what I know.'

'We met in Taylor's on Thursdays. We'd been doing that for years. Lunch. Girl talk. India enjoyed it as much as I did. If something else came up I'd always put it off. Thursday lunch was one time in the week when we'd put the world to one side. By the time we'd finished it would be around three. But then, a couple of weeks before she died, India wanted to be away around two o'clock.

'The last Thursday I saw her was when I asked her if she was having an affair. I couldn't understand what was so important all of a sudden. That she'd let it take over our time together. I could only think it must be a man.

'But like I said, she denied it.'

Marie had settled herself into the ladder-backed chair and listened to Naiomi's confession without interrupting.

'I didn't believe her. She left Taylor's just after two and I followed her. She fairly flew along Stonegate. She didn't have a clue that I was behind her. I'm sure it never crossed her mind that I might follow her. She was so fixed, so intent on her target destination that there wasn't room in her mind for anything else.

'She went to the Coppergate Centre. It was busy in there, people queuing to get into the Viking Museum, a couple of buskers, and children and young people running around. There were some homeless people juggling with fire clubs, and India collided with one of them, so he dropped his club and gave her a mouthful, but she hadn't seen him, and she didn't hear him shouting after her.

'I followed her into Fenwick's, the department store, and almost lost her there. I saw her get on the escalator, but by the time I got to the bottom of it she'd already disappeared off the top. The first floor there is dresses, suits, underwear, and I wandered around for a few minutes, but didn't see India anywhere. I thought she'd given me the slip, gone up the escalator and back down the stairs. I was ready to give up. But then I remembered the cafeteria, and took a peek in there.

'They were holding hands across the table. India had her back to me, but I had a good view of him. He was small, dark. He was looking at her with that look that men have, you know, right at the beginning, when they're hungry, when they stare and shake their heads, like they can't believe this is really happening.'

Naiomi shrugged her shoulders. 'That's it,' she said. 'He didn't look like he was going to murder her. He didn't look big enough for a start.'

'What did you do?' Marie asked.

'I came home. I had a couple of stiff gins and went for a jog along the beck.'

'Weren't you curious? Didn't you feel like waiting to see what happened next?'

'Yes, of course. But I was too bloody angry. India had cut our meetings short to meet this man. I think if I'd stayed there I might have confronted her. Caused a scene.'

'Can you remember anything else about him? Would you recognize him if you saw him again?'

'Yes. He was small with dark, piercing eyes, and he had a broad forehead with eyebrows that met in the middle. I remember that because we used to say that was a sign of madness. Slimly built, I could imagine him being a dancer. But he looked vulnerable, somehow. As though life had been a disappointment. And India had walked into that disappointment, and she was beautiful, so he was confused. Those feelings, of someone who was confused and disappointed, they're somehow stronger than the physical details of his face. Whenever I've thought about him since, I don't remember his features as well as I remember the feelings.'

She walked over to the window and looked out at her garden. She looked back at Marie, who was scribbling in her notebook. 'Oh, God,' Naiomi said. 'You don't think . . .?'

Marie stuffed the notebook into her pocket and got out of the chair. 'I don't know,' she said. 'But I'm glad you told me. And yes, it could be that this confused and vulnerable looking man transformed himself into the monster that killed India Blake.'

28

You open your eyes. Where's Sam? Your lips clog. You ask the question but no sound comes from your throat.

Diana understands. 'He's ringing the doctor.'

The iron bar is still there, lying across your body. It has always been there, Dora. Only you did not notice.

'Do you feel any better?' Diana has layers of concern on her face. Concern and fear. You have a dim desire to communicate. If she moistened your lips with the sponge you would be able to speak. But there is not a lot left to say. After everything she loves you. You love her. That is obvious, at last. In the end neither of you has any freedom about it. You are together. All the anguish, the self-recriminations, the guilt; it was all in vain. Maya. Illusion.

Sam's hand on your cheek, then he disappears. Diana watches the panic in your eyes. She takes your hand. 'It's all right,' she says. 'He'll be back in a minute. He's gone to the bathroom.'

Yes. It is all right. He is back with the sponge. He holds it to your lips. His free hand brushes the wisps of hair from your forehead. The iron bar shifts a little, recedes.

'Did you get through?' Diana asks.

Sam glances in her direction, but his eyes come back to yours when he speaks. 'Yes. He's out. They think he's on his way.'

'God,' says Diana, impatiently. She looks at her watch. 'It's been hours.'

'The doctor,' Sam explains. 'He's on his way.'

You shake your head. You don't want a doctor. You

don't want anything to do with doctors. You speak through the sponge, and Sam withdraws it. 'No hospital.'

He smiles. 'No,' he says. 'No hospital. Don't worry. I won't let them take you.'

Diana stands. 'Shall I make a drink?'

'Yes.' Damn that croak, Dora.

'Fruit juice?' asks Sam. Then to Diana. 'Dora wants fruit juice, I'd like coffee.'

When she has left the room he leans forward and kisses you on the forehead.

'Wait.'

He leaves his face close to yours.

'Sam, when I've gone—'

'Dora. Dora.'

'When I've gone, Sam. You should marry again.'

'OK,' he says. 'Three days of mourning, then I'll pop round the marriage bureau.'

'Don't joke. You should marry.'

He shakes his head. You have planted a seed in it, Dora. You have planted a seed in his head, and he tries to shake it out. 'I love you,' he says. 'You're not going to die, Dora. I love you.'

'Yes.' It is true, Dora, what he says. He does love you. But you are going to die. That iron bar is never going to dissolve. It is time for the reckoning, time to face everything that never needed to be faced before.

Sam has been a gift to you, a blessing. He came to sweeten the last months, to fulfil the girlhood dream of a man, a real man. You are a medium, Dora, a witch. You conjured him into existence. You let the dream go, and allowed it to be born.

No more fears, now. He was a gift to you, a blessing. And it is only through you that he can find his way back to life. You can show him the way. You have shown him the way.

189

29

Going to work on the morning of his honeymoon was not exactly what Geordie had envisioned. That kind of thing probably didn't happen to too many people. But then again probably not too many people had their honeymoon at home, and if they did have their honeymoon at home they probably didn't have their mother-in-law with them in the same house. And, and this was the final probability, if they did have their mother-in-law in the house, it was probably a mother-in-law who liked them. Not a mother-in-law who hated them and spent every moment of her life looking for mean things to say and do.

'I don't want to go to work on the first morning of my fuckin' honeymoon,' he'd said to Janet. 'And that's swearing.'

Janet had gritted her teeth. Looked as though she might cry. She wasn't going to give in to it, dissolve into wimpishness, but the desire to do it was shining in her eyes. She'd pulled her jeans on and fastened the zip, but she was barefooted and bare-breasted. Her wedding dress of the day before was hanging over the back of a chair. 'Geordie, if you stay at home that stupid old woman will make our life a misery. Just give me today, and I'll get rid of her.'

The prospect of life without Janet's mother was almost too sweet to contemplate. During the three days of her visit Geordie had been transformed from an optimistic extrovert to a cowering, almost speechless recluse in his own house.

'If I'm here I can help,' he'd protested. 'You'll have to get her to the station, carry all her suitcases.'

Janet had reached over and put two fingers against his

lips. 'She's my mother, Geordie. I know her of old. I can manage her. If you're here she'll divide us, and then it'll be twice as hard. On my own I can manage her.'

Geordie thought about it. 'But it's my fuckin' honeymoon, Janet.'

She shook her head. 'And it's my fuckin' honeymoon as well, Geordie. I want you to go to work. And when you come home tonight she'll be gone. I'll get some beer in, and we can slob out in front of the television. Not answer the phone. Pretend we're the only ones left in the universe.'

'OK. I'm giving in. You can do it your way. But if that silly old bag is still here when I come home tonight I'll set the dog on her. I don't like her, Janet, and I'm glad I don't, because if I liked her I'd have to let her stay, and I'd just hate it.'

Sam was at the office by himself. 'Didn't expect to see you today,' he said to Geordie. Barney put two front paws on Sam's leg, and waited there until Sam had finished fondling him. Then he walked slowly over to his basket. Looked worn out, like *his* mother-in-law had come to visit.

'I wish you hadn't, Sam. I wanted to stay in bed all day with Janet, but we've got a crisis on with her mother.'

'Celia rang in. She's staying at home, thinks she might've eaten something bad at the reception.'

'It was the dope,' said Geordie. 'When you're using it you think you're sorted, but then it carries on sorting you when you get in bed and try to sleep. In the morning you're so sorted you sort of wish you hadn't started in the first place.'

'The boy's a poet. I'm going down to Betty's. Get some decent coffee. If you wanna talk mothers-in-law I've got about an hour.'

They got a window seat in Betty's, and the waitress brought them a pot of coffee. There was a small tray with milk and cream and sugar, and Sam pushed it away. Geordie retrieved it and added all three to his coffee. 'Dunno how you can do that,' Sam told him.

'Dunno how you can do *that*,' Geordie replied, indicating Sam's cup.

'Looks like an infection.'

'Christ. This is my honeymoon, Sam.'

Sam smiled. 'Didn't expect to spend it with me, eh?'

'No. And I didn't want to. I still don't want to. Specially if you're gonna be sarky.'

Sam sipped at his coffee. Sighed. 'OK. Sorry. I can see I'm no substitute for Janet. Tell me about the mother-in-law.'

'What I don't understand,' Geordie said, 'is why she's like she is. I mean my mother pissed off with the landlord and left us behind, not a word, just a note I couldn't even read. And now all my life from that day I've been wishing she hadn't done it, or that she'd come back, because everybody else in the world except me've got mothers that look after them, or that you can give a card to on Mothers' Day. You can buy flowers for your mother, even after you've left home and got married, you can visit her on Sunday afternoon, have some roast beef and Yorkshire pudding. Hell, Sam, you know what I mean.'

'Yeah. It's a dream. It's a load of old bollocks, and you know it's a load of old bollocks, but you dream it anyway, because it's a substitute for not having a mother.'

'Yeah, it's crap when you haven't got a mother or, even worse, when you had one but she didn't think enough about you to stick around. Not even enough about you to send you a card, ever, in your whole life. A postcard with a second-class stamp on it and two words: "Hello. Mum." Not even that. I mean, what's the good of a mother like that? I tell you, Sam, there's times when I think it would've been better if I'd come out of a test tube. Then at least I wouldn't have all these thoughts in my head, like can I remember what she looked like, or am I making it up, grasping at ideas of what she might have looked like if she'd been a proper mother?'

'You're not gonna get morbid on me, are you?'

'Fuck off, Sam. It was your idea. You said you'd listen for an hour. We haven't had ten minutes yet. If it's too much, you can get up and walk away.'

'Sorry. I'm all ears.'

'So when Janet said her mother was gonna stay with us, I thought it'd be like *my* mother as well. That we'd get married and sort of share her. You know what I mean? But what happened was Janet's mother came and she didn't look at me. I was there when she got off the train and she looked at Janet and didn't even glance at me, and it was obvious she'd made up her mind that I was a pile of shit before she'd even met me.' He picked up a sugar lump and crushed it between his thumb and forefinger. 'It brings it all back, for Christ's sake, all the things I used to think about my own mother, but since I met Janet I haven't been thinking about her so much. Now it's all come back. There's been times these last three days when I've thought about breaking her scrawny neck. It'd be so easy. I could do it with one hand.'

'Just as well she's going home then.'

'So what is it with mothers? Celia told me in Islam they say paradise is under the feet of your mother. Where does that put me, Sam? I've only met two real mothers in my life, mine and Janet's, and both of them were crap. I look at these pictures they have in galleries, Christ and his mother, motherhood, fuckin' angels flutterin' around them, and it's like a huge confidence trick. Same as the Tories. Or any governments.

'All these painters, Reubens and Raphael and all those old guys, somebody must've paid them to paint angels around mothers and babies, because I reckon it never happens in reality. What happens in reality is your mother ups and goes with the fuckin' landlord as soon as he gives her the eye. Or if she doesn't get the eye she hangs around for ever and makes your life a total misery. There's no paradise under her feet. There's nothing under her feet. She might have shit on her boots. That's a possibility. But no paradise. That's what I think.'

'Yeah,' said Sam.

'Yeah, what?'

'Yeah, I don't agree with you.'

'Nobody's *allowed* to agree with me. I know nobody'll agree with it, because everybody's been brainwashed with the fuckin' propaganda. First of all history's full of it, with the painters and the angels, like I just told you. And that's in place, waiting for you even before you're born. Like an animal trap, that one. Then when you're born she's there. Your mother. Got to be, right? Like most of the time I bet if she didn't absolutely have to be there, at the birth, your mother'd be absent. There's a million places she'd rather be. But she's got to be there, so she is. So that's the first thing you see when you open your eyes. And from that moment on she and everybody else you ever meet in your life is gonna tell you what a wonderful woman she is, and how she's your mother, your best friend, and that as long as you live you're always gonna remember her. If you grow up and go off to war and get killed, your dying words will be "Mother".

'I mean you can say your country is shit, like England is the shithole of the world, or whatever country it is you live in. You can say that and there'll be some people who agree with you. And the people who don't agree with you, they'll forgive you. Maybe. Unless they're fuckin' crazy nationalists. "My country right or wrong." Patriots with loony attitudes like that. But if you say the same thing about mothers, you might as well kill your*self*.'

'Can I say something now?'

'Yeah. What do you think, I wanna monopolize the whole conversation?'

'What you're doing, you're taking something that's specific to you, your experience of your mother and Janet's mother, and you're trying to apply that to the rest of the world.'

'So?'

'You're not allowed to do that. Most of the people I know in this town are alcoholics. I try to go to an AA meeting twice a week. Sometimes, when I'm really down I go every day. They're all alcoholics. But that doesn't make me think the world's full of alcoholics. Just because my world, the world of my experience is peopled by alcoholics, it doesn't prove that there isn't anything else in the world.'

'What does it prove?' asked Geordie.

'It proves that there are some people in the world who, if they take alcohol, just one drink, they won't be able to stop. And if they don't get some help they'll go on drinking until they kill themselves. Governments and organizations have taken that on board, and some of them have tried to ban alcohol because of it. But that isn't the way to deal with it.'

'Hang on,' said Geordie. 'I'm trying to apply this to mothers, but what happens is I see my mother and Janet's mother with corks for hats. Like bottle-shaped women.'

Sam laughed. 'I've had bad experiences with drink,' he said. 'I can't handle it. You've had bad experiences with mothers. I've had to force myself to recognize that not everybody has a bad time with drink. Some people drink in moderation, and they have a good time with it. They're not addicted. They don't get drunk or spend the whole family budget on it. They manage their lives reasonably, and they drink. It's a fact of life. It's not part of my experience, but it happens.'

'OK,' said Geordie. 'So there are mothers who act like real mothers?'

'I'd think it would be a fairly safe bet to say that, wouldn't you?'

195

Geordie nodded reluctantly. 'What, they take care of their kids, and look after them when they're small?'

'Yeah.'

'And later on, when the kids've growed up and got married, the mother'll come and visit and act normal and be nice?'

'Yeah.'

Geordie picked up another sugar lump and popped it into his mouth. He ground it down with his teeth and reached for the remaining cold dregs of coffee in his cup. He swilled it around and swallowed it. 'I wish mine had been like that,' he said.

Sam smiled. He didn't have to say anything.

'If she walked in here now,' Geordie said. 'Say if she came up to the table and said, "Hello, I'm your mother. D'you wanna buy me a cup of coffee." And she was normal about it, and wanted to be friends. If she said she wanted to forget the past, and for us to carry on as though nothing had happened. Something like that. I'd agree to it. I'd say, "Yeah, mum. I'll get you a coffee. What about a piece of carrot cake?" Then after she'd drunk the coffee, eaten the cake, I'd take her round to see Janet. It'd be great.'

'Not likely, though,' said Sam.

'No, not likely at all. About as likely as angels.'

The allotment shed where India Blake's body had been found was still there. It stood apart from the other sheds around it with an aura of neglect. The outer walls were clad with tarred canvas, and the windows had been boarded up. The whole edifice was raised up on red bricks, three high. The roof timbers were bare. There was an eerie feeling about it. As though the suffering it had contained had somehow pervaded the timbers. Geordie walked along the rough grass pathway and pushed open the door of the shed. There was a roll of scene-of-crime tape, left behind by the police. The shed floor had been taken up completely, and every inch of the earth underneath had been dug up and sifted. Geordie didn't go inside. He thought it would have been like walking on India Blake's grave.

Next to the shed was something that looked as if it might have been a greenhouse. There was no glass left and the structure looked dangerous, as though it was about to fall in on itself. It was boarded up with rusty, pitted corrugated iron, wire mesh, and the base of it was formed from stone paving slabs. Alongside it were a couple of worn car tyres, different sizes.

'You looking for something?'

The man was stocky, sergeant-major build, with thinning hair and floppy ears. He had a bristly moustache and lived in his shoulders and upper chest. He was carrying a spade. Geordie showed him his ID. 'We're retained by the insurance company,' he explained.

'Nobody'll take it,' the man said, nodding towards the length of the garden. 'There's a waiting list for plots, but nobody wants this one. Not after . . .'

'. . . the murder?' Geordie prompted.

The man nodded. 'Makes me feel strange coming here now. After that. I used to enjoy coming before.'

'Which is your plot?'

'Right here,' the man said. 'Next door.'

Geordie looked along the length of the plot. This man's shed was completely different. One end of it was built out of corrugated perspex, the other end with boards encased in a bitumen sheath. Between the two sheds was a sheltered alcove with a corrugated iron roof and an open front. Along the back wall was a seat taken from the back of a car.

'And you never heard anything?' Geordie asked. 'Saw anything?'

The man shook his head, as though he couldn't believe it himself. 'Never dreamed,' he said. 'You don't. It's a garden. You plant seeds and watch the vegetables coming. Keep the weeds down. I come here to get away from the telly. All that violence.' He looked up at the sky, as though someone up there had played a dirty trick on him.

'What about the other gardeners?' Geordie asked. 'Didn't anyone see anything?'

'We've talked about it,' the man said. 'And the police have been here. We had to give statements. They had a picture of her husband, and wanted to know if we'd seen him around. But he wasn't the type you get round here. I don't think anybody saw anything. Sometimes somebody will walk through, taking a short cut, or maybe looking to pinch some tomatoes or sprouts. We lose a lot of sprouts in the winter. People just come in and help themselves. Cheeky buggers. But that, what happened in that shed, that was something else.'

'You think there's any point in talking to the other gardeners?'

The man shook his head. He stuck his spade in the earth and leaned on the handle, scratching at the growth of hair under his nose. 'They'll tell you the same as me. Whoever it was done her in was real quiet about it. While that woman was dying in there we didn't have a clue about it. The police, their forensics people, they say she was there for weeks, and we can't do anything but believe them. But gardeners on the allotment couldn't hardly believe that. What we thought was, she'd been killed somewhere else, and the body dumped here. Maybe if someone brought it here one night and dumped it, that might explain it.'

'Thanks, anyway,' said Geordie. He left the man leaning on his spade and walked towards the gate of the allotment. All the other plots looked as though they were being used. There were stacks of timber, green and blue plastic water barrels, cloches, heaps of cow dung and horse manure. Some of the plots had their own lavatories, just big enough for one man and a newspaper. Each plot was defined by wonderfully inventive fencing, the intrepid gardeners seemingly ready to use whatever came to hand. Geordie identified

198

asbestos sheeting, car doors, hardboard and cardboard, woven string and electrical flex, plywood, pallets, tree trunks, plastic sheeting, and even offcuts of carpet. Geordie stopped to admire one beauty of a shed, made up entirely of old window frames. Many of them had been relieved of their glass, boarded up; but nevertheless there was nothing identifiable in the make-up of the place that at one time or another hadn't been a window frame. And stacked beside it, waiting for their destiny, were another two dozen window frames. From the road he watched some horses exercising on the Knavesmire, a grey and a chestnut mare, being galloped. Geordie turned his thoughts back to Janet, hoping her mother had gone home.

He stood at the gate to the allotment, wondering what to do next. Maybe he should talk everything over with Marie, see if she'd come across anything that would lead them in another direction. He'd already decided to go back to the office, when the sergeant-major type called out his name. Geordie turned and watched the man leave his spade behind and stride out towards him. Geordie walked back to meet him.

'One thing you could try, is old Malc,' he said. 'He's here at night sometimes. Or he used to be. He kept budgies on the other side of me, in his shed, he'd had it kitted out as an aviary in there. Bred them and sold them to pet shops. And he took them to shows and won prizes.'

'But the police'll've spoken to him?'

'No, I don't think they did. He's been having heart attacks and surgery all year. Had another one a couple of days before they found the body, and he was laid up in hospital. His son came down and took the birds away, but old Malc himself was hit bad. We don't expect to see him down here again.'

'Is he fit enough to talk?' Geordie asked.

'If he is, he is, and if he isn't, he isn't,' the man said. 'You'll find out if you go round his house.'

'You got the address?'

'No. He's in South Bank. 'Bout halfway down. Everybody knows him. Ask for old Malc.'

The guy in the corner shop knew the house number. When Geordie knocked, the door was opened by a woman with a fresh perm. She looked like Janet's mother. Not exactly like her, but she was the same size and age and class, and the sound of her voice was almost the same. The thing that was different was that the woman who opened the door had a smile on her face, whereas Janet's mother's face had never managed to put a smile together. Not in Geordie's experience, anyway; and as far as he knew, and suspected, not ever.

Old Malc was sitting in a huge armchair in the back room. There was an open fire burning, and the room was too warm. He looked like an old sailor, mainly because of the tattoos on his forearms, a curled python on one, and a skull and crossbones with a galley on the other. He noticed Geordie looking at them. 'Got a gorilla on me chest,' he said. 'Been there forty-eight year.' He began pulling his shirt out of his trousers, but the old woman stopped him.

'Give over, Malc,' she said. 'Nobody in their right mind wants to see your chest.' To Geordie she said, 'It's not a gorilla anyway. It's a monkey.'

'Supposed to be flying through the trees in the jungle,' old Malc said. 'When I was younger I could make it wink. Flexing me muscles.'

His wife shook her head and raised her eyes to the ceiling. She went to the door. 'If he takes his shirt off give us a shout,' she said to Geordie.

Old Malc watched her leave the room. 'Did you see my shed down the allotment?' he asked.

'Yes. I didn't go inside.'

'Next time you're there, have a look inside. Let me know what it's like. 'Spect it's been vandalized.'

'I don't think so,' Geordie told him. 'It looked fine from the outside. Most of the sheds down there look as though they're on their last legs, but yours's been painted regularly. Looked after.'

'Yeah. I looked after it. Spent all my time down there. Get away from the old woman. Used to, anyway. Now I have to sit here all day, 'cept when she wants to take me for a walk.'

'I'm sorry,' said Geordie. 'You can't get out, then?'

'Never mind sorry. You've come to see if I saw the murderer? And you've come to the right place. I told her I'd seen him hanging round. She could've rung the police but she doesn't believe what I say. "They've arrested the husband, without your help," she says. "Well, I don't know if it was the husband or not," I tell her. "I only know it was a young chap, hanging round in the street, then going over to that shed when he thought no one was around. The police'll be looking for witnesses."

' "And a lot of good you'll be as a witness," she says to me. "Laid up on your back, half dead." Because that was just after I had the attack. I was in no state to argue with her. Even when I was fit I couldn't argue with her. Couldn't be bothered, to tell the truth. Arguing with a woman who can't ever be wrong. I'd rather eat bird shit.

'Then the next thing we hear they've let the husband go. And when I see his picture in the paper, he's nothing like the young chap was hanging round the allotments. Then I thought she should ring the police, tell them to come round here. But she's: "It's too late now, after all this time. They won't want to be bothered with something you might've seen and not seen. Police tramping through the house, I can't be doing with it." So I just think to me self, Oh, to hell with it, I'll watch the telly instead. It's nothing to do with us. But I thought somebody would come round enquiring sooner or later, and here you are. What's your name?'

'Geordie Black.'

Old Malc took Geordie's card and squinted at it. 'Geordie Black, private investigator.'

'This man you saw,' Geordie asked. 'You didn't see him with a woman?'

'No, he was always by himself. He came at night. He'd walk up and down the street a couple of times if anyone was around. Then, when he thought the coast was clear, he'd be over to that shed sharpish, like. Inside, and he'd be in there twenty minutes, half an hour, then he'd be away again.'

'How many times did you see him?'

'Three nights on the trot he was there, before I was taken bad the first time. I couldn't work out what he was up to. I was going to have a peek inside the shed after he'd gone, but then I had the heart attack, and that was that.'

'Can you give me a description? What did he look like?'

'It was always at night when I saw him, but I watched him good, because I couldn't work out what he was up to. He had a broad forehead. He was young, like I said, and he was thin. When he moved it was more like a woman than a man. I don't mean he was a woman. He was a boy. Not sure of himself. He was small and dark, not a working man, more like somebody what works in an office.'

'Like me?'

'Could've been, I suppose. But you're taller.'

When Geordie glanced back to say goodbye, at the door of Malc's room, the old man was smiling. Didn't improve him, though. Looked as ancient as God.

30

Joni Prine was the kind of girl who'd squeeze her friend's blackheads in the street. The village pub in Wheldrake had, of course, seen her like before, but had not become enamoured through the exposure.

Marie tried repeatedly to get Joni to keep her voice down, but it seemed like a physical impossibility. Even when Joni whispered, the locals took in every word. Eddy had been nice to her in the beginning, when they had first met. But for the last year she'd felt trapped, ever since he'd got her pregnant with Jacqui. Now the physical violence was getting worse. Eddy also threw his weight around with the younger girls. One of the ones in the cottage tonight had a cut lip. Almost impossible for a girl to work with a cut lip.

Marie had a miniaturized recorder, which she kept running while Joni talked. But at eleven o'clock they drank up and walked to the outskirts of the village where Edward Blake's cottages were situated behind a tall beech hedge. In the drive was a sleek Hertz rental with tinted windows, a sure sign that the gentlemen had arrived.

They were playing music inside the cottage, sounded like Cliff Richards' 'Summer Holiday', which put a certain vintage on the politicians, and pointed up the absence of taste which had led them, ultimately, into the hands of Edward Blake.

'I want to get this right first time,' said Marie, taking a small video camera from the bag on her shoulder. 'We don't go in unless we know we'll get some good footage.'

Joni held up a bunch of keys. 'We can go in the back way,' she said. 'Through the kitchen. They'll all be pissed anyway, and we'll be able to watch without them knowing we're there.'

Marie followed her round the house. They crept into the darkened kitchen, where Joni pushed open a serving-hatch. A tangle of naked and semi-naked bodies was revealed in the room beyond. A portly man with silver hair on his head and chest was kneeling on a cushion on the floor. He was the owner of a short, fat penis, which was fully and comically erect. The girl on his left, who was dressed in a pyjama top, was holding his member between thumb and forefinger. The girl to his right, who was tall and thin and brown, seemed to be licking out his ear. When the serving-hatch opened he was caught squealing with laughter, his red face blotchy with alcohol, and his mouth open in a roar of abandonment.

'Bobby!' he shouted. 'Tina wants us to make a daisy-chain.'

Bobby wasn't fully visible. He was stretched out on his back on the floor. Like the first man, he was completely naked. Only the base of his penis and a few red hairs were visible, the rest of it being subsumed in the mouth of a girl with a badly cut lip who knelt between his thighs. At the other end there was nothing to recognize, as a dumpy blonde with long nipples and a bored expression was sitting on his face.

'Let's get to work,' said Marie, flicking on the video camera. Joni kicked open the door, and the two of them tumbled into the room.

'Wheeeee,' screamed the silver-haired man. 'More girlies. Hey, Bobby, we've got more girlies.'

Bobby moved the blonde off his face and peeked out between her buttocks. 'More the merrier,' he said. 'Have a drink. Take your clothes off.'

Then he disappeared again under the blonde. Marie only caught a glimpse of him, but his face was almost a national icon. Robert 'Bobby' Neville was only a junior cabinet minister, but heavily tipped for one of the major jobs in the not-too-distant future. The Home Office and the Treasury had both been mentioned by political speculators.

His swift rise to prominence had been accomplished by a couple of veiled racist speeches, in which Bobby had partially concealed his misanthropy behind the cloak of patriotism.

But, like others who used flag-waving tactics, Bobby's only real love was himself. Marie reflected that patriotism was nothing more or less than the conviction that a country is superior to all other countries because you were born in it.

She let the camera run. Who knows, she might be making history, recording the formative moments of a future prime minister. Not exactly an in-depth interview, but revealing nevertheless.

The girl with the cut lip drew back from Bobby's sex and left it standing there, glistening with saliva. She looked at the camera. 'What the fuck's going on?' she said.

Bobby must have picked up on her tone, because he sat up quickly, and his engorged member went down like a pricked balloon, disappeared into that red bush real fast.

'Minister,' said Marie, zooming in on his face, 'is it true that when your dick gets hard, your brain gets soft?'

The minister's reply would have been censured in Hansard. His choice of words was not exactly considered, and there were far too many adjectives for the one sentence.

31

Before he went to the paper shop, Sam looked again at the photograph album Diana had found for him. They were all there, Arthur and Dora, Diana and Billy. There were a couple of photographs of Dora's parents, portraits gone yellow with age, people with spines so straight and rigid that today they would be regarded as abnormal.

The wedding-day photographs. Arthur standing tall with his bride on his arm. Dora smiling at the camera, her young face bursting with anticipation, her eyes innocent of the complications and hardships that the years ahead might hold. She looked too young to be married. Like a schoolgirl in a pageant that had nothing to do with real life, a child dressing up, pretending to be adult for the cameraman. Looking hard at the wedding photograph Sam couldn't detect much of the woman he now lived with. The girl in the photograph remained static, gazing into the dark aperture of the camera, fixed in the moment, unaware that another husband far in the future was looking back down the years at her through the same lens.

Sam sighed and flicked over a couple of pages. There was Arthur with Billy. Father and son in a studio portrait. Arthur would be around forty, the young Billy five or six years old. Billy had long curly hair and was dressed in a short linen coat, white ankle socks, and tiny sandals. Arthur was looking down at his son, who was standing on a chair. There was no physical contact between the two, but it was as if they were one being. The man's gaze encompassed the totality of the child, so that Billy was unaware of the precarious nature of his perch. He was aware of the undivided attention of his father. He was too young to recognize that the camera was there to make a statement, but the core of him, reaching out a tiny hand towards his father, illuminated an action that perhaps still continued down to the present day.

Sam picked up the *Yorkshire Post* and read the Stop Press headline on the back page. He paid for the paper and took it outside to a bench on the main road. He knew what it was going to say before he began reading it. It was like an epiphany, something he'd known was going to happen all along, something that he might have averted if he'd known it consciously. But he'd known it instinctively, with a kind of tribal knowledge. Until he'd seen the headline he hadn't even known that he knew.

The Surgeon Strikes Again?

Police were called to a house in York last night, after an attack on a young woman, believed to be the fourth intended victim of the serial killer known as the Surgeon.

A spokesperson said that the attacker was interrupted by the victim's boyfriend as he was attempting to strangle the woman. The attack took place at a flat in the Fishergate area of the town.

The woman is recovering in hospital.

The Surgeon, who has struck three times before in the York area, is known to use a distinctive modus operandi, and the attacker last night seemed to be following the same pattern.

The police spokesperson confirmed that no one had been detained. Various leads were being followed and investigated. An incident room was being established.

There will be a further statement later today.

It was the woman Billy had followed. Sam played it back in his head, the night he had followed Billy following the woman to the flat in Fishergate. He could see Billy watching from the shelter of the bus stop as she pressed the bell and was let into the flat. After she'd disappeared inside, Billy still waited, watching the building, looking up at the windows. He'd locked on to her and followed her halfway across the town, and now she had been attacked, nearly killed.

Dora had asked Sam to find Billy, her son, because she missed him, and because she was dying and wanted to see him one last time. What was he supposed to do? Go back and tell her Billy was a serial killer? Brighten up her last days with that?

Or should he do nothing, let Dora die in peace? Leave Billy free to kill again?

It was the kind of problem that made Sam Turner want to find a friendly pub. Get a high stool next to the bar and order a little glass of Scotch. Watch the world and all its problems recede into the distance.

It was always there, that thought. Have a drink and forget. Sam nodded at it inwardly. It was a demon he didn't need, but a demon he had to deal with.

Was Billy the Surgeon? Circumstantial evidence seemed to point that way. But circumstantial evidence wasn't admitted by the courts. The state wouldn't convict Billy on that evidence, but Sam Turner the great liberal had already judged him guilty without hearing what the guy had to say for himself.

And although in theory the state didn't convict anyone on circumstantial evidence, Sam knew from first-hand experience that in reality that was often the only kind of evidence available. And the fact that it was circumstantial had never stopped a good copper from going for the conviction. When he was a young man in Liverpool, the local filth had fitted Sam Turner up with a quantity of dope, searched him, found it, charged him, and sent him down.

He shrugged. So, slow down, Sam, he said to himself. You weren't a dealer when all the evidence said you were. It's at least possible that Billy isn't the Surgeon, even though it looks as though he is. Be suspicious. Don't close your eyes. But don't hang the guy until you're sure.

I've got a suspect, he told himself. That's all. A prime suspect.

Billy came out of the house in St Mary's and walked up to Bootham carrying a black holdall. Sam followed. Over to the east the sky was darkening, and violent squalls blew paper bags and bus tickets along the street. Billy crossed over the road and walked the length of Gillygate, eventually disappearing into a launderette on Clarence Street. Nothing sinister in that, Sam thought, the guy doing his weekly wash. Unless, of course, the black holdall contained clothing stained with the blood of the girl who had been attacked in Fishergate.

Sam watched through the window while Billy unloaded underwear and socks, a shirt, a single sheet, a pillow case, and a pair of jeans. None of them seemed unduly stained. Billy put money into the machine and sat down on a bench to wait. He was small and dark. He wasn't paler, or markedly more drawn. He hadn't turned into a slobbering Mr Hyde overnight. Didn't have a twitch. Sam tried to imagine what someone would look like who had recently attempted to murder a young girl and gouge out her eyes with a knife. It was an impossible exercise. Try as he might, he couldn't imagine that someone who'd done that would casually turn up at the launderette.

Sam didn't plan what happened next. He'd vaguely thought of tailing Billy for a couple of days, get to feel how the man lived, observe his habits before approaching him. But without thinking about it, he found himself pushing open the door of the launderette. He walked across the floor and sat down next to the young man. Billy tried to ignore

209

him at first, affecting the studied indifference of a frog on a lily leaf.

'Hello, Billy,' Sam said.

Billy slowly turned his head. He looked at Sam long and hard before saying: 'I'm sorry. I don't know you.'

'That's right. My name's Sam Turner. I'm married to your mother.'

A brief smile crossed Billy's face, but he didn't attempt to sustain it. 'Ah,' he said. 'One of Dora's fancy men.'

Sam suppressed the urge to break his neck. 'Dora's ill,' he said. 'She's going to die soon. She'd like to see you.'

The smile flitted across Billy's face again. 'Die?' he said. And he looked through Sam as he said: 'My father would have liked to see me before he died.'

Sam shook his head. 'I'm sorry. I know you were close to your father. But Dora, your mother . . . You'd make her happy if you came to see her.'

Billy turned his head away and watched his clothes going round in the washing machine. Sam looked at his profile. He'd changed from the night Sam had followed him across York. Then his hair had been slicked back and black, reminiscent of Elvis Presley. Sam remembered thick lips and a swarthy appearance. But today Billy's hair was short and auburn, and his lips were thin. He was paler, too. A different person. The Billy he'd followed across York had been wearing a wig and make-up.

'How did you find me?'

'By chance,' Sam said. 'It wasn't easy. You live like a recluse, like someone who doesn't want to be found. But at the same time you live in York, fairly close to your mother and sister. That smacks of ambiguity to me, on the one hand you don't want to be found, but on the other you don't want to get totally lost.'

'What are you? A psychologist?'

'No. I'm a messenger. I came to deliver a message from Dora.'

'Tell her I'm not coming.'

'Why?'

The smile again. 'So many reasons. She'll know why.'

'Maybe she will,' said Sam. 'But you could forgive her, whatever it is you're punishing her for. Just come and sit with her for a few minutes. That's all it'd take.'

'Is that part of the message?'

'No. I added that to the message. I'd like you to come as well. I'd like to get to know you.'

'Know me?' Billy shook his head. 'Nobody can know anyone else. You can only know what I want you to know. Same with Dora, you only know what she wants you to know. I know other things. A different Dora to yours. I could tell you about her.' His words were certain, but underneath he had all the foundation of a house boat.

'And if I listened,' said Sam. 'If I let you tell me about the different Dora, will you then come and see the Dora I know? Soon. Before she dies?'

'No. I don't want to see her. She's no good.'

'It can't be that simple, Billy.'

'People don't call me Billy. Nothing's simple. I don't want to open the floodgates.'

'What shall I call you?'

'William, that's my name. After my father. Arthur William Greenhills.'

'OK, William. What do you mean, "Open the floodgates"?'

'Let it all come out. What she did. How she planned it. The destruction. It's all contained. If we let it out where will we be then?'

'I give in,' said Sam. 'Where will we be?'

'Lost,' said William. 'I want to keep him alive.'

There was a deadness in the tone of his voice, and there was that vulnerability around his eyes that Diana had mentioned. But apart from those two things you wouldn't have picked him out in a crowd. Mister Normal, Sam thought. No distinguishing marks or tics. Little body language. In a line-up you'd walk right past him. Everybody's brother and son.

I want to keep him alive. Sam remembered saying exactly that about Donna after she was mown down by the drunk driver. 'I want to keep her alive,' he'd say, and people would think he meant he wanted to keep her alive in his mind, not let the *image* of her slip away. But he didn't mean that at all. He meant something much more literal, something that slipped away between the words. It was during that period, when he wanted to keep Donna alive, that he began the serious drinking.

'I think I know what you mean,' he said.

Billy, William was going to laugh. He'd heard it before and he knew it to be hollow. But something of the truth or the reality of Sam's words got to him. He suppressed the laugh. He looked straight ahead of him for several seconds, not moving, apart from a slight flexing in his hands. Then he said, 'If I could I would like to rewrite my life story.'

'That's not possible,' Sam said. 'But it might be possible to interpret it a different way.'

'I'll talk to you,' William said. 'I won't see Dora, but I'll talk to you. So long as you realize that no voice can reach me.'

32

A call from Celia. 'Dora, are you still living in that enormous house by yourself? Sam Turner's looking for somewhere to stay temporarily. Why don't you offer him a room?' Remember, Dora? Celia needs *her* spare room for her niece.

And two days later a lost white man in a white suit on your doorstep. 'Hello, Dora. Celia said—'

'Yes, come in. You can have Billy's old room.'

'I hope it's all right,' he says. 'I don't want to crash in if it's not convenient.'

You don't want a permanent lodger. You make that clear from the beginning. A few weeks will be OK. Until he can find something.

He brings a quietness into the house. For some weeks now you have been tired. All the time you are tired. In the morning it is an effort to get out of bed. You trudge through the days. At night you lie awake, staring at the ceiling.

Three days after Sam comes to live in your house you find the first egg on the underside of your left breast. You are lying in bed in the morning. You listen to Sam leaving his room and going downstairs to make coffee. The egg slips to one side as your fingers travel up towards the nipple. It is not a sparrow's egg, not the smallest possible egg; it is a blackbird's egg, embedded in the fat of your breast, close to the surface. Your skin begins to crawl, and a dank coldness grips you from inside. The egg is not perfect; it is almost perfect, but there is a ridge towards the narrow end. A mother blackbird sat on this egg would be worried.

You sit up and dress. You decide to ignore it. You go downstairs and drink coffee with Sam.

He prepares a meal for himself in the evening, and offers to make it for you as well. Why not, you think, he does not pay that much rent.

The house slowly grows brighter. Sam has a meal ready when you finish teaching. During the day he takes over the running of the house, does the washing, tidies up the garden. He spends two days repairing the cupboard doors in the kitchen. The hinges have been hanging off for years. He suggests repainting the hallway, brings home colour cards for you to look at. After the meal you spend two hours together pondering the relative merits of Coral Pink and Astley Hue.

Despite yourself you find yourself watching the clock during the day, waiting for the time you will return home. And it is not the house that calls you, Dora. It is definitely not the house. Through that autumn, after the hall is repainted, you walk together in the park. He tells you of his time in London and California, about his first wife, Donna, and his daughter, Bronte. You tell him about your job, about the intrigues of the department.

He plays you his Dylan songs and you listen to them, hear what he hears. You play him Lady Day, and he ends up playing her himself. Especially the Gershwin, 'They Can't Take That Away From Me'. He plays it over and over again because he's a sensualist.

The egg in your breast does not go away. You ignore it for a while, but you cannot forget it. You decide to tell Sam, work yourself into a state, and are then struck dumb in the breakfast room. It is impossible to look him in the eye. He places his hand on your shoulder. 'Something wrong, Dora?'

'No.' You have not yet fully recognized this egg in your breast. You have not yet accepted it yourself. It is too early to tell the world.

'Sure?' He lifts your chin towards him, forcing you to engage his eyes.

'It's nothing. I feel queasy.'

'Might be the beginning of a cold,' he says. 'Have a day in bed.'

But you get up, Dora. Go about the day as normal. Try to ignore it. If you ignore it it might go away.

The next day it has grown again. It grows every day. It is still an egg, but larger, larger than a blackbird could lay. You have to tell Sam now; the egg is too large for you to cope with alone. He explores it with gentle fingers, and it slips away from him as it slipped away from you. A cloud envelops his features as he tries to locate it again. You hold your breath, waiting for his verdict, hoping he will explain it away.

'It might not be serious,' he says. 'You'd better let the doctor see it.' You two are alone together under heaven. There is no explaining an almost perfect egg in your breast. Sam knows what it is. You know what it is, but even after breathing the word to yourself, after naming it, it is still not explained. It is not enough to know *what* it is, you need to know *why*.

But no one will tell you why, Dora. You join the unconscious merry-go-round of doctors, specialists, X-ray technicians. 'Don't worry.' That is the advice they have. 'Don't worry, these breast lumps are often non-malignant.'

They cut it out.

Sam takes you to the Radium Hospital and the two of you are lost in a maze of wards and corridors. Everyone is dying, the walls are porous, impregnated with hopelessness. The eyes of the patients no longer see. You are one of them, Dora. You will be welcomed here. Sam will go home, and you will remain. Sam will come for an hour every day while you grow weaker. You will take the treatment and vomit, the foundations of your face will crumble away and Sam will pretend not to notice. Nuclear science will gain an infinitesimal gram of understanding. And then you will die.

215

As you walk the corridors with Sam looking for the Reception Ward, he grips your hand tighter. You feel his nails digging into the heel of your hand.

You imagine what it would be like if the tables were reversed. If you were going back home without Sam. If you were, a few minutes from now, going to leave him here and return to your life in the avenue alone.

'Excuse me,' Sam asks a man with a concentration camp in his eyes. 'The Reception Ward?'

Your legs stiffen, Dora. You lead Sam to a side door, through it, and out into the gardens. You walk away from the building, and Sam follows, still hanging on to your hand. He does not ask what is happening. The buildings and the garden fan out behind you, and you train your eyes on the horizon, walking towards it, a thin line dividing earth and sky.

After some time Sam begins to laugh. You have climbed another fence and are struggling across a ploughed field on a hillside. Sam trips over a furrow and rolls about laughing. 'Do you think this is the right way?' he asks.

You sit on a ridge of earth and look down at him. It is as if your whole body is smiling. The right way? It is the only way, Dora. It is the way you have sought all your life. The way you never expected to tread. You brush earth from Sam's face and pull him to his feet. The light is beginning to fail, and the thin red line of the horizon has moved away from you. You still have a long way to go.

The park blazes with colour. The trees riot through browns, and yellows, and golds. Squirrels take on the rush of the approaching winter, seemingly working through the nights. You wonder that with their sense of urgency they have not yet invented arc lights.

Sam tells you about his marriage to Brenda. He does not blame the other man for the break-up. 'It was already doomed,' he says. 'He just happened along at the right

216

moment. If it hadn't been him it would have been somebody else.'

You do not speak about Arthur for a long time. When you finally do tell him he stops on the grass. He stands under a beech tree, fallen nuts around his feet. He watches you for a while, then he takes your hand and begins to walk again. The following weekend he brings Geordie, his young friend, and the three of you eat together. Geordie is shy, withdrawn, and dressed ridiculously in leather trousers, plastic shoes. They are running a private detective agency. You look at them and you don't believe they are private detectives. Then you look again, and it's obvious that they couldn't be anything else. Their last house was blown up by a psychopath. That's why Sam was living with Celia. But he's living with you now. Sam touches Geordie all the time. He cannot keep his hands off him. Eventually Geordie relaxes, chatters constantly about his friend called Janet. Janet is a cousin of Philip. Small world. Whatever happened to Philip? Some people are like that, insubstantial. They disappear.

When Geordie has gone you sit together with Sam in silence. He has something on his mind, but you do not prompt him. When he is ready he will speak. 'Have you ever thought of marrying again?' he asks.

You laugh. Of course you have thought of it. You thought of nothing else for years. But not now. It was something to think about, to dream about ten years ago, even five. But not now. Men are not interested in old women.

'I'm not interested in old women,' he says. 'But I'm interested in you, Dora.'

Your heart sits up inside your chest. It pumps blood at a breakneck speed into your head. You see Sam for the first time. You see him in a flash of light, and then he has gone. He is younger than you, but he has migrated across generations. In the space it takes to blink an eye you lose sight of him and something inside and outside of you pulls you to your feet. You are running from the room, as if pursued by a demon. You run over the garden, beneath the starving pear tree and out of the back gate. You are in the alley, lined with garages. It is night, pitch black apart from the stars. He has proposed marriage to you, Dora. This ... man; this young man.

You stop to catch your breath, pressing your back against the rotting wood of a garage door. The stars, which meant everything to the ancients, mean nothing to you. You try to put them in place, casting around for the Plough, but they will not take form. They strew the sky like spilled silver, and they remind you of people, of humanity itself, of the millions of isolated human beings sprawling over the planet, never touching, never coming within range of each other: your father in his perpetual sick bed, your cold mother, your dead husband, and your absentee children. They remind you of everyone you ever knew. Smiley and Philip, as far apart as the sky can reach, sailors and cowboys, Dylan Thomas and Sam Turner, your first and last lovers.

You walk back towards the house and Sam comes to meet you. He drapes your coat over your shoulders and takes your hand. You walk for a long time in silence, under the trees in the avenue, over the road to the park, alongside the lake.

'You came back,' he says.

'You came for me.'

He laughs and shakes his head. 'No,' he says. 'I wanted to meet you halfway.'

33

Over the years, piece by piece, William had refurnished the first-floor front room of the house in St Mary's. The size of it had started him off, the height of the ceiling, the proportions. It was now an exact replica of the room his father had used as a study when William was a child.

Some of the furniture had been easy. For a long time he had carried in his mind a picture of his father's favourite chair. The chair had a shield-shaped back, made of carved and inlaid mahogany. Although he looked for it in antique and second-hand shops he never found an exact replica until he managed to draw a picture of it for a dealer in Harrogate. The man looked at the picture and smiled. 'I'll find you one,' he said. 'Now that we know what we're looking for.' It was a chair in the style of Hepplewhite, and was the first piece of furniture in the transformation of the first-floor room. The desk came next, and through the same dealer. It was a writing-table, not a desk, French with reproduction Riesener marquetry, ormolu mounts and Sèvres plaques from the end of the Louis XV period.

Those two had been the most expensive items William had purchased in his life, and they had depleted his funds considerably. After that he had had to resort to desperate means to put money back into the bank. The bookcase and shelving had been discovered in a second-hand shop in York, and he had got them for a song. William smiled at that, the thought of buying things with songs. William knew a singer, a professional singer – he'd done his make-up for him from time to time – who bought everything with a song.

In another second-hand shop he'd found the picture of

the sailing ship. And the pens and the penholder almost completed the room. There were some books missing; books, the titles of which had gone from his memory. His father had had some large books, some of them so big that Billy, the child, had been unable to lift them.

For the carpet he had again had to use a dealer. It was Polish, with bold arabesques and long curved serrated leaves in reds and blues. Called Polish, but probably made, the dealer had told him, in Istanbul, back when it was Constantinople. An original would have been impossible to find, and would have cost more than a small country. But the dealer knew a woman who could make up a passable copy for three hundred pounds.

Black woman. She spoke with a Leeds accent but lived out at Escrick with her three children. She'd trained as an interior designer, but had turned to working with her hands. William couldn't remember her name now, but he could remember her face, and that she was thirty-five years old. He'd remember her name later.

He got a headache after he'd met her. An early indication that she was like Dora.

The same woman had decorated the room for him. The wallpaper that his father had used was no longer available. It was lemon coloured, with tiny blue florets, and the woman had mixed pigment and painted directly on to the wall. For a while William had not been happy with it, because he knew it wasn't wallpaper. But eventually he forgot about it, and now it felt exactly as he remembered the room when his father was still alive.

And there were times, more and more recently, when his father was there in the room. It was a ghostly presence, but none the less real for that. He couldn't see his father when he was in the room. But he could feel him. 'It makes me feel cold,' he told himself, trying to analyse it. 'Yet sustains me.'

That room and the attic room were the only furnished rooms in the house. William lived in the attic. The remainder of the house was a wasteland. There was a kitchen down-stairs, somewhere to heat water or fry sausages, but it was not a pleasant place to be.

William sat in the room he had furnished like his father's study when he was depressed, or when he wanted to feel close to his father, or when he needed to think. Today he needed to think over what Sam Turner had said to him. And he needed to think about his mother.

She was going to die at last. It was a flaw in the universe that she had managed to live so long after she had caused his father to die. Now, if he could believe what Sam Turner had told him, Dora was going to die soon. It would be good when she died. The world would be a better place. When he was still a child, living at home with Dora and his sister, Billy was the smallest. He was the smallest in the house, and he was the smallest at school. The smallness made him angry. And when he felt his anger it made him physically bigger and powerful. When that happened he could make Dora disappear, and Daddy come to life.

Now, if she died soon, that would become a reality. She would disappear from life. And if she disappeared from life his father would find it possible to live. Because they were opposites, those two. They had always been opposites. She was stupid, aggressive and intrusive. Billy, as a child, after the death of his father, had hated her, and now William, the man, hated her. His father had been loving, gentle, intelligent, and interesting. She should have died, and his father should have been the survivor. That would have made sense, had meaning. Now, after all these years, meaning was coming back?

William had told Sam Turner about the funeral. He'd wanted to show Turner what kind of woman Dora was, that was one thing. But he'd also felt able to talk to the man. He'd never see Dora again, but it was useful to have a go-between, then at least she'd know that William hadn't forgiven her.

Funeral? Fiasco, more like.

Dora was not going to take Billy with her. She and Diana were going to go to the burial alone, and leave Billy at home with a neighbour. But Billy wouldn't hear of it. He was going to be there, to listen to the service, to sing the hymns. To watch his father being sent up to heaven, to be there with the angels.

'Billy, there won't be any hymns,' Dora had told him.

'I don't care. I want to go.'

The three of them left the house at ten o'clock that morning. There was a priest and some people who had worked with Billy's father, but there was no coffin. The coroner's office had forgotten to send it. The priest had telephoned, and someone was trying to sort it out. After sitting in the church for nearly an hour, all the other people left. Then the priest explained to Dora that the coffin would arrive, but he couldn't wait for it. He had to be somewhere else. Some of his parishioners were sick. They were waiting for him. He'd return as soon as he could.

They went to the churchyard and found the hole in the ground. The gravediggers were still finishing it off, putting pieces of wood by the edge to stop the earth running back in. They walked off when Billy and Diana and Dora arrived. They didn't say anything.

It was cold there. There was no sun, and the wind was whistling through the shrubs, round the gravestones. The hole had been dug at the very edge of the graveyard, under the wall where everything was in shadow. In the centre of the graveyard, there were graves with marble angels, and others with white and green pebbles and tiny wrought-iron barriers. Billy would have liked to see his father's grave in the centre there, where there was light and air. But it seemed it had to be here in the gloom.

No bells rang in the church. Billy stood with the women and watched the earthworms in the newly dug soil. From time to time Dora or Diana shivered with the cold. Stamped their feet. Billy didn't shiver or stamp his feet. He gritted his teeth and waited.

The hearse ordered by the coroner's office came through the gate and drew up a hundred metres from the grave. Two men got out and loaded the coffin on to a wheeled gurney, which they pushed along the grass path to the edge of the grave. The plain wooden box containing his father's body rocked and teetered as if it might crash to the ground. The main man nodded at Dora, glanced at Billy and Diana. Then the two gravediggers returned, one of them flicking a cigarette end into the bushes.

The priest returned, breathless, and commended Billy's father's body to God. *Trusting that thou wilt in all things surely ordain what is best for thy creation; through Jesus Christ thy Son our Lord.*

'Do you want to say anything?' the priest asked Dora. She took Diana's and Billy's hands and stepped forward. She said the Lord's prayer: 'Our Father, which art in heaven . . .' She said it right through to the amen. Then she stepped back again, and looked at the priest and the gravediggers and Arthur's coffin. Billy pulled his hand free from his mother's grip.

They had a green rope which they put around the coffin so they could lower it into the hole. It seemed heavier at one end than the other, and it swung dangerously for a moment, as though they would lose it, banging against the top edge of the grave. But they controlled it and lowered it to the bottom. They threw the ends of the green rope down there too.

They stood quietly for a moment, then the main man said they'd be off. 'We'll leave you with yours,' the priest said to Dora. She nodded at him.

After a while Dora collected a handful of earth and threw it into the hole. Billy heard it rattle on top of the coffin. Diana did the same. Billy watched his sister, thinking she would have to copy Dora, pretend she was grown up.

And that was it. They walked away from the grave, and the gravediggers began filling it in before they'd reached the gate of the graveyard. The priest came out of the church then, and stood there while they walked past him. He had a black cassock on, and he had his hands tucked inside the sleeves, like a muff.

He called round later in the day, to see if he could be of service. Dora swore at him.

The church service had been different for Arthur because he had 'laid violent hands' on himself. That's what they called it. Billy would never go into a church again after that day. If he lived to be a hundred he would never forgive them. The church was happy to give the proper service to idiots and lunatics, murderers and rapists, almost anyone who needed to be buried. But not William's father, who was a truly good man.

William carried the candle into the room next to his father's study. The room was unfurnished and faced the back garden. There was nothing covering the floor, just the bare boards. Along the wall behind the door was a long chest, and inside the chest was a busybody. Only he wasn't busy any more.

Charles Hopper, secretary of the Fulford Players. His hands were tied behind his back, and his legs were trussed with the same rope. It was green, and new, and could have been used to hang out your washing on a windy day. Except William never hung out his washing. He took it to the launderette.

Charles Hopper had mad staring eyes. When William opened the lid of the chest, those eyes started blinking, and Hopper made sounds in his throat. He couldn't speak, though, because of the clear parcel-tape over his mouth. He'd peed himself. William could smell it, and it was just as well he'd thought to put some newspaper in the bottom of the chest before he put Charles Hopper in there. Sooner or later, when Charles Hopper stopped all his blinking and making noises with his throat, William would have to dispose of the body, and then he'd have to clean up the mess in the chest. Not a pleasurable task. Not something to cheer a chap up on a rainy day.

That was the kind of thing his father might have said. William smiled at the thought. His mother would never have said anything like that. She would have said something about history. Something dry and uninteresting, like about her own father or her mother. Or all that nonsense about Dylan Thomas. 'You're ten today, Billy. I remember my tenth birthday. Your grandmother had made me a dress in green satin. I wanted to climb a tree, but it was completely out of the question for a girl ...'

History. That's all she knew.

Whereas his father would take him on his knee. He'd lift him clean off the ground with his strong arms and hold him there. Billy would struggle and squirm, but his father was invincible. A man of iron and steel.

Then he would take Billy by the hand and they'd go to the park with a ball, leaving the women at home. They'd kick the ball around on the green, and other boys would join in for a time. And the other boys would be jealous because they didn't have a father with them who took them out with a ball. Billy would feel sorry for them, because they had to put up with the history and all the silly talk, and then go to the park by themselves.

And that's what Billy had to do himself, later. After his father was taken away from him.

He engaged Charles Hopper's eyes and held the contact for a few seconds. He widened his own eyes and reached for the lid of the chest. He pulled it forward and balanced it on the thumb of his right hand. Charles Hopper glanced away from William's eyes for a moment, saw that the lid was going to fall, and appealed to William with his own eyes. There was a silent eloquence about him. A supplication in his gaze worthy of any of the saints.

William smiled and took his thumb away from the lid of the chest, letting it fall heavily into place. It crashed downward, plunging Charles Hopper back into darkness and isolation.

It was a nuisance having Charles Hopper in the house. It was necessary, of course, as it was necessary and inevitable that Hopper would deteriorate, become weaker, and finally die. It would follow the same course as the woman, whatever her name was, India Blake. The woman he'd kidnapped for the money. William hadn't planned on the woman dying. He'd intended to let her go after the ransom was paid. But when he got the money he realized that he couldn't let her go. She'd seen him. She knew him. If she identified him the floodgates would be opened.

He had to keep her. Watch her fade away.

He'd fed her for a time. Made sandwiches for her, brought her a bottle of water and let her drink it through a straw. But then he'd left her quite alone, to fend for herself.

Now Charles Hopper would go the same way. William had no choice in the matter. If William hadn't put Charles in the chest, Charles would have talked to the detective, the woman detective. Marie Dickens.

If she'd talked to Charles Hopper she'd probably talked to other people as well. She was close, and getting closer. She'd have to be stopped.

William had seen her already. He knew the house where she lived, down by the river. She was living with a man, but she wasn't a mother. If he waited until the man went out she'd be alone.

It would have to be soon.

There it was again, that word. *Soon.* Dora was going to die soon, and so was Marie Dickens.

34

J.D. said, 'How was it for you?'

Marie had heard the line in films. She'd read it in newspapers. But she'd never expected to hear it live, right on cue, just after having finished doing it with a guy you thought you liked right up to that moment.

'Great,' she said, managing to sound not quite so fazed as she felt. J.D. was lying back on the headrest of the bed. He wasn't wearing his glasses, and there was a neat and sizeable dent in the bridge of his nose. His hands were clasped over his white stomach. He was smiling.

'Like clockwork?' he said.

Marie connected with his eyes. 'Well, no, actually. Not like clockwork at all. Just the opposite.'

J.D. shook his head and broadened his smile. 'It was OK, was it?'

'Yes.'

'Thing is, Marie, my old didgeridoo down there doesn't work like it ought to.'

She moved closer to him, placed a hand on his arm. 'Well, it did fine this time. A girl couldn't have asked for more.'

'No. You don't understand. It's prosthetic.'

'Prosthetic? Artificial?' She could feel her eyes getting wider, and could do nothing to stop them. Her heart put in an extra beat, then another one, and eventually went into a flutter. 'Jesus, you mean — ?'

'Well, no, not quite. I mean it *is* still there, it's just that it doesn't work without help.'

Marie took deep breaths, calmed herself down, hung on

to those words: *It is still there.* So that was OK, then, wasn't it? If it was still there, then she hadn't just been entered by something else. Something he'd strapped on specifically for the job.

'You understand what I mean when I say prosthetic?' J.D. asked.

She nodded. 'I'm a trained nurse. It means artificial.'

'Yes. But in this case it's an implant.'

'Not a transplant?'

J.D. smiled, more to himself than Marie, though she noticed that he was amused. If there was something funny about this, she hadn't discovered it yet. 'Not a transplant, no. It's a penile implant. A device that I can inflate and stiffen with fluid. Very like the original in fact. Except with this one I have a reservoir of fluid and a small pump implanted lower down.'

'Lower down?'

'In my scrotum.'

Marie wanted to cry. Men were always a disappointment. In theory you had to, eventually, meet one who was straightforward and uncomplicated, a strong, gentle man. But in reality they never happened along. It was always the same, you thought you'd got a man, but what you'd got was a bundle of problems. They were such pricks. Ha bloody ha.

Celia listened. She was good at that. She sipped at her coffee in Betty's, then she replaced the cup on the saucer and placed her hands in her lap. She didn't interrupt, let Marie explain all the intricacies of organic erectile dysfunction, and the various methods that the medics had introduced to deal with it. She managed to encourage Marie with various facial contortions, but not a sound came out of her mouth until Marie had finished.

'Poor man,' she said. Then she added, 'And poor you.'

'I feel like I've been an experiment, Celia. A sacrifice to modern technology.'

'I do understand,' said Celia pensively, 'from other friends, and from a catholic reading of the classics, that there are men in the world who do not have the ability to make a woman feel good about herself.'

Marie laughed. 'You can say that again. But thank goodness we can talk about it. I feel better already.'

'You've forgiven him?'

'No, but I've forgiven me.'

'Ah, yes, Marie. You have a good grasp of what's important. I'll buy you another coffee.'

'You know the fairy story about the frog and the princess. Where she kisses the frog and he turns into a handsome prince? That's never really been my experience. The story is always there, somewhere, at the back of my consciousness. So as I come across these frogs I have the right attitude. I mean, I expect them to turn into princes. But they don't.

'What happens is precisely the opposite. Whenever I kiss a frog, the frog gets decidedly worse. D'you think there's something wrong with my kisses?'

Celia asked a waitress to bring them more coffee, then turned back to Marie. 'I'm sure there isn't, my dear. It's the men, they make as much sense as a square toilet seat.'

Marie and Sam arrived at Edward Blake's office fifteen minutes before the cabinet minister was due. Blake's blue-rinse secretary was not in evidence, maybe she'd been given the day off, or perhaps she'd already found something better.

Blake let them in and locked the door behind them, leaving the key in the lock. 'You don't want us to be disturbed?' asked Marie.

He snorted, leading the way through the reception area to his own inner office. 'I presume you're here to ruin me,' he

229

said. 'I can't say that the prospect of visitors arriving during the actual operation fills me with joy.'

'The cabinet minister has already been in touch, then?'

'Five minutes after you left him. He got me up in the middle of the night.'

Marie smiled. 'Life's hard sometimes.' She placed a video cassette on Blake's desk, tapped it once with the tips of her fingers, and sat back in her chair. Blake fixed his eyes on the cassette, stared at it for so long that Marie wondered if he'd forgotten they were there. She glanced over at Sam, and he smiled but didn't speak. He was wearing a black trilby and he tipped it forward so it fell over his eyes. This was Marie's show, and he was only there because the cabinet minister's barrister had requested his presence.

When the other party arrived, Blake made the introductions. Robert 'Bobby' Neville, the cabinet minister, looked completely different with his clothes on. Almost respectable. His hair was sleek and black. Marie was now among the few who knew the truth: that he was a natural redhead.

His barrister was all bustle and feigned good humour, overweight and anxious to get the proceedings under way. Keen to show that he was worth his two-thousand-pounds-a-day fee. It was he who introduced a professional cough, just loud enough to gain everyone's attention.

'As far as I can ascertain,' he said, 'we are primarily gathered here to negotiate the purchase of a videotape.' He picked up the cassette that Marie had left on Edward Blake's desk. 'In fact, this must be the object in question. My client' – a glance towards the cabinet minister – 'is prepared to offer a nominal sum for the purchase of the tape, so long as the proceedings can be finalized immediately. He is not prepared to enter into protracted negotiations. Our bid is five hundred pounds, cash.' He flicked a catch on his briefcase and extracted a plain brown envelope, which he waved at Marie.

She shook her head.

The barrister smiled and extracted another envelope. 'One thousand,' he said. 'But that's final.'

Marie shook her head again. 'No deal,' she said.

'My client is in a position of some privilege,' said the barrister. 'I can assure you that the police will not look lightly on an attempt to extract money from him by means of blackmail.'

'No one's blackmailing him,' said Marie. 'I don't want his money. The videotape's not for sale.'

'But I thought—' said the barrister.

'Never mind.' Marie cut him off. 'We're here as a kind of industrial tribunal,' she said. 'To discuss the redundancy of one of Edward Blake's employees, Miss Joni Prine.'

Blake got to his feet. 'Now, just a minute,' he said. 'Joni's got nothing to do with this.'

'On the contrary,' said Marie. 'Joni Prine has been made redundant, and she is due a substantial payment to compensate her.' She paused to let her words sink in.

It was the barrister who got the message first. 'I think I see,' he said. 'The lady in question is obviously due some compensation, and my client, the right honourable Robert Neville, is here as a representative of government, unofficially, of course, to see that fair play is observed. He is not to be asked to contribute financially, and at the conclusion of the meeting he can leave with the videotape in his possession. Am I on the right track?'

'More or less,' said Marie. 'Give or take an inch here, a tuck there.' She smiled as if she'd swallowed a mouthful of sugar.

'Quite,' said the barrister. 'What terms were you going to propose to compensate the lady in question?'

Marie took a breath. 'Mr Blake is about to receive an insurance pay-out in excess of two million pounds,' she said. 'Joni Prine, who has been an invaluable aid in building up his present business, requires to be settled in her home town of Sunderland. We estimate that a one-off payment of one hundred thousand pounds should cover her moving expenses and allow her to purchase a moderate property for herself and her daughter.'

The blood began draining from Edward Blake's face.

'Another one-off payment of the same amount,' continued Marie, 'would ensure that Joni's daughter receives a decent education. And a final, smaller one-off payment, say fifty thousand pounds, would allow Joni's elderly and frail mother to spend her remaining days free from financial constraint and worry.'

The barrister looked at Edward Blake. Blake's features were immobile, but his whole body was shaking. 'What is your response to the proposals, Mr Blake?'

Blake brought his body under control and let a thin smile cross his lips. 'I'll not pay a penny,' he said. 'Joni Prine is a slag and a thief who's never been in my employ. And no one can prove otherwise.'

'OK,' said Marie, 'the alternative course for us is to solicit offers from the tabloid press for a certain videotape. One way or another Joni will be compensated.'

Robert 'Bobby' Neville leaned forward and touched Blake's arm. He smiled with a mouthful of teeth. 'Edward,' he said, 'I do believe you'd like to reconsider the proposals to compensate the lady.'

Blake glared at the cabinet minister with undisguised hatred. 'A quarter of a million,' he said. 'I'm screwed for a quarter of a million, and the rest of you go home with everything intact. Is that justice?'

No one replied. Sam Turner made a squeaking sound from underneath his hat, but he didn't actually say anything.

'I'm not going to fall for this,' said Blake. 'If I go down you all go down with me.'

'What you have to realize, Edward,' said the cabinet minister, 'is that the tobacco industry will immediately pull its cash out of your operation. And even if you are lucky enough to retain a new client, there will be very few politicians willing to listen to your arguments. If that tape ends up with the tabloids you'll be joining the dole queue.'

'We'll be there together, then, minister. There's no way that I'm going to pay everyone's fare out of this.'

Bobby and his barrister went into a whispered conference. Scratching of chins. Shaking of heads. Slow dawning of resignation on their faces as they came out of the huddle.

Bobby looked at Edward Blake and said, 'Fifty-fifty?'

Blake took his time, let the minister sweat for almost a minute. Then he said, 'You're a fucking prince among men, Bobby.'

The barrister did his cough again. He rubbed his hands together. 'Well, then, everything seems to be settled, er, amicably.' He collected the videotape and put it into his briefcase.

'A moment,' said the cabinet minister. 'What happens if for some reason Mr Blake doesn't honour his part of the commitment?'

'We'll go to the tabloids,' said Marie.

'So there's another copy of the videotape,' said the cabinet minister, almost to himself.

'Ten, actually,' said Marie. 'Lodged with different solicitors and banks. Just in case anything happens to Joni Prine or to anyone connected with her.'

Marie got to her feet. 'Coming, Sam?' she said. She waited until her boss had shaken hands with the other gentlemen in the room, smiling and nodding his head, occasionally raising his hat, but still not speaking. Then she followed him out of the office and down into the street where they both collapsed against the wall of the building.

'Unbelievable,' she said. 'I didn't think they'd buy the whole package.'

'It's true what they say,' said Sam, when he'd got his breath back, 'if it wasn't for the government we'd have nothing left to laugh at.'

*

233

A quick celebratory coffee and back to work. When she had spoken on the telephone with Charles Hopper, secretary of the Fulford Players, he had sounded as though he might be helpful. Marie had expected him to get back to her, but there had been no word from him. She decided to visit his house rather than telephone again. You got more information from a man if you could establish eye contact.

He lived in a three-storey Georgian town house off the Fulford Road. The place was well maintained, the mortar sharply pointed, the windows cleaned, and the three steps up to the front door had been recently scrubbed. The weather was electric. When Marie had started out the sky in the east had been black; now it was clear over there, but the air was heavy with pressure. There were sudden gusts of wind, shaking the trees and sending people running for their hats, then just as quickly the wind would die away and leave behind it an apparent calm.

The bell jingled merrily inside the house, but no one came to answer the door. Marie rang again and waited long enough for a man to get out of bed, find a dressing-gown and descend from the top floor. But there was no sound from inside the house.

She walked around the side, to the back of the building. Startled herself momentarily when she saw her own reflection in the glass of a conservatory. She wasn't totally put at ease, either, when she realized that it was her own reflection. Her practised eye detected that she was packing several pounds more than she had at her last visit to the bathroom scales.

She peered through the windows. The place was dust free. There was an easy chair in front of a television, a small table to the right of the chair. One wall was covered with books. And nothing was out of place. The surface of the table was uncluttered, polished. There was a framed photograph of a man, presumably Hopper himself. The floor of maple panels was naked apart from a rug. Charles Hopper was an unusual and fastidious man. Either that or he had a housekeeper.

Oh, hell, though, putting on weight. As soon as you take your eyes off it, it starts to creep back. Soon as you relax. She'd been so involved with J.D., so intrigued by him, she hadn't noticed the fat making its comeback. Now it had several days' advantage, which meant she'd have to suffer for twice as many *weeks* to get back to normal. She'd read an article by a Christian saying you could pray yourself slim, that Jesus would dissolve all the fat and leave you trim and ready to fight the devil. You just had to believe.

Marie didn't.

And it also confirmed something she had known all of her life. Jesus had no weight problems whatsoever. If he had been a fatty he'd never have got Christianity started. Or if he'd been a fatty and somehow managed to get Christianity started, we'd have heard about it big time. Like Robbie Coltrane, say. It would have been a feature.

But then the whole script would have been different. If he'd been fat they might not have crucified him, they'd have found some other way of getting rid of him, maybe drowned him in a barrel instead. Because you can't have a fat man on a cross, it would make the whole thing top heavy, end up toppling over. You just couldn't found a religion on a scenario like that. But if they'd drowned him in a barrel the iconography, everything, would have been different. Instead of wearing crosses round their necks, people would have barrels.

People with stigmata would never have been heard of. Never have been thought of. Hysterics the world over would not bleed from their hands or their sides. Instead you'd get occasional cases of *bloated* fanatics, their lungs filling up with fluid.

And the last supper would've been a fat man's supper. The last *banquet*, at which bread and wine would simply have been incidentals among a gluttony of nourishment;

hors d'oeuvre, cheeses, meats, succulent steak, beef, mutton, pork, veal, lamb, roast and boiled potatoes. They would have had stew, mince, broth and soup, a variety of suet puddings. And all the disciples would have been fat as well. In fact Christianity would have been a fat person's religion. A society of bellies and fleshspots getting together to race through the fish course and the entrée so they could bite, champ, munch, crunch, chew, sip, suck, and swill their way through a mountain of pastry, sweets, doughnuts, pancakes, mince pies, blancmange, and ice cream. While on the side would be chocolate, liquor and liqueurs, claret and coffee to ensure that everything was well washed down.

Holy Communion as we now know it wouldn't exist. It would have taken on a totally different face. When the priest asked the congregation to come forward to taste the body and blood of Christ, a vast catering conglomerate would go into action to feast the faithful.

Marie smiled. Religion would really mean something then.

'You looking for somebody?' The woman's voice dragged Marie back from her reverie. She turned to face a stout woman in a turban which was designed to hide a mixture of pink and white plastic hair-curlers. She was standing at a wooden gate which connected her garden to the garden of Hopper's house. The woman's face had been scrubbed with the same relish and zest as the front steps of the house, and, Marie concluded, with the same hands.

'Yes. I'm looking for Charles Hopper. Do you know if he's at home?'

The woman's top lip curled slightly. 'If he was at home he'd have answered the door. Who's looking for him?'

'My name's Marie Dickens.' She stepped forward and offered the woman her card. 'And you are?'

'Dawson's the name. Clara Dawson.'

'I spoke to Mr Hopper on the telephone a couple of days

ago,' Marie said. 'He was helping us with an investigation. Do you know when he'll be in?'

The woman studied the card, narrowing her eyes to read the small print of the address and telephone number. 'You'd better come in for a minute,' she said. 'I'm at the end of my tether.'

She opened the gate and Marie followed her into a small cottage that was attached to Hopper's house. Clara Dawson's legs were criss-crossed with varicose veins.

The door led directly into a Formica kitchen. The surfaces were all clean, and a whistling kettle gleamed its aluminium sheen from the top of a gas hob. A solid pine table took up the centre of the room, and the floor was covered with earth-coloured tiles. On the door of the fridge was a photograph of the woman, taken perhaps twenty years earlier. In the photograph she was surrounded by five small children, each of them with a striking resemblance to her, and she peered out at the camera with a permanent expression of amazement.

She noticed Marie looking at the photograph. 'They've all gone now,' she said. 'When they're that age you think they'll never leave, then you wake up one morning and they've all flown.' Marie couldn't tell from Mrs Dawson's expression or tone if she was happy or sad at the loss of her brood. 'You got any, yourself?' the woman asked.

Marie shook her head. 'Don't suppose I shall have now. Left it all too late.'

They lapsed into silence.

'You said you were at the end of your tether, Mrs Dawson. What do you mean?'

'It's Mr Charles. Sorry, Mr Hopper. He's not been home for a couple of days. It's not like him to go missing. He always says, even if he's just nipping out for an hour.'

'When did you last see him?'

'Friday. I look after the house for him. He was reading

237

the newspapers when I went out to do some shopping. When I came back he'd gone, and I haven't heard from him since.'

'Friday,' said Marie. 'And it's Sunday now. Have you informed the police?'

'No.' Mrs Dawson shook her head. 'I didn't know what to do.'

'I think you should tell the police,' Marie told her. 'They'll check the hospitals, at least. If he's had an accident, something like that . . .'

Mrs Dawson began shaking, and Marie led her to a chair. 'You're sure he didn't mention anything? Where he might have gone? If he had any phone calls or visitors?'

Clara Dawson put both hands flat down on the surface of the table. She shook her head from side to side. She wasn't listening any more. Now that she'd finally voiced her fears they came to the surface, hollowed out her eyes, and hung like gargoyles in the ploughed furrows of her lumpy face.

William followed her. He watched Charles Hopper's house, and he saw the woman arrive. It was as easy as that. He was wearing his lucky socks. Charles had said she was a private detective, but he hadn't seen her, only spoken to her on the telephone, so he couldn't describe her. William thought she looked like a journalist, but journalists and private detectives looked alike. They were snoopers. This one was thirty-five years old, something like that. A bit of a fatty. She wouldn't be easy to overcome, except she'd be surprised. Usually they didn't fight, anyway, they went to pieces, gave up almost immediately. Started begging.

He tried to think of her sexually. Imagined that he found her attractive. But he couldn't do it. William had never found women attractive. He'd told himself that Pammy was attractive, all those years ago. He'd told himself that he wanted to have sex with Pammy. But he hadn't wanted to. Not really. And for a while there, when he was in London

238

he'd thought that he might be gay. He'd tried looking at men, then, and young boys. But it was the same as looking at women. They disgusted him.

They were weak. They let life and events overwhelm them. Humanity was like insects. William called them *The hordes*. He watched them every day. He had studied them for years. They queued up outside shops before they opened, and at the doors to theatres and cinemas. They formed orderly lines and they waited. They sat in stationary cars, and on buses. They sat there and they waited. They lived in their houses, little boxes, side by side, stretching like ribbons along drab or twee roads. Even their clothes were the same, their crimplenes and their nylons and mixed fibres. How could you pick one of them out and say you found him or her attractive?

They weren't attractive. Not at all. They were ugly.

Ugly and pointless.

Getting born, eating, fucking, and dying.

Physical actions taking place in a vacuum, an impenetrable silence.

She rang the doorbell a couple of times, then she stood back and looked up at the house. After a few minutes she went around the back. William's first thought was to follow her. He could stride over the road and down by the side of the house. Charles Hopper wasn't at home, he knew that, because Charles Hopper was in a chest back at William's house. So the woman, the private detective, would be alone now around the back of Charles' house. No one at home. The house deserted, quiet. He could come up behind her, take her by the throat, shake the life out of her. Punish her.

But for what?

William didn't move. Why should he punish this woman? She wasn't Dora. She was no one. Nothing.

And yet, there was a reason. Otherwise William would not have followed her. Now it was like being in a dream. The day had set itself up around him, it had placed him at

239

the centre of the scene, painted in Charles Hopper's house, provided the private detective. Somehow the opportunity had arisen to get rid of this woman detective, and deep within William there was a voice nudging him towards the conflict. *Take her. Take the woman. Do it.*

And he would do it, too. If he could remember why.

If she was Dora he wouldn't hesitate. But something was wrong. Dora was a mother, and this woman wasn't. Even that wasn't clear in William's mind. He didn't know if this woman was a mother or not. And it was important to know that. If she wasn't a mother there would be no point in taking out her eyes.

The woman called Marie Dickens left Charles Hopper's house. Suddenly she was back on the street and walking towards the town. William followed.

He followed her home. He watched her take a key from her pocket and put it into the lock of the door of her house by the river. He sat on the grass verge about eighty metres away and waited, watching her house. After an hour a man arrived. A man with a raggedy beard. The man tried the door, but it was locked. The man knocked on the door lightly, twice, and Marie Dickens opened the door and let the man with the beard in.

The wind came back again. Gusting along the river and the bank so that birds wheeled in huge arcs to maintain their positions. For a few moments William thought it was out of control, a tempest, a hurricane, he narrowed his eyes and grabbed hold of the sods of grass. But it blew itself out as quickly as it had arrived. There was a puff and a sniffle and a catching of the breath and the earth returned to its previous calm.

William went home to his house in St Mary's. While he'd been sitting on the grass verge by the river he'd managed to clear his head. Now he was tired, weary, and felt that if he got on to his bed he'd fall asleep. But he didn't want to do that. He wanted to sort out what had happened to him this morning.

There were two things he had to do. The first thing was to kill Dora. William smiled. Not literally, of course. If he killed his mother he would be arrested by the police and locked away. Everyone would know, the whole world would know that he had done it, and if there was a court case they would all know *why* he had done it. For his father. Revenge for his father. But then they would all forget. Within weeks, days even, the world would forget. William would be locked away, Dora and his father would be dead, and there would be no one to remember. The newspapers, the television, all the reporters would find another story. Reality would be swamped by illusion.

So that was clear, then. That's what he had to do. Kill Dora, over and over again. He had to find a suitable stand-in. She had to be similar to Dora, that's all. Not identical. William was a make-up artist. He could take any woman and transform her into Dora. Provided she was around the right age, and that she had the right kind of experience. She had to be a mother.

Theatre.

All the world's a stage.

The play's the thing. The play allows the artist to subjugate his desires. It is a safety valve. Dora can die a million deaths, and never know she has died. The violence that William feels towards his mother need never be given rein. Within the cosmic theatre it can find free expression. The violence is contained within the play, and Dora's life is never threatened.

That's what William did. It was something he knew, something that was easy and clean and simple. His father was revenged. The formality of the operation, the twist of taking out their eyes, like she had taken out Arthur's eyes, gave the play symmetry, the fatal gift of beauty.

241

Between acts. Between the repetition of the same act over and over again. William could forget and relax.

Almost.

Anyway, that was the first thing. The main thing. The second thing that William had to do was connected to the first thing. It was the same with every production. In the theatre nothing was possible without finance. Many of the actors, the scene-changers, the little people associated with the theatre didn't realize that. It was not their realm. But the producer, the writer, the director, they knew. Nothing happened without a budget. Every production needed money.

That's how the business with India Blake came about.

She wasn't a mother; she was a meal ticket. The plan had been to hold her there, in that garden shed, until her husband paid the ransom. Then she would be released. But it didn't work out, because William realized that she would give his description to the police.

When he got the money, William thought about killing her. But he couldn't bring himself to do it. Just to kill someone like that, in cold blood. She wasn't a mother, she wasn't Dora. She didn't fit into the pattern of vengeance, of revenge. She wasn't suitable as a sacrifice. And anyway he'd done the sex thing with her. As an experiment. To see what it felt like. He'd brought her water and packets of crisps, and watched her eat and drink. He wouldn't have been able to kill her. So it was good that she died eventually, of natural causes. That had solved the problem.

And it would be the same with Charles Hopper. There was no way that Charles could be used as revenge for William's father. He would have to live in the chest in William's house until he died.

All that was clear.

The Dora stand-ins had to die; they had to have their eyes taken out. That was written into the script all those years ago. The others, India Blake and Charles Hopper, they knew too much, they would stop the play being performed if

242

they had their freedom. They had to be imprisoned. They didn't have to be killed. They had to be stopped.

What had happened today, when he had felt impelled to kill the private detective woman, was that he had temporarily got the two categories mixed up. Up to now he had been able to keep them apart. He had understood from moment to moment exactly what was happening. He had been in control. Then suddenly, today, when Marie Dickens had gone to the rear of Charles' house, he'd lost sight of who she was. He'd thought she was Dora. And she wasn't, she was just someone who knew too much.

And something else. In the instant that he'd mistaken the private detective woman for Dora he'd lost sight of himself. His self had slipped away from him. There was a moment there when he had almost taken her. A moment when he had been on the verge of becoming a common murderer.

William scratched his head. The top of his skull was prickly. There was a dull ache behind his ears and behind his eyes. Tension in his neck.

It was absolutely necessary that he keep a clear head about this. The issues were straightforward. There was no need for things to become confused. It was a matter of concentration.

There was a loose end. The loose end was called Marie Dickens, the private detective. She was getting too close. William would have to get her inside his house, put her in the chest with Charles. They could be company for each other.

That's what he had to do. He had to remember that she wasn't Dora. At all times he had to remember that. He would keep saying it over and over to himself. *She isn't Dora; she isn't Dora.* But when he'd said it five or six times he had to shake his head, because suddenly there was too much to remember, too many processes to control. And his head hurt, both inside and out.

Felt like it might explode.

35

Diana comes in with a tray of drinks. Outside the wind is buffeting the windows. There may be a storm brewing and you wonder what it would be like to walk in a storm. To have that hard rain in your face; to watch the drops bouncing off the pavement; and return home dripping, your hair in rat's tails, your neck and back sodden. You could ask Sam or Diana to open the window, but it would be a waste of breath. 'Shall I lift you?' Sam asks. He places his hand beneath your head. 'Lean on my shoulder.'

You shake your head. You do not want to disturb the iron bar. To lean on Sam's shoulder would be good, but time is running out. You do not want more pain. He holds the glass to your lips and the liquid trickles into your mouth. 'Not long, now,' he says. 'The doctor will be here soon.'

The doctor. That's what happens next. You are still here in the physical world. You lose track of time and space. Only one thing you know. As you get older less and less happens more and more often.

Sam holds the glass to your lips, but this time the liquid trickles from your mouth. You hear yourself making a sucking sound, but this simple act, drinking, is beyond you. You catch concern in Sam's eyes as he watches the droplets clinging to your chin.

You're dribbling, Dora.

And Sam's watching.

Dribbling.

Like Billy did after Arthur died.

He began bed-wetting. He'd sit and look at you while he soiled his pants. Loss offers opportunities of maturity or regression. For you and for Diana the loss of Arthur meant a kind of maturity. But for Billy it was different. The death of his father revealed an unequivocal opportunity for regression. Because Billy didn't grieve, Dora. You knew he should grieve, and you tried to make him.

But he wanted to suffer. His father's life had gone. Now Billy seemed to want a living death.

'I want to give Daddy his eyes back.' This child, this tiny son of yours looks at you from his bed, and he says that. *I want to give Daddy his eyes back.* You go to him. You enfold him in your arms, crush him to your breast. Because he is taking on more than his scrap of a soul will ever manage to carry. He has too much knowledge, Dora. The weight of it will swamp him.

You watch anger, hostility, and guilt growing in the child. You explain over and over again that it is not his fault, that Arthur loved him, but that Arthur's pain was too much to bear.

Billy's eyes glaze over.

From time to time the child's anger is directed against his dead father. He cries out in his sleep: 'Daddy, don't leave me.' But when he wakes he is ambivalent about Arthur and Arthur's death. He wants to carry the weight. And he wants to put it down.

Ambivalence is guilt.

As he grows, the guilt grows along with him, sometimes disproportionately. It is always there, in his eyes. He looks at the floor. He doesn't engage your eyes or the eyes of his sister. In an end-of-term report his Geography teacher mentions this strange phenomenon. *Throughout the length of the period I have had to teach this child, he has never looked me in the eye.* It is as if the only eyes he engages are the eyes of Arthur, the eyes that have been eaten by the birds. He thinks about his father. He thinks about what was said, and what was not said. And he feels, increasingly, that he can only achieve relief for his guilt by paying restitution for the rest of his life. That's what he means when he says: 'I want to give Daddy his eyes back.'

He has lost his father, and nothing will ever replace that loss.

The best he can do is idealize the man. Idealize him and identify with him. And as Billy grows, you watch him become more and more like Arthur. Every day there is another facet of his father's character being reborn in Billy.

The child grows, and as he grows a kind of sickness grows with him.

The only person in the world who could have stopped that happening, Dora, is you. And you failed.

You failed because, as he got older, Billy wanted you to be clean, good, and hardworking, like the idealized version of his father, and he told you so. And you, Dora. God forgive you, but you didn't want those things. You wanted to live. That placed you at a distance from your son. He couldn't hear what you had to say. You weren't a proper mother; you were greedy, bad, and sexual.

You wished on the moon.

What happened there?

'You were sick,' Sam tells you.

There is that stench of vomit. You can taste it on your lips. Sam and Diana have changed the pillow and the sheet.

Weary.

You want to talk to Sam but you are too weary. Floating away to that dream state between living and dying. There is so little of substance in your world, Dora. You are like a spirit.

When you began sleeping with Sam the world was still made of iron and steel. That inner smile fills you when you remember how he called you Donna in the mornings. When he was tucked in that space between sleeping and waking, you would feel his arm snaking around you, pulling your body close to his. Then he would say, 'Donna, Donna,' and you'd snuggle up closer to him as if you were her. His dead wife from long ago.

You didn't mind, Dora. You knew he loved you. He could call you anything he liked, so long as love was there.

You and your Sam. You were ravenous, voracious. Those first weeks and months you were always hungry together. Always eating, and yet never satisfied. What do they call it, that open-mouthed hunger and thirst which is unquenchable? For ever eager, burning, and yet for ever unsated?

You couldn't remember the word, because you'd never experienced it before. But Sam knew. Didn't even have to think about it.

'Lust,' he said with a laugh your mother would have called obscene.

36

Dear Sam Turner,

Just a note of thanks for allowing me to sit in on the investigation. I would have liked to thank you personally, but I understand that you are indisposed because of your wife's health.

The information I need for my next novel does not necessitate my spending more time on research, and I feel that I have been less than professional in allowing myself to become emotionally involved with one of your operatives.

In the circumstances it is in everyone's interest that I withdraw without further delay.

If in the future I can repay you in any way for your kindness, please do not hesitate to contact me.

Yours sincerely,

J. D. Pears

37

Geordie picked up the phone and listened. 'Yes, it's me,' he said. He listened some more, nodding as he did so, at the same time keeping his eyes fixed on Janet. If he didn't know he wouldn't have been able to tell she was pregnant. Not from looking at her, and not from running his hands over her stomach, or putting his ear right up close. Doctors could only tell because they had all the gear, and they could calculate when it would be born to the day, as long as the woman knew when was the last day of her period. And the other thing they could tell by sound waves and computers, was, they could tell if it was a boy or a girl. But Janet and him didn't want to know.

They wanted to guess.

He put the phone down.

'Who was that?'

'Marie. I've got to go out.'

'Trouble?'

He shook his head. 'I hope not. Marie thinks she's being followed.'

'What about her boyfriend? J.D.? I've cooked us a meal. It's nearly ready, Geordie.'

'J.D. and her have fallen out.'

'Why? Last time I looked they couldn't keep their hands off each other.'

'Dunno. They prolly didn't look long enough before they leapt. Far as I can tell she's told him to commit sodomy with himself.'

Janet laughed. 'And Sam?'

'He's with Dora. They've had to call in the doctor.'

'Yeah. And it's your case.'

'Mine and Marie's. Yeah, we said we'd take it on. I'm sorry, Janet. I'd rather be here with you.'

'But you've got to go.' She followed him into the alcove by the front door, watched as he put on his leather jacket. He embraced her, felt her arms slip beneath the jacket and her fingers knead the flesh on his back. 'Listen,' she said. 'I can slow the cooking down. It'll be ready in about an hour. If you're not back by then I'll get a taxi and bring the whole lot to Marie's house.'

'Can't wait,' he said, 'I'm starving,' and he kissed both of her eyes. Janet didn't always let him do that. Sometimes she'd say it made her feel like a doll, and she didn't like feeling like a doll.

He opened the door and went out, looked back twice at Janet standing there watching him go. The third time he looked back she'd gone inside and closed the door. Barney went into someone's garden and Geordie whistled for him.

There were many things Geordie didn't understand about women. And that thing about feeling like a doll if somebody kissed you on your eyes was one of them. Seemed unreasonable somehow, kissing eyes was something important in life, that shouldn't be denied. He'd talk to Sam about it, see what the great thinker thought. Sam'd say something like we'd never understand why people denied certain things for themselves. He'd say it was nothing to do with women, that there were plenty of men who had phobias. He'd come up with examples, like men and women he'd known who'd been totally unreasonable. Then he'd say: *Go fathom.*

Geordie walked along the riverside path. There was a strong wind blowing, which suddenly abated, as if God had changed his mind and hit a button up in heaven to switch it off. There was a huge harvest moon sitting on the horizon, pale orange. J.D. said it was called a harvest moon because it helped ripen the corn, but Janet had turned her nose up at that, said it was an old wives' tale. And Janet had taken her mother to the station and put her on a train. Geordie wondered if Janet's mother could see this huge moon, and if his own mother could, and his brother, wherever they all were.

Barney came face to face with a duck and both of them stopped dead, staring. Barney's tail went between his legs and the duck hissed. Geordie wished he had a camera so he could take a picture of it. Barney and the duck and that big ol' moon shining down on them like the dawn of creation. But the only camera he had with him was his memory, and he stored it away in there, hoped he'd never forget it. It was something he'd never be able to explain to anyone, even Janet. A moment with a dog and a duck and the moon. A scene that could've happened any time in history, down through the ages. If there was a picture of it, you'd be able to look at the picture and say, that could've happened any time, fifteenth century, fourth century, even BC.

And when you said that some people'd think you was crazy.

But fuck them. What did they know?

For the rest of his life Geordie would remember it, and when he thought about it he'd know that it happened round about the time Dora was getting ready to die, and just after the time he got married to Janet, and before it showed that she was pregnant. And he might never be able to explain it to anyone else, or to fully understand it himself. He'd just know that it was connected to poetry somehow. Poetry and music.

That was close. Though there was no sound of music, no song in his head. A faint whisper from the river, maybe? That hissing sound the duck had made.

When he was much older, and he tried again to describe it all to his daughter, he'd say, *It was the moon and the dog and the duck, nothing else. All the other thoughts came later, about the wedding, and Dora getting ready to die. But the moment itself was just the dog and the duck and the moon. It was poetry and music and ghosts.*

Marie was sitting in the window. She waved as Geordie approached the house, but did not move. She passed out of sight as Geordie walked around the side of the house, to the back door. He joined her at the window. Barney put his front paws on her knees and waited for a pat.

'I've got coffee going,' she said. 'It's getting to be my favourite thing in the world; sipping coffee in the evening and watching the river. Have you seen the moon?'

'The door was open,' Geordie said. 'I can't believe you left the door open.'

'I meant to lock it,' she said. 'When J.D. went. Must've forgot.'

'Jesus Christ.' He went through to the kitchen. 'I'll pour the coffee.' He found mugs and semi-skimmed milk. Looked for a jug to put the milk in, but couldn't find one. Looked for a tray to put the mugs and the milk bottle on, but couldn't find one. He wondered if his love-bite showed. 'Yeah,' he shouted through to her, 'great moon. Barney met a duck on the path, and they were both framed in it.'

Marie didn't answer. 'There's a tray beside the cooker,' she said.

'I thought J.D. was your favourite thing in the whole world.'

'Things aren't always what they seem.'

'But you liked him. You two was all over each other.'

Marie looked up and smiled at him. 'Yes,' she said. 'We were searching for something. But whatever it was I was after, J.D. didn't have it.'

'And the other way around? Did you have what he was looking for?'

Marie shook her head. 'Maybe an approximation of it,' she said eventually. 'If people've got a gap in their life, it's not possible for someone else to fill it. All those hollow places we've got, the bits that make us feel lonely and frightened, they're there because we have to deal with them ourselves. It's not a job you can give to someone else.' She shrugged her shoulders and grinned. 'What I mean,' she said, 'J.D. offered me a job as a saint, but I didn't like the hours.'

Geordie let her words stand there by themselves for a while. It seemed like they needed space. If they'd been written down he'd have underlined them.

'Tell me about the guy,' he said. He placed the tray on a low table and turned a chair slightly, so that he could watch the river. The surface reflected a million winking moons. Imperceptibly, inside its ears, the corn grew ever riper.

'It was him,' she said. 'He was young, small and dark with the broad forehead. Thin.' She explained about Charles Hopper, how she had spoken to him on the phone, and then gone round to call on him. 'I noticed this guy following me when I was halfway home. But he could have been waiting outside Hopper's house. He looked like the guy Naiomi Leaver described, and it matches the description of the guy at the allotment.'

'Then what happened?'

'I came in the house and he walked on by. But when I looked out the window he was sitting on the grass, by those trees. He was sitting there for about an hour.'

'And then he went, and he hasn't come back.'

'Yes,' she said. 'I didn't see him leave. He could be watching from farther away.'

'What would Sam do?' Geordie asked.

'Flush him out,' said Marie. 'The most important thing is to find out who he is, where he lives. If I go for a walk, you hang back but keep me in sight, then if the guy follows me, you follow him.'

'Better still,' said Geordie. 'I'll leave now, so if he's watching the house he'll think you're alone. But when you go out stick to main roads. Don't go anywhere quiet, or where there's no one about. We know the guy's dangerous, and we don't want him having a go at you.'

There was a small floating pier and a cluster of rowing boats a hundred and fifty metres downstream. Geordie sat on the pier and let his legs dangle over the edge, listened to the boats rubbing up against each other as he kept half an eye on Marie's house. She was going to wash-up before she left the house, change her clothes, give Barney something to eat. She'd be out in about twenty minutes. Alone. Barney would remain behind as a guard dog.

No one was taking an undue interest in the house. Geordie kept an eye on the people who were strolling the path, dog owners, the odd tourist or two, mainly couples. Two lads on bikes, doing wheelies. Something that looked like a student, dressed in a black cloak, head to foot, couldn't tell if it was male or female. Nothing to worry about there.

The wind returned with little warning. There was a rushing sound on the river, as if the fish had all come to the surface and were doing the breaststroke. A cloud blew over the face of the moon, and in no time at all the river bank was deserted.

Geordie zipped up his jacket and toyed with the idea of going back to Marie's house. There was no point in her coming out in this weather, no one would follow her on a night like this. The wind whipped up white caps on the river and set up a moaning through the trees that was almost human. Like women and children screaming, wailing for something that had once been wonderful but was now lost for ever. The willows lashed the surface of the water and one of the women in the wind, her voice falsetto in the cacophony, was crying herself blind.

As Geordie decided to give up and go back to the house the wind dropped, the voices died into a distant dirge. Some of the light of the moon returned and a large planet – no, two of them – Venus, with Mars above it, winked down at the earth. The goddess of love and the god of war forever tied together. Over to his right a door slammed and as the elegy in the wind anchored itself to the calm he watched Marie walk from the shadow of her house into the ineffectual fire of the moonlight.

She was dressed in a lilac suit, the skirt with a stylish cut that emphasized her stride. At the neck of the jacket the moonlight picked out the satin collar of her blouse. He waited until she had passed him, let her get a hundred metres ahead, then he followed, keeping close to the wall, so he was hidden by the shadows. She walked through the Museum Gardens, which was exactly what Geordie had told her not to do. She kept the ruins of St Mary's Abbey on her left and was hooted at by a peacock sitting on the ancient watergate. She slowed her pace after that, so Geordie had to adjust his own to maintain the correct distance between them. There was a moment when something dark and flowing caught his attention, looked like a witch or a spectre, over to his right, by the river. Something over there flapped between two trees, but when Geordie turned his attention to it there was nothing to see. Just fancy and the moonlight.

Marie left the gardens and crossed the road to Lendal. She walked past the post office and looked in the window of Betty's, at the people inside eating and drinking. Geordie closed the gap between them. He wished he was inside Betty's, with a cup of that good coffee in front of him. There was a pianist in a spotlight, playing around with 'Danny Boy'.

Marie crossed into Stonegate, walked past the Punch Bowl, and then turned around and looked back at Geordie. She looked long and hard, made sure he saw her, then left the tourist area behind by turning quickly into Back Swinegate and the maze of passageways and arcades between there and Grape Lane.

'Jesus,' Geordie muttered to himself, 'this is asking for

trouble.' And even as he said it a gust of wind returned and flung out the folds of the black cloak of the man who followed Marie into the alley. Bat-like in the moonlight, silent, but obviously not blind.

Geordie covered the distance to the mouth of the alley in a few seconds, but when he turned the corner there was no sign, either of Marie, or her pursuer. The moonlight didn't penetrate into these passages, they were narrow, and the walls that bordered them, high. There was the occasional lamp, and as Geordie ran through the maze, there was also the occasional tourist or passer-by. After a few minutes he stopped and listened. Instead of running blindly, he reasoned, he might hear footsteps, and explore the direction from which they came. But he heard nothing.

He made his way back to Stonegate and started again. Taking a different route, and making sure he explored every alley and cul-de-sac along the way. His heart was pounding loudly in his chest, and he was breathless with anticipation and fear. The wind had returned now, and was whistling around the arcades and threatening to lift tiles from the rooftops. It was roaring and clamorous, blowing dust and mortar from the medieval walls and buildings. Geordie strained to hear any sounds above or below the wail of the wind. And there was something there, close by.

It didn't sound like Marie's voice. It was a long, piercing scream, the kind of anguished cry that took Geordie back, momentarily, to his time in the children's home. He would hear cries like that from time to time in the night, from new boys and girls, or from someone dreaming of the past or the future.

But this wasn't about the past or the future, it was of the moment. He turned into a small yard, and as he did so the scream that brought him there died a series of deaths and broke up into whimpers. There was the back of the black cloak. The man who was wearing it had the hood up, and his arms outstretched, so the cloak looked like a pair of ribbed wings. Marie wasn't visible at first. Geordie had to move to one side before he saw her huddled in the corner of the cul-de-sac. Her face was white like the moon, her eyes large and staring up at the face of her attacker. She was transfixed and didn't notice Geordie at all.

The cloaked man moved forward a step, and Geordie caught sight of the green rope that trailed from his right hand. The wind fell and rose again, whipping the black cloak around the figure of its wearer, and Geordie screamed something unintelligible, even to himself as he hurled himself at the man and tried to hold him back from Marie.

But Geordie didn't make the contact he had hoped for. The black cloaked figure heard or felt him coming, half turned and ducked as the force of Geordie's body came towards him. Geordie glanced off the man's shoulder, and although he grasped for the material of the cloak, he found himself falling away, and landing in a heap on top of Marie. As he fell he put out his right hand to save himself, and he saw and heard his forearm snap twice as the weight of his body came down on it. There was no pain, only a sinking feeling as he realized that the hand would be useless to him in the fight that lay ahead. Then there was nightmare agony, a rush of blood from the sleeve of his jacket, and his body writhed, his head twisting up and back.

Maybe he lost consciousness for a moment, he couldn't remember, but the next thing he knew was the black-cloaked figure had the rope around his neck, and was dragging him over the cobbled yard. Geordie's lungs were roaring, his eyes popping. He reached up to the rope with his good hand, but could get no purchase on it as it was already biting into the flesh of his neck. The man in the cloak was not large, but he had tremendous strength, and he was twisting the rope and cutting off Geordie's life with surprising speed and agility.

Geordie could see the slumped figure of Marie on the far side of the yard. As he watched he saw her move, then his vision began slipping away. What had been the figure of Marie turned into a swirling mist. The sounds made by the wind merged with the rasping sounds coming from his own lungs. There was a continuous wailing now, and Geordie unaccountably thought of storm damage, of insurance claims. Briefly he wondered where Sam was, and what the baby would be called when it was born. He thought his injured arm should hurt more than it did, was glad he'd seen Barney and the duck against the harvest moon, and way off in the distance he heard a wild cat growl.

Marie picked herself up. She hadn't realized the man in the cloak was there until he'd grabbed her by the arm and spun her into the cobbled yard. He'd been muttering something, a kind of rhythmical chanting, *Che, che, che, che*, on and on like rolling stock. He never varied the volume, his voice harsh, and as he closed in on her his chanting increased in pace, like a death train. The sound was designed to remove all compassion from the man, as if he was consciously squeezing the humanity from himself, and leaving behind a function, an operation, a machine.

He pushed her back against the wall, and it was then that she looked up and saw his face. He was hooded, but within the folds of the hood was the face of a ghoul, red skin, puckered as if burnt, black eyes against a white leprous background. It was a face both savage and dangerous, the face of a serpent about to strike. Marie screamed, then she felt her legs give way, and her skirt rode up her back as she crumpled to the ground.

It wasn't clear what happened next. She heard Geordie's voice, though could not make out what he was shouting. Then Geordie was flying over the thing in the cloak. He landed on top of Marie and she heard bones break, quickly, like twigs. The cloaked figure had a rope around Geordie's neck, and for a moment Geordie appealed to her with his eyes.

Marie got to her feet and rushed across the yard at Geordie and the man or beast who was choking the life out of him. She'd had karate lessons, and was experienced in self-defence, but she forgot everything she'd ever been taught. Instead she turned herself into a wailing banshee. In place of the stiff fingers or the fist, she attacked the cloaked figure with fingernails, claws. She scratched at his face and pulled at his hair. When he put up a hand to defend himself she grabbed it and sank her teeth into it, feeling the flesh crumble and tear, and tasting the fresh salty blood as it ran into her mouth and down her chin. She kicked out at him with both feet, feeling the connection of his shins with the toe of her boot.

She never doubted for a moment that she would vanquish this monster, and in a remarkably short period of time, she realized he had let go of Geordie and was running for the entrance to the yard. She followed for a few metres, determined to stop him, but then realized that Geordie needed her help.

She unwound the twisted rope from his neck. His face was blue, and his head and limbs were limp. Marie said his name, felt for the carotid pulse on his neck. He was breathing and his heart was working, but he was unconscious.

She placed him in the recovery position and ran to the entrance to Stonegate. 'I need a doctor,' she yelled. 'A doctor and an ambulance. And bloody quick!'

She got neither. What she got was four big lads from the Punch Bowl, all smelling of beer, and a Suzuki jeep. The biggest of the lads drove the jeep along Stonegate, and unloaded a plank of wood. Then all four of them loaded Geordie on to the plank, made him comfortable in the back of the jeep, and drove him and Marie to the emergency ward of the district hospital.

When they arrived there he still hadn't regained consciousness, was looking just like a ghost.

38

The bell rings downstairs and the door opens. You hear Dr Hillerman shout from the foot of the stairs and Diana goes to meet him. He bustles into the room and listens to your heart through his stethoscope. Bushy eyebrows, sprouting every which way. The iron bar has almost gone from your body. You feel light, like one of Mother's sponge cakes.

'You've had some pain?' he says.

You look him in the eye and shake your head. He turns to Sam questioningly.

Sam laughs. He can't believe you've looked the doctor in the eye and told a big lie. He turns back to the doctor. 'It seems better now,' he says.

The doctor holds your wrist. He is not taking your pulse. He is trying to reassure himself by physical contact. 'We don't want to take any chances,' he says. 'We'd better have you in the hospital.'

'No.'

'Have you a phone?' This to Sam.

'She's all right here, doctor. There's no need for the hospital.'

The doctor makes a face. 'Impossible.'

Sam crosses him and stands by the bed, his hand on your arm. 'She's all right here,' he repeats. 'She doesn't want to go.'

Silence.

The moment of decision.

'We can cope,' Diana tells him.

The doctor dithers on the spot, but he knows he has lost. He turns his face to you. 'You're a stubborn woman,' he says, but the tone of his voice has softened. He closes his bag. 'I'll be off,' he says. 'Some of my patients need me.'

You listen to his footsteps on the stairs, and the front door closing behind him. You catch Sam's eye, and return his smile. He strokes the side of your face.

Diana places both hands on the bed and shakes her head. 'You two,' she says. 'You two against the whole bloody world.'

39

William stood back in the shadows of the street and watched Dora's house. He saw the Daimler arrive and the man get out with the doctor's bag. A few minutes later he watched the man leave the house, get back into the Daimler and drive away. Every room in the house was lit. The ground-floor rooms were unoccupied. Upstairs, the curtains to Dora's room were drawn, but figures, silhouettes, could be seen moving behind them.

It would be possible, simple even, to go around the back of the house and gain entry through the kitchen door. Then creep up the stairs, give Dora a big surprise. He had a length of green rope in the pocket of his cloak. A warm knife nestling next to it.

He smiled to himself, then replaced the smile with a furrowed brow. Because things were going wrong now.

His attempt on the woman in Fishergate had gone wrong. Badly wrong. He had planned it exactly like the others, and the others had gone according to plan. The man wasn't supposed to return when he did. William couldn't understand that. He had thought about it over the last couple of days, and it still didn't make sense.

Everything had been going right up to that point. He had stalked the woman. Watched her, he knew how she organized her life. There was a man there, a man who lived with her, but when he went out to his club he stayed out of the house until midnight. Always. As long as William had watched them the man had never returned before midnight. And when he returned he staggered and sometimes sang, as the alcohol boiled inside his brain.

But when William had the rope around the woman's neck, when her eyes were bulging with disbelief, the man had returned. It was still not ten o'clock. And the man was not staggering or singing, he was quick and alert. He was strong. William only got away because he heard the door to the flat opening. If he hadn't heard that the man would have trapped him in there.

That had been the first thing that had gone wrong. Not counting India Blake. The India Blake thing had gone wrong, but it had come out all right in the end.

The second thing that had gone wrong was Charles Hopper who was still in the chest in William's house. William had not wanted to put Charles in the chest in his house. He had not wanted Charles to be involved in any way at all. Charles was work, business. William didn't want to mix business and pleasure. He wanted to keep them separate, like everyone else did.

And what had made Charles Hopper get involved was the woman detective who was asking questions. William had thought about that as well. And what he had thought was simple. Get rid of the woman detective and everything would stop. Almost. There would still be Charles to deal with, or his body when he died. But that was all. The woman detective was the one who had started things going wrong, so if William dealt with her that would signal the beginning of the end of his troubles.

Only it went wrong again.

He'd trapped the woman detective. Was closing in on her. She already had that look of resignation in her eyes. She was whimpering in the doorway, reconciled to the fact that her life was to be sacrificed when the man in the leather jacket had arrived.

William didn't like fighting. He especially didn't like fighting with men. He knew all about it, of course, how to do it. He'd learned all that when he worked as a bouncer. But he didn't like it. It was true that the man didn't put up much of a fight. Probably because his arm was broken. And it was also true that William'd won the fight. He'd killed the man, or nearly killed him when the woman detective had begun her attack.

William had had to flee again. What should have happened, he should have been able to frighten the woman detective. He should have killed the man who had come to her rescue, and then killed her. But it all took too long. By the time he'd subdued the man, the woman detective had turned into a fireball. William looked at his right hand. There was a clear outline of her teeth there; you could see where she had sunk them into the flesh. If William hadn't wrenched himself free at that point she would have bitten part of his hand away. He explored the perimeter of the bite with the fingers of his left hand. It was sore. The blood had begun to clot now, but if he applied a little pressure it would start to flow again.

He should go home and treat it. He had a first-aid kit, with antiseptic ointment, sterile pads and plasters. He could take something for his headache.

He looked up at Dora's window.

There was a choice to be made here.

Something he had to decide. Only he couldn't remember what it was.

He had played this part in life. There were no parts like this in the theatre. Not that he'd been offered, anyway. The parts that were on offer in the theatre all required a leading lady. And William didn't want a leading lady. That's what had led him to specialize in make-up. All those leading ladies he did not require.

The problem was the words in all the plays, the words where you had to tell the leading lady that you loved her. William had been able to say all the other words convincingly. But those words where you tell the leading lady that you love her had stuck in his throat.

At first he'd told himself he had to conform. That other people managed those words, and that he should be able to manage them as well. He'd tried with Pammy. With Pammy he'd said the words, spilt them out, so they stood there between them. And the words had given rise to a huge silence. The words had been unconvincing. Pammy didn't believe them at all. And neither did William. The words were empty shells, filled with the sound of the world's oceans. The silence had risen up and engulfed William and Pammy. And that was the moment when Pammy began to fade, to gradually metamorphose into Dora.

William realized that people didn't love and hate. There were no passions. He realized that nothing mattered. That it was all play. That there were good actors who survived, and bad actors who fell by the wayside. And he decided that he'd be a good actor.

A good actor was one who played the parts he was best at. William was never going to be a romantic lead. He knew that. He had insight.

He was going to play a loner.

An invisible loner with his own script. He would be a man who lived by night, a man who was unremarkable. Occasionally, from time to time he would audition a leading lady. But only for a very short part. She would not have any lines as such. What you might call a walk-on part.

William held two images in his head. The first was of a howling wind, his cloak whipping around his legs. The second image was of a black Daimler. He promised himself that he wouldn't move until he'd worked out what connected these two images. He couldn't remember how long a time had passed since he'd made that promise. It might have been a few minutes, or it might have been several hours.

He knew why he couldn't work out the connection between the two images. It was because the images were decoys. They had been put there to distract his attention from something else that he should be concentrating on. He didn't know what the something else was. Once he'd worked out the connection between the wind and the Daimler he'd be free to concentrate on the other.

The light in Dora's room shone. The silhouettes behind the curtain moved.

The promise that William had made, about not moving. There had been a reason for that, but the reason wasn't obvious any more. He pushed his left foot forward, and took a step toward the light in Dora's room.

They called him the Surgeon.

Because he cut out his mother's eyes.

Who would stop him?

There were silhouettes in the room with her, but the Surgeon would remove them. That's what a surgeon did. He cut away the bad, the evil, so that the good could grow and flourish.

William stepped into the road. The rope and the knife were there, safe in his pocket. She'd be drinking up there, he thought. Sucking on a bottle. William didn't like his mother drinking, but it was the only thing she could do.

He had the house in his sights now. The very house where everything had happened. He remembered seeing his daddy hanging there, outside in the garden, and how he had been so small at the time, and frozen with grief. And he remembered thinking it was the end of the world, because his daddy was dead, and how it would be impossible for the world to carry on without him.

Almost everything about his mother disgusted him.

A car turned into the street and William retreated back into the shadows. It wasn't a Daimler. It was a taxi, and it parked outside Dora's house. William watched and saw the woman detective get out of the back. She was wearing the same lilac-coloured suit as earlier. She paid the taxi driver and went into Dora's house.

266

William was paralysed again.

He looked up at the harvest moon and tried to remember what happened next.

He listened for a prompt.

His head was like a bucket with holes punched in the sides. As soon as he thought something the thought slid through one of the holes and was gone. There was a real connection between the woman detective and Dora, there had to be. But what was it?

The taxi got to the end of the street, turned the corner and was gone. He looked back at the house.

An ordinary house in an ordinary street. There was nothing to distinguish it from the houses on either side. People passing by would not give it another look. But behind it, hidden from the world, was a pear tree. And in the branches of that tree William had discovered the knowledge of good and evil.

His mother had hired the woman detective. In phase one his mother had killed Arthur. Phase two would be the death of William.

Unless, somehow, Arthur and William together could devise a plan to wipe her from the face of the earth.

40

Sam watched the bedroom door open. Celia was standing in the doorway. She mouthed the word: 'Marie.' He looked down at Dora, who was sleeping. He smoothed the cover near her shoulder and left the room, closing the door quietly behind him. 'It's Marie,' Celia said. 'Sounds important.'

He looked at Celia, placed his hand on her shoulder. 'You look worn out,' he said. 'Why don't you go home? Get some rest?'

'I'll hang on a little longer,' she said. 'See what Marie wants. If you have to go out you'll need me here.'

'What about Diana?'

'She's sleeping.'

Sam followed her down the stairs. Marie got to her feet as they walked into the living room. She was dishevelled, her hair stuck to her head, her skirt and tights scuffed and torn. He went to her and put his arms around her. 'You all right? What happened?'

'Yeah. I'm fine. But Geordie's in the hospital.' She quickly told him what had happened. How she'd gone to enquire at Charles Hopper's house, and how she and Geordie had been attacked by the character in the cloak.

'Geordie,' said Sam. 'Is he conscious?'

'Yes, Janet's with him. It's a compound fracture, broken two bones in his forearm. The radius and the ulna; it's nasty, the upper part of the radius came through the skin. No wonder he passed out.'

Sam flinched. 'But it'll mend?'

'Yes.'

'And what about his neck?'

'It looks terrible where the rope has burned the skin. But it's superficial. He'll come through.'

'Did he say anything?'

Marie smiled. 'Yeah. He said, "Tell Sam I'm sorry, and tell him to nail the bastard."'

'And Janet? She can cope?'

'I got them a private room. She can stay there with him. Be like a honeymoon. I told the hospital you'd pick up the tab.'

'I'm stunned,' Sam said. He cocked his head to one side, listened to the sound of a distant cash register.

'I thought you'd want to make a gesture.'

He shrugged his shoulders. 'What the hell. It's better to give than lend, and it costs about the same.'

'We didn't get a look at the guy,' said Marie. 'He wore a hood. Like a medieval monk. But he was deadly serious.'

Sam turned back to Celia. 'Get on the phone to J.D. Tell him thanks a lot for his letter, but I need him over here now. I don't want to leave you unprotected. As soon as we leave, lock the doors and make sure the windows are all fastened.'

'We going somewhere?' asked Marie.

'The guy who attacked you,' Sam said. 'I know where he lives. You game for a bit of house breaking?'

'Will I need a note from my mother?'

They detoured to the hospital. They walked through the main entrance and took a lift to the second floor. Marie led the way on to the ward, past the nurses' station to a private room. Geordie was flat on his back, Janet sitting in a chair by the side of his bed.

'Great security system here,' Sam said.

Marie laughed. 'Yeah, you can walk in and smother all the patients. Kill the doctors if you like. No one will stop you unless you're smoking.'

Sam went to the bed and placed his hand over Geordie's, looked down into his face.

'It was weird,' Geordie said. His voice was faint and hoarse. Didn't sound like him at all. 'I knew I was dying and I was really pissed off. I didn't see all my life pass in front of my eyes. Nothing like that. It was like being drowned, like being in an ocean, being dragged down into the depths, all alone. Up on the surface there was Janet and Barney in the sunlight, you and Marie and Celia. And down below it was pitch black. I didn't want to go but there was no way round it. It was so disappointing.'

Marie took a step towards the bed. 'But you didn't die, Geordie.'

He put something like a grin on his face. 'Thanks to you.' He reached out his good hand and she took it, leaned over the bed and put her cheek next to his. When she pulled away Geordie looked exhausted.

'We'd better be on our way,' Sam said.

'You gonna get him, Sam?' Geordie asked. His face was whiter than snow, his eyes huge and black.

'Yeah. We'll wrap it up tonight.'

'Careful. He's Radio Rental. He's not big but he's stronger than you think. I tried to kick him in the grapes.'

Sam nodded. Glanced at Janet, then snapped back to Geordie. 'You gonna be OK?'

Janet said, 'The doctors and nurses are really good. They could put scrambled eggs back into the shell.'

Geordie did something with his face, another stab at a smile, but not much better than the last one. 'I could use some grapes,' he said. 'I thought that's what's supposed to happen. People come and visit you and tell old jokes and feed you grapes.'

Sam got up and headed for the door. 'Don't be a sprout,' he said.

*

St Mary's was quiet. The moon was bright but the wind had dropped away. Billy's attic room was lit with a flickering glow that could only have come from a candle. The other windows were in darkness.

'We'll go in the back way,' Sam said. He led Marie through the pedestrian passage to Marygate Lane, and from there to a brick wall and tall wooden gate which led to the back of Billy's house. The gate was locked from the inside. Sam asked Marie to hold his torch. He put a dustbin against the wall to give him a start, went over the wall and unbolted the gate so Marie could follow. The bolt on the gate hadn't been used for some time.

They stood together in the dark and listened. There was no sound from the benighted house, no sense of life or movement from within. The concrete floor of the yard was little used, there was moss growing in the cracks and a smell of cat piss. An old bicycle was leaning against one of the walls, both of its tyres flat, all of its moving parts rusted and crusty. Sam felt Marie tremble next to him. He took hold of her arm and squeezed it gently. 'You OK?' he whispered.

'I'll manage. It feels weird.'

'You can wait out here if you like. Watch my back.'

She shook her head. 'I wanna be where the action is. I'd shake to death out here.'

He smiled and moved over to the door. He turned the knob slowly and eased back on the door, but it didn't give. 'I'll take the window out,' he said. And he turned his back to the window and hit one of the small panes sharply with his elbow. There was a loud crack as the glass shattered, and a marmalade cat which had been sitting on the garden wall watching the break-in did an open screak followed by a sudden scattering run.

Sam slowly withdrew his arm and brushed shards of glass from his sleeve. They reflected the moon as they fell to the ground. He put his hand through the jagged opening and turned the key in the lock. When he next turned the knob on the door and pulled gently, there was a creaking sound as the dry hinges allowed it to swing outwards.

Sam looked at Marie, and together they gazed into the impenetrable darkness within the house. Stale cooking smells were evident. Burnt fat, toast, and something rancid, fetid. 'What's that?' Sam asked, sniffing gently, unwilling to let whatever it was into his head.

'Smells like rotten meat,' Marie said.

'Yeah.'

He moved into the kitchen, Marie following close behind. He flicked the torch on and off to get his bearings, noticed a grimy kettle to his right, sitting on a two-ring gas stove. He reached out and touched it, wondering how long it had been since Billy had been down here. The kettle was cold.

On a table were two bottles, each with stumps of candle stuck in their necks.

Underfoot had changed to sticky and damp. What had once been a carpet was now like a thick dough, partly cooked, a breeding ground for sucking insects, worms, maggots and disease-producing microbes. Billy was keen on the launderette, but as far as housework went he was still in nursery class.

Sam flicked the torch on again, noticed there was a step up from the kitchen to the next room. He reached behind him and found Marie's hand. 'Stay close,' he whispered. 'And as quiet as you can.' He felt her grip his hand tightly, and they edged forward over the floor like a single being. The room was almost empty. There was a large cast-iron frying pan on the floor, the butt of a candle standing in it; and there was a carpet runner which looked like it might once have been a stair carpet. In the glance he had of it in the flick of his torch Sam couldn't tell if it was patterned or plain, and he suspected that the answer to that one, even in daylight, would require the aid of a forensic scientist.

From that room the next door led to a short corridor. To the left was a staircase with cupboards underneath it, and to the right was the front room of the house. The front room was also unfurnished, though it had curtains, seemingly stuck to the windows by cobwebs. There were mice droppings on the floor, and several of the floorboards had been taken up and removed, leaving dangerous, jagged holes, and a means of access for vermin.

'Are you sure anyone lives here?' Marie whispered. And while her words were still hanging there in the dank space of the room there was a single thud from the ceiling above their heads. A footfall? Something being dropped? It wasn't clear. But someone was up there. Someone or something who might or might not know that Sam and Marie were in the house. Marie let her breath go slowly, and Sam felt a prickling sensation at the back of his neck.

He reached for Marie and pulled her head around so his lips were close to her ear. 'We're going up,' he said.

She didn't reply, but Sam felt a tremor travel the length of her body. He gripped her hand and made for the stairs. As they reached the first step a large longtail leapt through the wall of the balustrade and brushed Marie's legs as it scurried into the front room. Marie let go with a shrill and unrestrained scream. The stillness of the house was shattered and every brick, every mite of dust in the whole edifice echoed her cry. She smothered it immediately, dammed it up inside herself, and everything fell quiet again apart from the sound of Marie trembling, her teeth chattering, her lungs sucking in oxygen to augment the flow of adrenalin.

Sam hugged her to his chest. Her whole body was fluttering with panic. It was as though the effort of will to suppress the scream had transformed the sound into an inner force that was rocking her bodily systems to their foundations. Sam held on to her for several minutes, until the terror began to subside. At the same time he listened for other sounds in the house. But heard nothing.

'Come,' he said. 'We'll go. I'll take you home and come back later.'

Marie looked up through the gloom at him. She narrowed her eyes. 'We're going up these fucking stairs,' she whispered, her voice shaking but betraying an inner calm and determination. 'Both of us. Now.'

Sam flicked on his torch and eyed the staircase. There were parts of the wall where the plaster had been gouged out and left in lumps on the treads. It looked as though someone with a grudge against walls had come up with a revenge scenario involving an axe. Near the top there was one strip of burgundy-coloured flocked wallpaper which hung from the ceiling down to the stairs. It was patterned with Chinese dragons, and on either side of it the wall was covered in infantile graffiti which wouldn't have been out of place in a secondary school bog.

As they made their way up the stairs their shoes crunched on loose plaster, and Sam was aware of the taste of grit on his lips. There was an aura of decay and neglect about the house, but it wasn't like a house that was unoccupied. It was occupied by someone who didn't care. By someone who didn't care about anything except a half-buried driving force, a fanatical and twisted urge to survive in a world which was alien and inhospitable.

The house had something of the feel of those derelict, futuristic and wasted cityscapes that fascinated Ridley Scott in *Blade Runner*. Sam wouldn't have been surprised to see Rutger Hauer or Sean Young pass along the upper landing.

At the top of the first flight of stairs there were three rooms, all with closed doors. Sam hesitated, wondering if he should check them or continue up to the attic. It briefly crossed his mind that Marie could check these rooms while he went on up to the attic alone. But he didn't suggest it, because he suspected Marie might not manage on her own, and he knew *he* wouldn't. He remembered the flicker-

274

ing light in the attic room which was always visible from outside.

With Marie close behind, he began the ascent of the final flight. There was a thin carpet on these stairs, and the near-side wall had been painted once, a long time ago. Apart from their own breathing and the muffled whisper of their feet on the carpet there was no hint of movement.

The upper door was fastened with a wooden latch. Sam lifted it and let the door open into the room. Marie moved over to Sam's right, so she could see whatever might be in there. The light from the single candle was not very bright, but it was enough to disorient their eyes for a moment. When they adjusted to the changed light Sam moved into the room. Marie stayed behind in the doorway.

'Nothing,' she said. 'He isn't here.'

Sam picked up the candle from a low table and surveyed the room. It was a den. The floor was carpeted with several rugs. Billy had let some of the rugs run up the walls, and there were cushions scattered over the floor. There was a shelf on one wall, but nothing on the shelf, apart from the remains of a take-away meal. There was a coatrack with two shirts and a jacket suspended from it. And underneath them an assortment of clothes. Socks, underwear, a bright red sweater. An ironing-board was folded and stacked against the wall.

Marie stepped into the room and drew in her breath sharply. Sam watched as she moved over to the room's only chair. Draped over it was a long black cape. He watched her finger it, and caught her eyes as she looked towards him.

'That what he was wearing?'

She nodded. She lifted the hood, and looked back at Sam. 'Yes. That's why we couldn't see his face.'

'He's been back, then.'

Marie glanced around the room. 'But where's he gone now?'

'I don't know. We'll wait for him. Might as well see the rest of the house while we're waiting.'

He led her back to the first landing, Marie carrying the torch and, like Sam, only flicking it on occasionally. There was a bathroom sandwiched between two other rooms, with the bath full of dirty water, though the plug didn't appear to be the cause of the blockage. There was a bathroom cabinet with a razor, a bar of soap, and a face towel from hell.

The back room had bare boards and was unfurnished. Sam turned to leave but stopped when he caught sight of a long chest behind the door. Marie had entered the room behind Sam and walked over to the window, where she was looking out on the back yard.

'Jesus,' said Sam. He had lifted the lid of the chest, but still in darkness, so he couldn't see what was inside. His exclamation came from the stench that arose from the chest when he lifted the lid. Urine and faeces in a good quantity, and left to accumulate over a couple of days.

Marie came over with the torch and they gazed down on the still figure of a man. His arms and legs were tied with a new green rope, and his mouth was sealed with clear parcel-tape. The bottom of the chest appeared to be lined with old newspapers.

Marie edged Sam aside so she could get closer. Sam held his nose and willingly stood back. He watched her probing the front of the man's neck for his carotid pulse, then she leaned right into the chest and put her face next to his nose.

'He's still alive,' she said. 'It's Charles Hopper. Help me get him out.'

Sam took Hopper's shoulders, Marie his feet, and they lifted him clear of the sides of the chest, carrying him through to the landing and placing him carefully on the floor. Sam unclasped a penknife and cut the rope that was binding him. He pulled the tape away from the man's mouth. For a moment Hopper's eyes flickered and his cracked lips moved, but then he lapsed back into unconsciousness. Marie had gone into the bathroom and returned with her scarf dripping water. She held it to Hopper's lips for a few seconds, then squeezed a few drops of liquid into his mouth.

'He's dehydrated,' she said to Sam. 'We'll have to get him to a hospital.'

'OK. Let's find something to use as a stretcher.'

'You do that,' she said. 'I'll go ring an ambulance.'

She ran down the stairs to the front door. Sam watched until she disappeared outside, then turned to the other room on the landing. He glanced momentarily at the prone body of Charles Hopper, then opened the door to a blazing light.

There must have been two hundred candles burning in the small room. They were lined up along the top of the pelmet above the window, perhaps an inch between each one. There was a writing table, similar to one that Dora had in her room, and the surface of that was festooned with flickering white candles. The bookcases and shelving all housed similar legions of candles, all more or less the same size.

The lemon-coloured walls, picked out with blue florets, reflected the light and shadow thrown by the moving flames of the candles, and for a brief period the walls seemed to lose all solidity, so that instead of being made of brick and plaster they could have been woven from silk.

Near the centre of the room, angled away from the door was a distinctive antique chair with a shield-shaped back. A chair, again, which was identical to the one in Dora's room. Candles had been placed along the top of the shield, and were burning very close to the shoulders of the jacket worn by the chair's occupant.

As Sam watched, the man rose from the chair and slowly turned to face him. It was Arthur, Dora's first husband. Sam knew that it couldn't be Arthur, and that it must be Billy, but the illusion had been wrought with great skill and a total commitment to detail. Sam had studied the photographs of Arthur from Dora's album, and the figure that now stood before him was indistinguishable in every detail. Even the suit was authentic. Sam remembered wearing a suit like that himself. Something he wouldn't be seen dead in now.

Billy took a step forward and Sam saw the knife glint in the white light of the candles. In his other hand was a length of green rope, which he had fashioned with a noose.

'For Christ's sake, Billy, it's all over . . .' Sam said. He took a step toward Billy to disarm him, but Billy raised the knife and brought it slashing down like a rocket. Sam saw the movement but couldn't dodge away fast enough. The blade of the knife went into his forearm, just above the wrist. He saw it happen, found himself watching the blade penetrate his skin. And even as he watched it he was aware that the noose of green rope was looping toward his head.

Realizing that he had postponed his response for too long, Sam brought up his free arm to wave the noose away. He pulled his injured arm free of the knife and made a movement towards Billy's wrist, hoping to wrest the knife away from him. As they grappled together, the chair in which Billy had been sitting overturned, and the candles ignited a pamphlet that was lying on the carpet. Billy looked down at the flames, and something wild and uncontrolled entered his eyes. He turned and, with the rope, he swept the remaining candles off the surface of the writing desk. The room began to erupt in small torches of fire.

Through the light and the gathering smoke Billy sprang at Sam. Making a successful grab at Billy's knife hand, Sam hung on to it as he felt himself falling over backward. Billy was sitting astride his chest, and although Sam refused to let go of the hand which held the knife, he couldn't stop Billy whipping at his face with the rope.

Concentrating on trying to save his life, Sam didn't hear

Marie's footsteps on the stairs, and was only aware of her when she wrenched the rope from Billy's hand. In one movement Billy placed his knee in Sam's face and reached up to push Marie away. The full force of his body was behind the shove and Sam saw Marie topple backward into the landing and fall over the prone body of Charles Hopper.

She got to her feet again, and came back for more, shaking her head from side to side. Sam still couldn't manage to throw Billy off him, and he realized that the gathering smoke was affecting their ability to breathe. He rolled his left hand into a fist and punched upwards into Billy's face. It was a hard blow, and he saw Billy's head ride away with the force of it. In the instant after the punch Sam was able to roll Billy off his chest, and the two of them came face to face on their knees. Sam still had hold of Billy's knife hand, and Billy still grasped the knife.

'No,' Sam said to Marie, his voice breathless. 'Get Hopper down the stairs.' He had barely got the words out of his mouth when Billy butted him in the face. Sam went down again, but even as he went down he realized that Marie had begun dragging the body of Charles Hopper down the stairs. The antique furniture in the room was like tinder, already beginning to crackle, and it was becoming increasingly obvious that the whole house could go up in flames.

Sam felt his head crack against something hard on the floor, but he didn't dwell on the pain. He wrenched at Billy's wrist with all his might, and heard Billy cry out as the knife flew away to the other side of the room.

Where Sam had fallen the carpet was running with flames, and soon his hair was alight. He quickly smothered the flames and struggled to his feet. A stream of flame ran along the carpet, out into the landing, and began chewing away at the stairs. Billy had gone in search of the knife, but now the smoke was so dense that anything more than a metre away was invisible. Sam plunged into the smoke and found Billy on all fours, crawling around in what was quickly becoming a sea of fire. He grabbed him by the hair and the seat of the pants and lifted him bodily out of the room on to the landing.

Billy got him by the throat, but Sam quickly broke his grip. He pushed Billy up against the wall and gave him two hard punches, left and right, both of them low in the stomach, way below the belt. Billy sagged and as he did so Sam ducked and caught the weight of him on his shoulder. He grabbed Billy's wrist and hoisted him down the stairs. As he looked back the fire had spread from the room out on to the landing, and was now engulfing the upper staircase.

A window cracked and shattered and oxygen began to be sucked to the centre of the flames, giving more fuel and energy to the fire.

Sam stumbled out of the front door and dumped Billy on the road. Marie was there with the prone body of Charles Hopper, and a small group of neighbours had begun to gather and watch the burning house.

Sam pulled Billy to his feet and pushed him down against the hedge, but there was no longer any necessity for force. When Sam looked at him, there were tears rolling down his face.

The smoke curled out of the door and windows on the first floor, blackening the upper façade of the building. A house is like a head, a skull. Door and windows are like mouth and eyes. There was a definite sense of resistance to the burning. The house had held its form for close to a century, and it didn't want to let go. It was old and cracked, but it wanted to remain; it was stubborn and fought against the fire.

In a matter of minutes the outside bricks were warm. Inside it was like an oven. The fire acted like a bellows. It sucked air inside and consumed it in enormous gulps. In the tension between the resistance of the house and the greed of the flames there was rage, a spitting passion which split oak and cracked stone; and there was despair, a hollow screaming monarch of grief.

Someone was leading neighbours out from houses on either side. The street was bustling with life, as if a circus had come to town.

Sam knew it was a trick of light. The movement in the upper window. The head and the waving arms. A hand seemed to reach out and touch the sill, before drawing back from the heat and disappearing. Similarly, the distant voices above the howling of the fire. Ghosts. Nothing real.

Suddenly the house was a fortress of flame.

The siren of the fire engine or the ambulance, or both, came whining through the night.

Marie had retrieved the first-aid box from the car, and she got Sam to slip his arm out of his jacket while she bound it tightly to stop the bleeding. The wound wasn't as bad as it looked, but it was going to be sore for some time. While she was tying the final knot of the bandage Billy got up on his feet and walked back into the house. Sam chased after him, but the heat was too intense to follow. He tried winding his jacket around his head, but he still didn't get close to the front door of the house before the material began smoking. He fell back into the road and looked up at the building.

There was an aura just before the floor collapsed. The rage and despair of the blazing house ceased for a moment. Weight and time and motion were all suspended, and something akin to silence took over. The flames hid their fangs.

Then everything fell inward and the rage and despair renewed their crackling fury. The ghost at the upper window remained in view for an instant, and was then sucked inside.

The sirens grew louder and ambulance and fire engine both came into the street. The men in their uniforms jumped to the ground and began running back and forth with hoses and ladders and axes. Sam watched the paramedics from the ambulance tending to Charles Hopper.

When Hopper had been loaded into the ambulance, Marie came over to Sam. A police car had entered the street behind the fire engine, and the two officers were questioning residents about the cause of the blaze.

'Head them off for a while,' Sam said to Marie. 'I'm gonna get back to Dora. Give me an hour.'

Marie half turned to look at the policemen. 'You've got it,' she said. 'It was my fault, Sam. I should have left the bandaging till later.'

He touched her arm. 'It's best like this. His job was done.'

41

She returned after your operation, Dora. You did not recognize her. You opened your eyes and looked around for Sam, but there was only a strange girl. Diana, your daughter. Gradually you put the parts of her face together, and managed to speak.

'Where's your cowboy?'

She smiled at you. 'They've taken him away,' she said. 'He went crazy.' He had developed an aversion to clothes. The police picked him up in a bar, stark naked, drinking stout. 'I was fed up with him, anyway,' Diana said. 'He was a fake.'

'Where's Sam?'

'Outside. I'll tell him you're awake.' She walked to the door and then came back to the bed. 'Sorry I didn't come to the wedding, Dora. If I'd known you were marrying such a lovely guy . . .'

Your life is spinning away from you now. The reality has been Sam and the last months. The rest was a bad dream: Arthur, your parents, the pear tree and the cement factory. You cannot remember if the parties and the drinking and the streams of young men happened or not. Perhaps they were all like Dylan Thomas, something that someone else remembered and projected on to you. But Sam, he was real, he is real, and you can hear his breath, feel his hand on the quilt. If you opened your eyes, Dora, you would be able to see him.

Time stops now. It is no longer a linear experience. It is a spiral. You drift in it, dream-like. The images of the past are insubstantial, phantoms. When you rise to the surface, to the present moment there is Sam. Without him you are dead.

He is dragging you back now. His voice is insistent in your ear. 'Dora. Dora, wake up.' His face is close to yours. You would not return from the spiral for anyone else. It takes all your strength to open your eyes.

'Billy?' You don't hear your own voice, Dora. It is far away. Sam Turner, your man, your great detective has been out looking for Billy.

'Yes,' he says. 'I found him.'

Sam has a black eye. You smile, remembering the time you had a black eye from Sam. Accidentally, when he couldn't get out of his own way.

You close your eyes again, back into the spiral. There is a smell of burning. They talk amongst themselves, Sam and Diana and Celia. You cannot make out their words, but it is good to have them around you. The spiral falters, changes into a lower gear, and continues. Sam has found Billy. He is back in town. All the way from ... You can't remember where.

You smile at the thought of him. Smile like he was sun on your face.

Sam leans over the bed and kisses you on the cheek. That smell of burning again. He has not shaved and his whiskers are rough on your face. You tell him: 'Figs and whiskers.' His face registers surprise, but he kisses you again. You remember with a start that you have never told him about Dylan Thomas. *Figs and whiskers?* The words are reflected on his face. He does not know what you are talking about.

The spiral falters again, shudders, and stops. There is a loud rustling sound, like wind filling the billowing sails of a boat. Or it could be autumn leaves, a dense swirl of them caught up in a stiff breeze. Then stillness.

Lady Day lifts her face to the lights. Her eyes are closed as she sings, 'What A Little Moonlight Can Do'. You never heard her sing it so slow. Or with so much understanding.

284

You leave the bed and look back at it. The cadaver of the old woman is completely still. Sam is kissing it, but he draws away suddenly and looks around the room for you. He knows you have gone. He slumps in the chair and buries his head in his hands.

There are so many things he does not understand.